The Key to Secrets

Hearts in Hazard ~ Book 7

by

M.A. Lee

WRITERS INK BOOKS

The Key to Secrets
Copyright © 2018 Emily Dunn
Doing Business as M. A. Lee & Writers' Ink

First electronic publishing rights: January 2018

All rights are reserved.

NOTE FROM THE AUTHOR

This book is a work of fiction. The names, characters, places, and incidents are products of the writer's imagination or have been used fictitiously and are not to be construed as real. Any resemblance to persons, living or dead, actual events, locale or organizations is entirely coincidental. The author does not have any control over and does not assume any responsibility for third-party websites or their content.

Published in the United States of America.

Cover design by Deranged Doctor Design.

www.writersinkbooks.com
winkbooks@aol.com

Acknowledgements

My especial thanks to Diane and Steve, best first readers in the world. Best friends in the world, for honesty and caring and support. Best family in the world, for laughter and love and life.

To **Deranged Doctor Design**, whose artistic designers always create inspiring covers that keep me writing.

Novels by M.A. Lee

12 Books of the Hearts in Hazard series
A Game of Secrets
A Game of Spies
A Game of Hearts

The Dangers of Secrets
The Dangers for Spies
The Dangers to Hearts

The Key to Secrets
The Key for Spies
The Key with Hearts

The Hazard of Secrets
The Hazard for Spies
The Hazard with Hearts

Into Death ~ Post World War I
Digging into Death
Christmas with Death
Portrait with Death (coming soon)

Non-Fiction Works

Think like a Pro Writer series
Think like a Pro ~ 1
Think / Pro: A Planner for Writers ~ 2
Old Geeky Greeks: Write Stories with Ancient Techniques ~ 3

Discovering Your Novel ~ 4
Discovering Characters ~ 5
Discovering Your Plot ~ 6
Discovering Your Author Brand ~ 7
Discovering Sentence Craft ~ 8

*Just Start Writing ~ **Inspiration 4 Writers** :: book 1*

Other Books
2 * 0 * 4 Lifestyle: A Planner for Living

Contents

Chapter 1

Cold had settled into Bee's heart the way the snow had settled over the land, covering the fertile soil and sending the living plants into their wintry sleep. The blank whiteness stretched over the fields and pastures, a glory of ice crystals packed together, sealing the good earth under a vacant layer both lovely and deadly.

Her internal snow had fallen so quickly and so completely that she hadn't even noticed its danger. It settled first into the empty crevices of her heart and of her hopes. From there it spread to cover her life. Now she was trapped. She'd said "no" to her barren life and "yes" to a life with potential only to realize how iced over that life would also be.

Bee watched Mad Aunt Beth use her cane to knock snow off the frozen rosebushes. White clumps fell to the ground. A repeated *whack*, *suss* filled the air. No sound came from the garden or the air. The birds and little animals kept to their warm cover. No sounds came from the manor or the carriage house and stables. Sane people hovered beside their hearths. Only she and Mad Aunt Beth had ventured out, she reluctantly and the old woman with the defiance that became all the more obstinate when faced with reason. Bee had given up argument, bundled them both into wool shawls and cloaks, and followed into the garden.

Shivering, mittened hands held to her face, she watched Aunt Beth mutilate the bushes. The wintry sun hadn't strength enough to melt the new snow. She had lost her own strength to stand up for the life she wanted. Like a coward, she accepted the life chosen for her. A life she should never have agreed to. It had seemed an escape then. Now she knew it would be a prison.

Aunt Beth gave a hard whack to the largest rosebush. Bee stepped forward to stop her. The gardeners would complain about the damage once they ventured away from their cozy quarters. She faltered before interrupting Aunt Beth. The older woman could be vicious with her cane. Her usual nurse hid the cane that her charge didn't need but always wanted. Yet Nurse Gregg had catarrh, and Aunt Beth wanted sunshine after days of clouds. Bee was the family retainer who did the miserable tasks that no one else in the Chalmsley family would do. Her dogsbody existence had driven her to say "yes".

She should have said "no".

A rider emerged from the trees, following the drive that led to the main road and then Chalmsley Village. He came at a canter, the dark horse moving easily over the snow-covered gravel. The capes of his greatcoat lifted and fell, lifted and fell, like black wings. The wide-brimmed hat hiding his face added to the impression of a great black bird.

"Ha! One for sorrow."

Bee jumped. Mad Aunt Beth had quietly come to her side. She held the cane over her shoulder, like a cricket bat, and pointed at the rider.

"Carrion crow, out of the oaks, come to catch a murderer. 'Fol de riddle, lol de riddle, hiding do'." Her singsong of the nursery rhyme sounded as creaky as rusty hinges. "Come too late for you, that one. Come too soon for her." She sang that as well then grinned at Bee, revealing missing front teeth.

"Aunt Beth, what are you talking about? Too late for me? Too soon for her? Who are you talking about?" Then, she remembered the sordid murder discovered this morning. The old woman should have known nothing about the crime, for she would have been in the nursery with Nurse Gregg. "What do you know about the murder, Aunt Beth?"

The shrewdness of the deranged had the old woman looking around before she patted Bee's arm. "Poor little Bee. Buzz here, buzz there, never quite know where to go, never quite know what's to know, never quite know what to do with the truth. You know he didn't just die in the night, little Bee. You know she killed him."

He. William Kennington had died last night. The hullaballoo over finding his bloodied corpse had filled the house this morning. The chambermaid who found him had fetched Bee. Bee had alerted the butler and the housekeeper to the crime. Then Bee took on the unenviable task of waking her great-uncle to inform him of the murder of an important guest.

The hullaballoo eventually had abated to sobs from his fiancée Moira Fraser and whispers from the other guests. The Chalmsleys maintained a stoic front. After being the center of the maelstrom, Bee discovered that she now circled the outer edge. With Nurse Gregg pleading sickness, Bee was relegated through the noon hour and half the afternoon to the nursery with Aunt Beth. At the top of the house, the nursery was intended to offer quiet solitude to the old woman.

Yet how did Aunt Beth, cooped-up in the old nursery, know more than Bee did about the murder?

"Carrion crow you'll know, though," Aunt Beth said now. "Unless the snow has frozen your heart. I'm cold." The cane came down to help her cross the snowy paths back to the house.

Bee trailed her. "Who is he? Who is this carrion crow?"

"Most wanted. Least expected."

How was she to interpret that? Then she realized. Her heart thumped madly. "Hector? Is it Hector Evans? He's in London."

"Where are your ears, girl? He came back last Spring, appointed constable by my nephew-in-law. He straightened out that mess over at Helmesford."

"He came here to Chalmsley Court? I didn't see him."

"No, they were careful about that. He stayed over in Meadowbrook except for a couple of visits here. Lord Chalmsley's niece mustn't marry a lowly constable. A Seddars mustn't marry a clerk's son."

"Aunt Beth, Hector and I never—we were too young to expect—he left. I forgot him because he never wrote."

"Wrote and wrote, never answered."

She gaped at the old woman. She had written to Hector, several letters, awkward little outpourings of her heart. When he never responded, she had abandoned them. Had he written her, and those letters were confiscated? That last summer had seemed idyllic—until Lord Chalmsley decreed Hector would remove to London. Had more driven that decision than Bee realized?

Should she believe Aunt Beth? The old woman didn't sound deranged, even though her earlier comments seemed crazed. Aunt Beth's insanity had its own sense, skewed and riddling. She had a knack for prophetic announcements that most of the Chalmsley family ignored—until they were suddenly true. As her pronouncement that Sampson and his son would soon be traveling far had come true two years before.

Not an hour ago she claimed the two servants would soon return. Since Sampson and Daniel had escorted the son and heir to Vienna, was George also soon to return?

Aunt Beth did know things that others at Chalmsley Court did not. Especially Bee. Like Hector Evans now served as constable for Lord Chalmsley, the district magistrate.

She glanced again at the rider. Carrion Crow. He had reached the forecourt. A groom ran from the stables to take his horse. The black-brimmed hat still hid his features.

From her frozen stance in the side garden, she couldn't see enough to trust Aunt Beth was right. Bee vividly remembered the blood on the bed, the blood on her hands after she bent closer to examine the wound, the blood she had scrubbed and scrubbed to remove. She said the only thing that fit with the morning's uproar and the appearance of a carrion-crow rider. "William Kennington was murdered."

"Murdered. Stabbed with a steely pick. I'm cold. I want my tea." And Aunt Beth headed into the house.

Bee followed. She wondered how Aunt Beth knew that someone used a steely pick to murder William Kennington.

She wondered if she would have a chance to see Hector, to talk with him.

Was it too late to re-kindle the spark between them?

. ~ . ~ . ~ .

Cold as the chapel was, Hector Evans turned colder when he pulled back the sheet covering the corpse and saw the blood on the man's neck. The lantern wavered in the footman's hand. Shadows danced wildly. "Steady up, man," he said as he bent for a closer look at the wound.

A thin hole. Something small and sharp and long.

He'd expected some kind of violence when the message to report to Chalmsley Court arrived. Lord Chalmsley would not send for a constable unless violence occurred, and the only violent person at the Court was George, his lordship's only son.

He wished Lord Chalmsley hadn't ordered the corpse moved to the chapel. He wished a dozen things. Mostly, he wished he hadn't seen Bee Chalmsley as he rode toward the house.

The two women in the snow-covered garden could only be Bee and Mad Aunt Beth. Only Mab would ignore sense and venture outdoors. Only Bee or a servant extremely well paid would follow to ensure the crazy bat didn't hurt herself. Aunt Beth had never hurt anyone, though. With a shawl hiding the taller woman's pale hair and her shape enveloped by a cloak, she could be anyone—but he knew it was Bee.

Eight years away from Chalmsley Court, yet he still felt the old stirrings. She had broken his heart once. He'd heard that all the young Chalmsley ladies became engaged over Christmas. Hector had wondered if Bee was included, but he hadn't asked. He wouldn't. He didn't want anyone to guess that a too tall, too thin woman-child had captured his heart one long-ago summer and never given it back.

He refused to moon about looking for her, hoping for a chance to speak with her, not when he had a murder to solve.

He straightened and yanked the sheet into place over the corpse. The footman lowered the lantern.

"Who found him?"

"I don't know, sir."

Hector narrowed his eyes, but the footman continued to look ignorant. The man was new, not a servant that Hector remembered from his own years at Chalmsley. "You've been here since they brought the body to the chapel?" He didn't say 'corpse'. He'd learned during his London years not to use that word to people unused to murder.

"Yes, sir. Lord Chalmsley himself appointed me to this duty."

"Did Lord Chalmsley order that the body be brought to the chapel instead of leaving it in place?" Once again, the man looked blank. "While you have stood guard, did anyone else wish to come into the chapel, perhaps to see the body?"

"No, sir. Well, sir, Miss Fraser, she came with her parents. She wanted to see him. She didn't believe he was dead."

"Miss Fraser was Mr. Kennington's fiancée?"

"Yes, sir."

"I expect that Lord Chalmsley would like a report."

"I wouldn't know, sir."

Nor did Hector. His lordship left his constable to his duties, boring enough most of the time. His only excitement had come immediately following his return from London, over in Helmesford, when an arson exposed a decade-old murder. Although he narrowed his suspect for the arson to one man, he'd lacked the evidence needed to take the case to an inquest or to the magistrate. As for the ten-year-old murder, he wound up with three suspects: one he didn't think had done it, the second he wanted to pin the murder on but had no evidence, and the third and most likely suspect would never be considered seriously by a jury. Cat ladies never were considered for serious crimes. They reminded people too much of afternoon tea, buttered crumpets served with preserves and a cat purring away on the mantel. He would never have gotten a conviction of Aunt Sally.

If the old maid aunt had shot the man. Maybe she hadn't.

Lord Chalmsley would frown if Hector failed a second time. Any jack with a bit of sense could see the drunks home and find stolen articles and hurry vagrants along to the next shire. Murders needed cleverness—and Hector didn't know if he were clever enough.

He left the footman with instructions to keep everyone out of the chapel. The Kennington family would expect the body's return soon. He needed to investigate the murder scene and start interviews, especially of the man's fiancée.

Half hoping his lordship was elsewhere, Hector knocked on the door to Lord Chalmsley's study. The "enter" was muffled but clear enough.

Chalmsley glanced up but continued his writing. Hector stood before the desk, remembering earlier years when he had stood in this very spot, waiting to hear either compliments for his skill in his lessons or discipline for his multiple mischiefs. He had ceased fearing the discipline long before Chalmsley sent him to work with London's chief magistrate Sir Richard Ford.

He used the wait to study his lordship. Although his body appeared fit, dissipation showed in the pouches under his dark eyes and the slackness of his jawline. He wore a gentleman's country attire with the nonchalance afforded by wealth that could replace expensive clothing with ease. Silver streaked his dark hair, but he showed no other signs of age.

Lord Chalmsley set his quill in the stand then leaned back in his chair. "I expected you earlier, Evans."

"Yes, my lord. I have viewed the body. A clear case of murder."

"I knew that."

"Yes, my lord." He sounded like the footman and vowed not to fall into such dumb obedience. "I'll look for the murder weapon when I search the scene. Where was his chamber?" He wasn't surprised when Kennington's room was the second floor. The first floor was reserved for family and privileged guests. He himself had never rated below the second floor. For many years he'd had a room on the third, down the hall from the nursery, closer to the servants. "Another question, my lord. Can you tell me the reason his body was removed to the chapel?"

"Couldn't leave him lying there, could I? The Fraser girl was caterwauling in the corridor ,and her parents demanded answers I didn't have. Still don't. You'll need to speak with them. Lord Fraser plans to leave in the morning. Unseemly haste, I'd say, but he seems to think murder is contagious. When will you speak with them?"

"After I've viewed the crime scene, my lord. I understand you and Lady Chalmsley are hosting a week-long party? Did Mr. Kennington have any family members here? I would wish to question them as well."

"Is this an example of your new methods of investigation? Ask questions? Search about for things? No, Kennington has no family, not here. There's a mother living and an uncle. He's a diplomat, assigned to Prussia, I understand. A sister, I think, married. But no one here."

"Thank you, my lord. And the other guests? Do they have plans to leave?"

He huffed. "They'd rather stay and titter about whatever transpires. Who do you think murdered Kennington?"

"I will not say until I have completed my examination of the evidence and conducted several interviews. I apologize in advance for inconveniencing your guests—."

Chalmsley waved aside the comment. "They inconvenienced me by coming here at my wife's invitation. Her idea, to host a party to celebrate the engagements at Christmas. Then she has to drag in my daughters' friends and their fiancés and parents. At least we don't have schoolchildren running about. How long do you think you'll need?"

"I could not say, my lord. The evidence and the interviews will determine that."

"Learned to be cagey, have you?" Chalmsley gave a decided nod. "You'll be staying here. Taking your meals with us. After all, I raised you with my own boy." He picked up the quill and reached for another parchment. "You'll be wanting to start your investigation."

"Yes, my lord." Feeling as if he should have questioned Chalmsley—how did a constable interrogate a magistrate?—Hector bowed then retreated from the study.

Without thinking, he turned left, heading for the front hall and the main stairs. Fitting back into the house would not be difficult. Chalmsley Court never changed.

Fitting back with the family? He knew George was off on a reduced Grand Tour, abbreviated to avoid Napoleon's army. Lord Chalmsley's daughters Cordelia and Portia had never cared for Hector and had stayed out of his way. His presence at dinner would not please them. As for Lady Chalmsley—Hector had never managed to get a read on that woman. For many years of his time here, she'd taken laudanum so much that he suspected an addiction. Yet in his fifteenth year, when he'd returned from school, she'd been brighter and happier than he'd ever known her, with no signs of laudanum anywhere around.

And Bee—. He finally allowed himself to dwell on her. How would Bee react to his presence here at Chalmsley Court? Would she welcome him? Would she be happy to see him? Or had she forgotten him, a singular mark on the map of her life, a mark that had long ago lost any meaning for her?

He didn't know, but he desperately wanted those answers.

He had yet to see Richardson, the butler. Two footmen stood in the entrance hall, statues paired, with nothing to do until a Chalmsley gave an order. They didn't blink when he passed them and started up the stairs.

"My goodness! Cordelia, look! I do believe that's Hector Evans. Hector! Do stop, Hector."

Chapter 2

Hector turned. Seeing the two young women, he bowed. "Ladies" seemed innocuous enough.

All smiles and blonde curls, the Honorable Portia Seddars approached with blue eyes wide, a trick from her nursery days. After years of association with Portia, Hector immediately suspected her of machinations. In early days she needed the trick to deflect or misdirect punishment, either for snatching away a doll or hiding a pretty bauble that belonged to a visitor or kicking the maid who tried to restore the bauble to the visitor's chamber before it was missed.

Behind Portia came Cordelia Seddars, most often the owner of the snatched doll. She had her father's dark eyes, deepened even more by the dark circles under them. Her blonde hair lacked her sister's pretty curls but waved charmingly. Pretty on her own, she paled beside her sister.

Bee Seddars, with flaxen hair and a narrow face, had paled even more beside Portia. Yet she'd caught his eye and then his heart.

"Ladies," Hector repeated, not knowing what else to say. He was eight years from this house and any contact with the privileged daughters of Lord Chalmsley. What should he say?

"You're here for the murder, aren't you?" Portia quizzed. "I understand you're a constable now. You'll have to solve the murder, won't you?"

While he answered, he considered her question out of tune with the event. Cordelia had flinched. Although she said nothing, she stared at her sister's back. She had started rubbing her fingers, an old sign of stress that Hector recognized. "Did you have much contact with Mr. Kennington?"

"In London I did. He was mine, you know. All of them were." Portia came closer and lowered her voice as if she shared a secret. "I told him to pursue Moira. I didn't really think she'd accept him. Silly thing had said she wanted to live in Scotland, and Will lives in the fens, you know. Or he did," she added. "Then she accepted him, and he— well, Mama invited the both of them. Now look what has occurred." She rolled those blue eyes and snared his arm. "I suppose you have lots of questions to ask, and you want to see his bedchamber."

A flick of his gaze checked on Cordelia, standing as if frozen except for the rubbing down of her fingers. "Why would I want to see his bedchamber, Miss Seddars?"

"Oh, not Miss Seddars! Not from you! Do not pretend, Hector, that we are not old friends."

"An age has passed since we were children together. I have seven years on you."

"Papa wanted to betrothe me to the Marquess of Musgrove. We attended a party at his estate last year. He is over ten years my senior, so you needn't think seven years is such an age."

"We have not met Lord Musgrove." Cordelia's insertion rang as oddly as Portia's first questions. "We enjoyed the party at Grove Park. Neither of us found a suitor. Mama was displeased. Lord Musgrove did not attend his own party. We returned here in early March. We did not leave for London until Autumn."

"London in October when most people are home. I was beginning to think Cordy would never find a match. She's turned twenty-one, you remember, three years older than me. Quite on the shelf. Barrington Pierpont proposed, didn't he, Cordy? Barrington's a sweetheart." Those blue eyes widened a little to seem guileless. "Beatrice is older. Twenty-three. Yet even she has a fiancé now."

"My best wishes to you, Miss Cordelia." He glanced down at Portia. "I understood that both the Chalmsley daughters were betrothed."

She giggled. "Of course! Mama insisted that I attend the London Christmas parties, and I took immediately. Brougham Paton. The Devonshire Patons?" she quizzed, as if he kept up with Debrett's Peerage. "He has two years on you. He loves my eyes."

When she batted her eyelashes, Hector thought it safe enough to chuckle. He managed to disentangle himself in order to give both young ladies the approved bow. "All best wishes to you, as well, Miss Portia."

"Here is Beatrice," Cordelia announced. "You must tell her 'all best wishes' as well."

During his examination of Kennington's body and his brief conference with Lord Chalmsley, Bee must have returned Mad Aunt Beth to her normal watcher. She looked only a little frazzled as she glided toward them.

And glide she did. Her fluid movements had always fascinated him. She seemed to alight onto chairs, float down the stairs, and drift along wooded pathways, light as fairy-thistle. Even at fourteen, she had an otherworldly grace. The faraway look in her deep blue eyes, the flyaway nature of her flaxen hair, her long slender limbs—all combined into what he had once fancifully called 'elvish'. He fell in love with her laugh. Yet as the summer passed, she grounded at Chalmsley Court, and her fairy-thistle air dissipated.

Bee still glided, but she seemed less like dream and more reality. When he had discovered the tips of her ears were a little pointed, he teased her unmercifully. Her laughter at that naming had dispelled her faraway gaze. He later learned that memories of her deceased parents caused that far-distant gaze, and he had tried hard to dispel her sadness.

He had tried too hard, for Lord Chalmsley had noticed his ward's attention to his niece. October found Hector miserable in sooty London, trying harder to please Sir Richard Ford as he learned how to investigate crimes and arrest criminals, which had necessitated training in fisticuffs and weaponry that a youth at Chalmsley Court had never learned.

Bee smiled. "Hector, welcome back."

"You're the first to tell me that," and her smile brightened.

"You must flirt with him later, Bee. We were just going to take him to Mr. Kennington's room. Then you can flirt with him. Just the way you once did. That summer was idyllic, wasn't it? We were all here. George, too."

"I am engaged, Portia. I should not flirt with anyone."

"Engagements mean nothing. Marriage doesn't either."

"What on earth do you mean?"

"Haven't you noticed, Bee? Married people are never together. They're always with other people. Fiancés are the same. Mr. Kennington was engaged to Moira Fraser, but he flirted with me. So does Barrington Pierpont, and he will be my brother-in-law." She beamed, all angelic gold and white and blue. "You two can flirt while Edmund flirts with me. All afternoon."

"If you're busy flirting, Portia, you'll miss tea." Even as Bee issued her warning, the longcase clock under the stairs began chiming the four o'clock hour.

Hector started counting his hours. He had reached Chalmsley Village after noon. Expecting to be put immediately to his task, he had taken a quick pub lunch, then continued his ride to the Court. He'd already spent two hours here, and he had done nothing more than view the body and speak with the magistrate. He had the scene to view, interviews to conduct ... . He didn't need to waste time with the sisters. Or with Bee. Or his lordship.

Cordelia stopped rubbing her fingers. "We must not miss tea, Portia. Mama will be displeased. We have had too much disruption today, she said. You remember. Do you remember?"

Portia scowled. "I remember. We cannot go with you, Hector. A footman will have to direct you."

"I do remember my way about the house."

"It would not do to make a mistake, Constable," Bee said calmly, creating distance by using his job rather than his name. "I will direct you and then return for tea."

"Unless you wish to take tea with us?" Portia asked, her hand returning to his arm.

"I believe my time would be better served attending to my investigation, but I thank you for the invitation."

She pouted prettily. "You must sit beside me at dinner."

"Preference, Portia," Cordelia reminded her.

The younger daughter sighed dramatically. "Then you will turn my pages while I play the pianoforte."

The two sisters left, heading in the direction of the drawing room. He heard other people above stairs as well as along the side passages, one which lead to the library and the other to the conservatory that captured the cold winter sun.

Bee glanced up and spotted guests beginning their descent from the first and second floors. "You will no doubt face multiple questions as soon as everyone discovers you are the constable in charge of discovering Mr. Kennington's murderer. Shall we take the backstairs? That will delay the questions."

Her gaze skittered away from his, as if she felt guilty and tried to hide it. Why would Bee feel guilty about anything?

Unless she'd murdered William Kennington.

Hector didn't remember her having any homicidal tendencies, and he couldn't believe she might change so drastically. Yet London had taught hard lessons. The chief lesson remained the first he'd learned— *smiles disguise knives, and innocence is a cloak easily shed.*

A youth alone in London, Hector had clung to Bee's oath that she would write to him. He hadn't given up until Christmas when Chalmsley's letter arrived. He had refused Hector's request to return for the holiday season. *Other things to learn, young man,* his lordship had written, *and no one here of interest to you.*

Hector had spent Christmastide shivering in his single room, little more than garret space, invited only by his parsimonious landlady to her Christmas dinner. The day after Boxing Day he'd attended a dinner at Sir Richard's, along with a handful of other young men in training for Bow Street. Then he'd returned to his cold room and vowed not to write another letter until Bee wrote him. She hadn't written. The lack still broke his heart.

He watched her glide to the narrow servant's stairs. A maid plastered herself against the wall as they passed. At the start of the second flight up, another maid saw them climbing. Turning her face to the wall, she waited on the landing. Near the top of the second flight, they encountered a footman coming down the third flight from the nursery and the servants' floor. He stopped and opened the door to the second story corridor. Bee thanked the man then led Hector along the corridor.

"Where's George?" Hector asked, as much to slow her as to find out where the violent young man was.

She stopped and faced him. Her eyebrows had lifted slightly. "Was he your first thought, when you heard we'd had a murder?"

The mind of the Bee he'd known had worked much like his own. They had leagued together against the strongest irrationalities of the Chalmsley brood. Yet in eight years she may have transformed into a creature of Chalmsley. He chose diplomatic silence on her question. "Where is he?" he repeated.

"Not here. Not in England. He left two years ago, for Vienna."

"I did hear that. Two years is a long time to be from home."

She ignored the comment. "As much as possible, Mr. Kennington's room was left as we found it." She spoke over her shoulder as she resumed her progress. "I stopped one maid from cleaning up, but I'm afraid his valet refused to leave without packing Mr. Kennington's belongings. I believe he was in shock."

"Did he find the body?"

"No. That was the chambermaid Holyfield.. She came in with Mr. Kennington's morning tea and to stir up the fire. As soon as she saw that he was—that he was dead, she came to me."

"Why did she come to you? Why did she not report to Lord Chalmsley?"

"A lowly chambermaid does not interrupt Lord Chalmsley's sleep. Nor Lady Chalmsley's. That duty fell to me. Besides, my room is now on this floor." They had reached the landing for the great stairs that descended to the entrance hall. Bee stopped and faced him. "I have the room on the end, a much better room than that narrow little room beside Cordelia's on the family floor. I have a wonderful view of the gardens and the long lawn, all the way down to the river."

"You used to love the river walk."

"I still do. I will miss it." Her lashes flickered. She turned to lead him on. "When the maid came to me, I didn't quite believe her. After I ascertained exactly what had happened—."

He stopped her with a touch. "What do you mean by ascertaining what happened?"

This time she fully faced him. In the corridor's dim light, the dove grey of her gown reflected like ash on her pale neck. She swallowed then said, "I checked the body. I shouldn't have, I know. A carefully brought up young lady does not enter a man's bedchamber, not even when he is dead. My great-uncle has already scolded me for doing so. But he would never have countenanced being disturbed so early unless something untoward had truly occurred."

"Wait. You're telling me that the body was found early. How early?"

"The maid said that he wanted to be awakened at 7 o'clock, just after dawn. I don't know the reason. Mr. Kennington didn't ride, and he certainly wasn't one for tramping."

Remembering the man's flaccid shape, Hector nodded. "So you examined the body."

"Not truly an examination. I stood beside the bed. The tester curtains around the bed were pushed back on one side, and the sheets were in disarray, as if he tossed them out of his way earlier in the night. The blood—." She swallowed again, and Hector realized that she had paled even more. "It soaked into the mattress beneath his head and shoulders. I did examine the puncture wound in his neck. He was murdered at night, while we all were sleeping peacefully. How can a man be killed so violently and never make a sound?"

Hector knew multiple ways. "What did you do then?"

"I told the maid to stay outside the door and not let anyone else in. I dealt with the butler and the housekeeper. Then I awakened my great-uncle. He had to see for himself."

"When did the valet come in?"

"After my great-uncle left. The news was spreading by then, you see. He sent a messenger to find you and I dealt with the valet and the chambermaid."

"Who ordered Kennington's body removed to the chapel?"

Her gaze went past him. Her eyes widened then closed only to open immediately. "You must speak with Lord Chalmsley about that."

He heard the footsteps approaching behind him. "I will," he said grimly then turned to face the newcomer.

A man approached. He was tall and golden as a god, with a smile and an outstretched hand for Hector. "You must be the constable everyone is talking about. I understand you are a former ward of Chalmsley's. I am Edmund Tretheway, Beatrice's fiancé."

Hector shook the extended hand and controlled the desire to crush it. "Hector Evans, sir."

Tretheway stepped around him to take Bee's hand. "Your hands are cold, my dear." He looked back at Hector. "I understand you are the son of a friend of Chalmsley. A Mr. Arthur Evans, that was."

"A barrister and the grandson of the late Lord Bute."

"Bute. That's a good family. Old title."

"I thank you, but my connection to Lord Bute is on the distaff side, sir. The current baron is my second cousin. Our lives do not intersect."

"I imagine not. You were a Bow Street Runner?"

He avoided the whole explanation of how Bow Street worked and merely agreed. "May I wish you congratulations, sir, on your choice of

Miss Seddars for fiancée?" He met Bee's gaze. "She is a fine choice." The bland words hid his wish to punch that thin-lipped smile from the man's face and break his Roman nose. "Thank you, Miss Seddars, for guiding me this far. If you will point me to the correct door?"

"The third one down, on the left. If you need anything else? I understand that you may wish a more formal interview of my involvement in this. And I will inform Richardson that you must speak with Dowding, Mr. Kennington's valet, and Holyfield, the chambermaid. She might speak more freely if I am present."

"My dear, it is not necessary for you to involve yourself," Tretheway declared at the same time that Hector asked, "Who is the housekeeper now?"

Bee chose to answer him, and a petty glee had him internally pumping a mental fist in celebration. "Mrs. Lovell. She runs the staff quite competently, but she does not endear herself to the lesser maids. Holyfield will be more comfortable answering your questions if she knows I am watching out for her. Shall I have Richardson send her to the conservatory at half-past six? And Dowding as well. He can wait in the hall while you question the maid."

"I would appreciate that."

"Very well then. We will meet again in an hour." Her gaze drifted over her shoulder, likely at the door she had directed him to. "If that is sufficient time."

"It should be. Thank you for your assistance, Miss Seddars."

She nodded, and Edmund Tretheway lost no time in shepherding her back to the stairs.

Chapter 3

Bee listened to Edmund's complaints, one for every tenth step to the ground floor. She didn't see that he had a right to complain of her help to the constable who would solve a murder. He obviously disagreed. He disagreed all the way into the drawing room, although there his comments were muted.

Earlier, when he learned that she had seen Kennington's dead body, not only blood-covered but unclothed, he'd expressed shock. He expected her to be shocked. "Do you think I should swoon onto a fainting couch?" she had teased. From his startled expression, she guessed that was exactly what Edmund had expected.

Had part of Hector's surprise at her retelling of this morning's event been his expectation that she should have swooned? She had collapsed only once in her life, when the solicitor brought the news of her parents' deaths at sea. She had vowed never to swoon again.

Holyfield had nearly swooned. Lady Chalmsley certainly had. Portia was excited, feeding off the gossip about Kennington's flirtation with Phaedra Dunham when he should have focused on his fiancée. Portia once more repeated that he'd flirted with her before he had proposed to Moira. Cordelia had followed the typical Cordelia instinct—she hunched into herself and retreated to her chamber.

As Bee sipped her tea, she glanced around the withdrawing room. For once, Lady Chalmsley interacted easily with three of the ladies. She often merely stared, and everyone became uncomfortable. Over her years with the family, Bee learned that the Chalmsleys rarely involved themselves with their guests. In seeing them at teatime, dinner and afterwards, and occasionally during the day, they apparently believed they fulfilled their duties to any visitors.

Great-Uncle Hamilton took the occasional guest hunting or shooting. Following her husband's lead, Lady Chalmsley might embroider with like-minded ladies. The sisters did interact with their particular friends, but they never extended any welcome to other guests. And George—Bee was glad George was abroad. He would have lived like a hermit in a ruined forest chapel if his father had left him to his own devices. Great-Uncle Hamilton hadn't trusted what those devices would turn into. With George, drowning kittens had started early.

Mad Aunt Beth had said *"she* killed him". Who was that *she*? What did Aunt Beth know? How did she know it?

Hector needed to hear Aunt Beth's claims—if he would listen to them. He knew Aunt Beth's derangement was long standing, long before the Quenton family transported her to Chalmsley. To be taken care of, they had apparently said as they passed the duty to her niece Lady Chalmsley. Watched carefully and guarded was what they had meant. Aunt Beth was a fixture at Chalmsley Court long before Bee arrived.

Edmund muttered something in her ear then excused himself to speak with John Nashe. Bee attended to Lady Osgood. Having no care for fripperies like embroidery, that lady had avoided the hostess's circle. With her husband and the Herricks and Mr. Dunham in tow, she surrounded Bee.

Bee was surprised her fiancé had pretended his devotion for as long as he had. Lord Herrick formed part of his reason to stay, but that gentleman busily enjoyed the savory pastries at which the cook Mrs. Shelton excelled. He'd filled his plate twice.

Lady Osgood currently held forth on her plans to organize a church bazaar, "prior to Valentine's Day, I think, to assist the poor of our parish, you understand." Mr. Dunham nodded agreement while Lady Herrick handed her plate to her husband.

"Will you be selling items?"

"A few, of course, to fund necessities. We will also collect household items and clothing. Not outer garments. The poor received cloaks and coats at the first Advent service. We collected those in October and November and distributed them."

"You purchased these?"

Lady Osgood primmed her mouth. "A waste of money, my dear. I have discovered that poor people do not take good care of their clothing. Our parishioners donated items they no longer needed."

"It must be difficult," Bee inserted, as tactfully as possible, "to keep in good trim any clothing that has had considerable wear."

Lady Osgood stared. "I do see your point," she admitted. "How often do you distribute clothing to those in need at your home, Lady Herrick?"

Lady Chalmsley had turned the good-will duties over to Bee on her first Christmas here, but Bee didn't not inform Lady Osgood. She let her thoughts and gaze drift away. Edmund had finished his conversation with John Nashe. He stood listening to the group gathered around Missy Wilton, a beauty who outshone even Portia.

Sometimes, when Bee looked at her fiancé, doubts confused her. Edmund was attractive. When he proposed, he had spoken of his wish to start a family. She wanted children, to love and to guide into their lives, a house to maintain, a stronger purpose for her life. He spoke good sense. After eight years with the Chalmsleys, Bee wanted someone with logical reasoning powers. She wanted her efforts to benefit her own family, not others who often undermined her.

John Nashe seemed a man like Edmund. She wished Cordelia had shown interest in Mr. Nashe rather than being swayed by Barrington Pierpont's brooding looks. Pierpont seemed self-absorbed. Mr. Nashe did not. He didn't nobble on about his wealth. He wore subdued clothing, and his sole concession to ornament was a glittering stickpin in his cravat at dinner. Cordelia needed someone kind and calm, and John Nashe certainly didn't deserve to have snippy Tina Wilton hang upon his arm.

Mrs. Nashe, as subdued as her son, didn't deserve to have Silly Wilton chatter in her ear. But Mrs. Wilton's chatter about London society was better than rehashing the events of the morning.

John Nashe hadn't committed to Tina Wilton yet. Tina's sycophantic father seemed more interested in courting Lord Chalmsley's approval. Mr. Nashe might slip away from the Wilton talons.

Edmund left John Nashe and continued on to Brougham Paton, who sat beside his fiancée Portia as she chattered to Miss Herrick. Mr. Paton looked bored. He didn't join Portia's chatter. When Edmund approached him, he rose from the sofa and stepped aside to talk quietly.

Her tea had gone cold. Bee glanced at the clock then once more around the room. She saw Cordelia pleating her skirt, the lace-ruffled hem rising higher and higher, revealing more of her yellow stockings and buttoned shoes.

"Please excuse me," she told Lady Osgood when the woman broke her spate to breathe. "I must speak with Cordelia about this evening." She crossed the room and squeezed her way onto the cushioned sofa. Looking across Cordelia, Phaedra Dunham gave Bee a quizzical look that changed when Bee placed her hand over her cousin's nervous fingers.

Cordelia gave a start. She looked down at Bee's hand on hers, then she gave a shuddering sigh and released the pleated fabric.

Behind her, Lady Pierpont nattered on about embroidery to her hostess, a safe topic that Lady Chalmsley would happily pursue for hours.

"I understand that you personally know the constable, Miss Seddars." Missy Wilton's comment startled Bee, drawing her attention back to the group she had joined. Dressed in a pretty rose satin, the young woman looked a portrait of the proper young debutante. Over Christmas, the *haut ton* in London had declared her a diamond of the first water. With Alex Westover's ring flashing on her slender finger, she had the assurance of a much-older woman.

Cordelia's hand twisted. It turned and gripped Bee's hand, returning the comfort Bee had earlier given.

Bee sent the society smile that she hated around the circle. Whenever she saw that smile reflected in one of the multitude of mirrors scattered around the Court, she could see its falseness. Lady Chalmsley had reassured her, years ago, that no one else knew it was insincere. Bee had believed Mad Aunt Beth's reassurance more than Lady Chalmsley's. Drawing on long practice at serenity, she leaned forward a little to make eye contact with Missy Wilton. "We all know Mr. Evans, Miss Wilton. He was Lord Chalmsley's ward before he went to London. His father was a friend of Lord Chalmsley."

"My sister asked if you personally know Mr. Evans?" Tina Wilton gave a society smile of her own. Hers clearly looked false.

Bee let herself frown a little. "If I personally know Mr. Evans? I am not certain what you are suggesting. Cordelia and Portia and I all know Mr. Evans. He was here at Chalmsley Court for many years, long before I came. He and George had the same tutors. I understand Cordelia and Portia played pranks on him."

Cordelia relaxed more. "Hiding pieces to his favorite jigsaw puzzle," she offered. "Putting ink blots in his copybook. Tying rocks to his kite's tail."

"Oh, foul play," John Nashe said. "Especially the ink blots. My tutor had a standard count of the cane for every inkblot in a day's lesson."

"I daresay you became a master of the pen," Wallace Osgood judged from his place at one side of the mantel. The young man aspired to the Corinthian set. He wore a collar starched so stiffly that he couldn't turn his head which prevented him from seeing himself reflected in the shine of his boots.

"He has lovely handwriting," Daphne Herrick said then blushed.

Tina Wilton seized upon the comment. "How do you know what his handwriting looks like, Daphne?"

"I believe we were asking how well Miss Seddars knows Mr. Evans," her sister countered.

Why was Missy Wilton pursuing that question?

Mad Aunt Beth's *she killed him* echoed once more. Clarity chilled Bee. Aunt Beth's words were a puzzle and also a warning that the *she* was not one of the servants. *She* had to be a guest. Which of the women here had entered William Kennington's room last night? Which one had plunged a steely weapon into his neck? Which one had a reason to hate him that much?

She'd thought too long. They were all looking at her, even Edmund, who had left his conversation with Brougham Paton and rejoined the group. "I haven't seen him or spoken to him for eight years, Miss Wilton."

"Portia mentioned that you two seemed particularly close one summer."

"That was my first summer at Chalmsley. My parents were recently deceased. I felt lost, forlorn. Hector Evans was kind enough to try to lift me out of my melancholy. But he left that October and never returned." Her heart panged at the words. Why hadn't he written? If he had lost interest, the Hector she had known would have written a few lines to tell her that, at least.

"Hector is clever," Cordelia was saying to Phaedra Dunham, answering some question that Bee hadn't heard. "He will solve this murder. Do not worry."

"Likely some disgruntled servant," Mr. Westover guessed. "Perhaps that valet of his. Have you seen the man? Fancies himself a dandy."

"It would be safe if the murderer was a servant."

Bee glanced at Cordelia. Why had she said *safe*? What did she know?

No one else seized upon her choice of *safe*. They began dissecting William Kennington's character, his multiple flirtations before he had proposed to Moira Fraser, his obvious appreciation for the bounty Lady Paton had displayed last evening at dinner with her high fashion evening gown, the debts he apparently owed at several gaming clubs, and his attempts to borrow monies from Wallace Osgood and Alex Westover.

Richardson entered and stood beside the door. His steady stare focused on Bee, not Lady Chalmsley or her daughters. Bee released Cordelia's hand.

Cordelia grabbed her hand. Then she saw the butler. She didn't relax, but she knew Bee's role at Chalmsley, to manage anything that the butler and the housekeeper could not.

Dogsbody that she was, Bee interacted with the servants and the visitors to the house and the guests of the family more than anyone else. Richardson and Mrs. Lovell brought problems with the servants to her, hoping she would intercede. Lady Chalmsley did not wish to be bothered with what she called trivial concerns, nor did she need to be bothered by such. They distressed her, and my lady needed to remain on an even keel, as Bee's sea-going father would once have said. She dealt with the vicar and his wife, other villagers, tradesmen, and anyone else who came to the Court. She saw the guests first, directing them to their rooms, tending any concerns that arose, ensuring their stay was as comfortable as in her power.

Cordelia might have wanted Bee to remain beside her, might have needed her comfort when faced with the Wilton sisters, yet she withdrew her hand and clasped her own together in her lap.

When Bee neared him, Richardson stepped out of the drawing room and into the hall. When he also shut the door so the guests would not hear, a pit opened in Bee's stomach.

"Richardson, you have a difficulty?" *Not another murder, please God, not another murder.* "Has Holyfield gotten into the wine again?"

"No, Miss Seddars, the issue is not one of our employees. Rather, it concerns Mr. Kennington's valet. Dowding is missing."

"Missing? He has left the house? Knowing that the constable wished to speak with him about his master, he has left the house?"

"He cannot be found, Miss, and his personal items appear to have gone with him."

"That is definitely missing. Did he walk to the village? Or did he ride Mr. Kennington's horse to the village?"

"I believe he is still on the grounds, close to the manor, Miss. Mr. Kennington arrived by carriage, if you remember. His horses would not be suitable for riding. I do know that a footman saw Dowding not a half-hour ago, in the quarters assigned to the guests' servants. Nor have the gardeners seen anyone walking along the drive in order to leave the estate. Only a fool would hike cross-country in this weather."

"You are granting that this Dowding is not a fool."

"That may be a mistake," he agreed, "but I believe he remains here. He was very particular about packing Mr. Kennington's effects, Miss. After that scene, I do not believe he would just leave."

"Mr. Kennington's *baggage* still remains with us?"

"It does, Miss. It will be returned with Mr. Kennington himself. I did have a thought, Miss Seddars. Dowding was known to visit the stables every afternoon. In accordance with that information, I have sent someone in the hopes that he retreated there." The butler's stiffness proclaimed his disapproval of a valet keeping lower company than house servants. "I remind you that he expressed his wish to leave as soon as possible."

"That will not occur. Dowding will accompany Mr. Kennington to his family after Mr. Evans no longer deems either of them necessary to his investigation. What Dowding chooses to do after that is not our concern."

Her comment raised the butler's eyebrows, but he nodded agreement.

The long-case clock began chiming, preparatory to striking the five o'clock hour.

Bee twice re-worded her question before she managed a toneless "Has Constable Evans reached the conservatory?"

"No, Miss Seddars. Since the hour is striking, Holyfield should arrive there momentarily."

"Then I should be there before her. If someone asks—," but she didn't complete that sentence. Someone would be Edmund Tretheway, and she didn't want Richardson to know Edmund might check up on her whereabouts—or might not.

"I will inform any person who asks of your location, Miss."

"Will you inform me when Dowding is located? You are certain he has not left?"

"I am reasonably confident, Miss. We will locate him, I assure you."

"Then I will so assure Constable Evans. Thank you, Richardson. We could not manage without you."

The long-case clock had stopped striking. Bee glanced at the clock's dial with its moon slowly rotating into the window beneath the XII. Then she hurried to the conservatory. Holyfield might slip off if she had to wait alone for the constable.

Chapter 4

The outside cold had penetrated the conservatory's glazing. Hector couldn't quite see his breath, but he didn't want to linger in the plant-filled room longer than necessary. The maid had chosen a comfortable chair in a cleared space beside a low table. Bee had taken a chair near the glass, at angles to the maid's chair. He was clearly intended to take the basket-style chair across from the maid and the low table.

Obedient to the seating, Hector slid onto the seat, expecting it to creak and surprised when it held his weight without give. As he pulled out his notebook and pencil, he eyed the chambermaid. She was yet another new servant to Chalmsley Court.

When he'd lived at Chalmsley, the staff was stable, only age or infirmity causing changes. Since he'd arrived, however, he'd counted over a dozen new faces going about their work in the house, with more new faces at the stables. The servants who had accompanied the guests would be tending to their masters' and mistresses' necessaries. They would not assume the duties that kept Chalmsley running smoothly.

He had not seen one very expected face, belonging to the giant Sampson, the man who had taught him a few basics of fighting and fishing, stalking game and skulking about. He would have to ask about the man. Sampson was the face of the Chalmsley serf, absolutely loyal to the bloodline even if he had disdain for its current title holder.

As for the older woman before him, she was certainly a new face. The chambermaid wallowed on the cushioned seat, enjoying the luxury. Raw-boned and with a decided jaw, she looked neither attractive nor ugly. He wondered where she was from and how she'd come to her employment at Chalmsley.

Sitting in the fern-filled corner, Bee looked serene, as if his half-hour tardiness hadn't fazed her. Yet when he'd entered the conservatory, she was standing before the woman, ordering her to keep her seat or lose her position. The threat had worked; the woman had sat immediately. Then she'd seen Hector. Her gaze darted around, looking for an escape, but Bee blocked the entrance to the garden and Hector blocked the door into the house. She still had a nervy look that said she'd bolt at any opportunity.

Catching his gaze, the maid straightened in her chair. Hector didn't want her scared of him. He wanted honest answers clearly given.

Hoping to melt some of her fear, he looked at his notebook and wrote *Joan Holyfield* in careful looping script.

He cleared his throat. She jerked. Keeping his gaze on his pencil, he began his interrogation. "Miss Seddars informed me that you discovered Mr. Kennington, Miss Holyfield."

She giggled. Nerves, he knew and didn't look up.

"*Miss* Holyfield," she repeated, as if the naming had shocked her.

"Holyfield, be still and pay attention," Bee ordered. "Constable Evans needs you to answer his questions, and giggling when he questions you is inappropriate."

The chambermaid scrunched in her shoulders. "Yes, Miss Seddars. I didna touch nothin', Constable."

"I believe Miss Seddars said earlier that you entered his chamber at half-past seven." His memory of Chalmsley's hours served him in his point. "Half-past seven is especially early. Why did you enter?"

"It were before sunrise, which were what time he asked to get his tea. I were to take in his tea, an' open his curtains. He got up early. That Dowding, his valet, he were to come in after an' get up 'em togged up for ridin'. Cook were gettin' him his drink ready. Somethin' with a raw egg." She shuddered.

"Tell me exactly what you did when you entered the room. Did you notice anything unusual?"

"Right off I noticed that the curtains 'round his bed hadn't been pulled shut an' the coverings were all out of sorts, an' he was just layin' there. I put his tea beside the bed, like usual. That's when I saw the blood all over the bed."

"Excuse me, Holyfield," Bee interrupted. "If the bedcurtains were pulled, how did you see the blood?"

"I had me candle, Miss Seddars. I fair near dropped it on the bed. That would have been a trouble, wouldn't it? Catchin' that bed on fire."

"When did you open the window coverings?" Hector asked.

"I did that." Bee looked contrite. "I'm afraid my candle was shaking severely. I saw that he was dead but not the nature of his injury. I wanted to be certain, so I opened the curtains for a steady light. That was foolish, of course, for the light was still too faint."

Hector noted her reason, but he thought it odd that she had wanted to examine the injury so closely. What had she expected? He glanced up briefly to see the maid wringing her hands and Bee studying the tiled floor, as if she dared not meet his eyes. He turned back to Holyfield. "After you realized Mr. Kennington was dead, what did you then do?"

"I ran to tell Miss Seddars."

"Why go to Miss Seddars?" He had Bee's explanation. He wanted the servant's.

"Miss Seddars knows what to do."

Such a simple comment, but it opened Hector's eyes anew to the role that Bee had assumed at Chalmsley. The servants turned to her when emergencies occurred, not the butler, not the housekeeper, and certainly not their master or mistress. He remembered Lady Chalmsley as chatelaine, not wholly competent but not incompetent unless she were stressed. Her ladyship should have dealt with anyone who came to the Court, from high-ranking guests to mud-scraping tradesmen. When had Lady Chalmsley ceded her responsibilities to Bee?

"So, you went to Miss Seddars," he continued. "What did she want you to do?"

"She took me with her back to Mr. Kennington's room, an' she asked me to stand outside the room an' wait while she were in there."

His gaze lifted to Bee, who met it steadily. "Was she asleep when you reached her?"

"Oh, yes. She had trouble wakin' up, trouble hearin' what I were tellin' her. She made me repeat it three times."

"I couldn't quite believe her, you understand," Bee explained.

Hector nodded. "And you returned to Mr. Kennington's chamber with Miss Seddars? What did she do in there?"

"I don't know. I didn't look. I didn't want to look."

He glanced at Bee, but she remained quiet. Just gave him a nod to let him know she would answer his questions whenever he wanted her to do so. "And then, Holyfield, what then?"

"Well, she came back into the hall an' sent me fer Mr. Richardson an' Mrs. Lovell."

This time he did direct his question to Bee. "Why did you wait to inform his lordship?"

"We had an obvious murder. I wanted competent people to protect the scene, to assure me that I was taking the correct steps to discover who committed the crime. Rumors run rapidly through the staff, Constable, and the younger servants can be excitable."

"That's true," the maid agreed. "They go off at the least little thing. Fair wear me out."

"So, Holyfield, you awakened the butler and the housekeeper."

"They was already up, just comin' on to start their day. Down in the kitchen with Cook."

"How did they react?"

"They was shocked, sir. No other word fer it. Mr. Richardson, he were sippin' his tea, an' he just froze with it in the air. Mrs. Lovell, now, she dropped her fork. They followed me back up here right quick."

"And never more glad was I than to see their faces," Bee declared.

"What did you do then, Holyfield?"

"I waited at the door, as the Miss asked me, until a footman came. Then I went on with me duties, Constable. I got jobs to do, an' I were behind with 'em. If I don't do 'em, they don't get done, an' then our guests would have fretted about. As it were, I had to get fresh tea an' all before I continued."

"Did you inform anyone else what transpired?"

"Eh?"

"Did you tell anyone else that Mr. Kennington had been murdered?"

"Oh. No, sir. Miss Seddars asked me not to. But Cook knew, 'cause she heard me tell Mr. Richardson an' Mrs. Lovell. White were in there. An' I told Becky. I'm that sorry, Miss Seddars. She were the first person I saw after I left ya, an' it just came pourin' out."

"Do not fret, Holyfield." She turned to Hector. "Becky Clarkson is a first-floor chambermaid, and Johnnie White is the youngest footman."

Those names were new to him, not from his previous years at Chalmsley. More new people on the estate, when the long-time servants and tenants should have had children entering employment as the older ones become pensioners. That was a question to pursue when he didn't have a murder to solve. "You told no one else?"

"No, sir," Holyfield swore.

Once more, Bee clarified for the maid. "I doubt anyone else would be about at that hour. I pressed White to help Holyfield and Clarkson with the morning rounds. That usually begins about eight o'clock. The servants who came with their masters and mistresses are to take their breakfast trays to them unless they have expressed their wish to break fast in the morning room."

"As today has progressed, Holyfield, did you hear anything from other servants or overhear anything?"

"Only gossip, sir." When he queried for more, the maid settled into her cushion. "One said that Mr. Kennington were cheatin' with another lady while he were engaged to Miss Fraser."

"Which lady?"

"Now that I dunno, sir," but she looked at Bee as she denied any knowledge, and Hector saw Bee nodding approval. Had she coached the woman?

He glanced through his notes. "Do you have anything more to tell me?" When she shook her head in a decided no, he dismissed her. Hector stood when Bee did. "A moment more, Miss Seddars."

The chambermaid glanced back. Bee gestured for her to continue on, then she turned to Hector. "Shall I take the interrogation seat?"

"No, you can return to your seat." He dragged an iron chair around to face hers. After he sat, the cold penetrated his heavy wool tweed, just punishment, he reckoned, for suspecting Bee of withholding information or skewing his perception of the evidence. "When did you take on the role of chatelaine for Lady Chalmsley?"

Her deep blue eyes widened at the surprising question. "Two years after you left. I was sixteen. She couldn't cope with the preparations for the dinner for the local district, the one they hold every August, you remember? I had already assumed quite a number of the responsibilities she wouldn't pick up. Gradually, I took on more and more until—." She spread her hands. "She plans, and I give her the help she needs."

"A bit more than the usual help, I think."

One shoulder lifted then fell. "I give her the help she needs," Bee repeated, obviously not comfortable with saying more.

"Holyfield had trouble waking you."

"I stayed up late. I had a letter to write, and I reviewed my notes for the next days."

Letters. After she hadn't written to him. "Who were you writing?"

"My father's solicitor."

"You have financial difficulties?"

"No. He had written with questions about my—my upcoming marriage to Edmund Tretheway. My marriage will not substantially change my inheritance, only the management of it. I wish Mr. Cosgrove to remain in control, as my father's will stipulated. Edmund will only replace my great-uncle as a trustee. Mr. Cosgrove had questions about my request."

"You do not wish Mr. Tretheway to manage the remainder of your inheritance?"

"It's not that. It's—Mr. Cosgrove has been extremely conservative in his investments with my funds. He has grown the original inheritance. I would not be classified an heiress, not by any means, but it is an easy competency that I would like to retain."

Did she have doubts about Tretheway? Then why had she accepted his proposal? Unless Lord Chalmsley had driven the engagement to remove her from his household. Why would he want Bee removed from Chalmsley Court?

He wasn't here to pursue that point either. He didn't have this trouble tracking his investigations in London. *I know too much about Chalmsley Court. I know background, connections, personalities. In London I know only what I can see. I can focus on the crime, not side issues that likely have nothing to do with the crime.* Tucking away his notebook and pencil, he shifted on the cold iron and leaned back, trying to look at his ease, wanting to put Bee at hers. At some point she had become guarded with him. He didn't want that.

"I find it interesting," he said calmly, "that you wanted to see the injury closely."

Lips twisting, she glanced down. Her hands wrung together. Here, revealed only to him, was the reaction he had expected earlier. Did she exhibit it to him because she trusted him or because she wanted to manipulate his observations? She had seen Kennington sprawled bloody and naked on his bed. When Hector viewed the body, shrouded and on a cold bier in the chapel, he'd expected murder. She hadn't expected it. Why hadn't she swooned? Why hadn't she shown even a little discomfiture before now?

"I thought he committed suicide." Those deep blue eyes lifted to capture his. "Stupid of me, wasn't it, to think suicide? Murder is a greater fear, and I didn't—well, I just didn't expect it. Holyfield came blurting *blood* and *dead*, and I wanted it to be suicide. I was expecting slit wrists, not blood all over his neck and chest. There was all that blood, and the smell—."

The more she talked, the more her descriptions fit with what he had expected from her earlier. Hector relaxed a little.

"He had a puncture in his neck. You saw it, I'm sure. I cannot understand what would make it. I couldn't find what would make it."

"You looked for the weapon?"

She nodded. "I couldn't find it. I looked under the bed, everywhere close to him. Could he have stabbed himself in the neck then flung it away from him, away from the bed?"

"No," he said, as coldly as he felt. "That's what you were doing, looking for a weapon?"

She nodded. Her shoulders sagged as she gave up her hope that his death was suicide, not murder. "What could make such a wound?" she whispered.

"I won't know until I find it."

"You're looking for a specific weapon, aren't you? Some kind of dagger."

The conversation strayed too close into how he investigated a crime. He needed her on a different track. "Why did you delay informing his lordship?"

"I told you. I wanted competent people in place to preserve the scene. Great-Uncle Hamilton, he can be quite cantankerous when awakened early."

"That was early? You were reaching half-past eight, surely. I remember his lordship rising at dawn to be out on the fields hunting."

"He had a riding accident, you know."

"No, I didn't. When did this occur?"

"Two years ago. The girth strap on his saddle broke. Luckily, it happened when the horse was still cantering, not at a full gallop or when he was jumping. Great-Uncle Hamilton suffered a broken arm and collarbone. We think he was knocked unconscious briefly, but he would not admit that. He limped home on his own and met the searchers on their way to find him. His horse had run back to the stables."

"On the side of angels, then."

She winced. "Yes, that's one way of saying it."

"What happened to the groom who didn't notice the girth strap had worn out?"

"It wasn't worn out; it broke. Nothing happened to the groom. He retained his position."

"One of the few who are still here," he muttered. Was Bee, the de facto chatelaine, responsible for the change-over in the servants?

"What?" Startled, her formality dropped. "What do you mean, Hector?"

Before he answered, a throat was loudly cleared behind him. Hector twisted in his seat and saw the butler standing at the doorway.

"Miss Seddars, we have found him. Where I expected."

"Excellent. Will he remain there?"

"Coggins is keeping him there, Miss. I have had your cloak and gloves brought."

"Thank you, Richardson. We should go," she said to Hector. "Dowding has gone missing once. I would not want him to escape your interrogation a second time."

"Dowding is Kennington's valet? He went missing?"

"Yes. At least, he left the house without informing Richardson, even though he knew that you—or whichever constable came—would have questions for him. Richardson thought he might be at the stable, and as you have just heard, he is."

"And you're going with me?"

She looked startled. "Well, yes. I know you know the way to the stable, but I thought—we could talk—if you wish me to remain here at the house—."

"I would like you to accompany me."

Her consternation cleared, and he realized his answer meant more to her than he would have expected. *She is engaged,* he reminded himself, *to a man she doesn't quite trust with her money. Did she not want to marry him?*

"Your outerwear is at the back hall, Miss Seddars."

"Thank you, Richardson," and Hector noticed her color had heightened, either from her earlier disquiet or from the butler witnessing it.

Chapter 5

The clouds had that heavy cast of imminent snow. The wind bit sharply. Bee tucked her face into the knitted shawl draped around her cloaked shoulders. The shawl looked as blue as her eyes, a deep yet clear blue, not sapphire, not naval blue. Hector had never been able to pin the color. He thought of all he wanted to ask her and all he shouldn't ask her.

I have a job. She is engaged to Edmund Tretheway. Reminding himself didn't help.

He kicked himself to focus on his investigation. "Tell me about Holyfield."

Her face lifted. "Holyfield? What do you want to know about her?"

"I don't remember her being at Chalmsley before I left."

"She wasn't. She's new—well, she came about two years ago. She replaced—we hired her to replace a chambermaid who left abruptly."

"Servants don't usually move from family to family, not maids, not outside of London. How did she come to Chalmsley Court?"

"Oh. Her previous employers turned her off. Holyfield drinks. As long as we keep her away from any alcohol, she's reliable."

"Who were her previous employers?"

"I do not clearly remember. I have the letters she supplied as references in my files as well as their return correspondence from my queries to them. Do you wish to read them? You don't think Holyfield killed Mr. Kennington, do you?"

"I would like to read those letters. How many are there?"

"Four. Holyfield unfortunately likes gin. Richardson has learned to keep the liquor locked up. He actually keeps that habit without Holyfield creating the necessity, but he is doubly certain to do so now. Nor does he decant more than what will be served or used by Great-Uncle Hamilton or anyone else after dinner. Mrs. Lovell also keeps Holyfield to work on the upper floors where she's less likely to encounter alcohol."

"Has she had lapses here?"

"Two, but only before we learned to manage her work. Nothing in the last year. She does visit the pub on Saturday evenings, but we give her Sunday off. I believe she spends her Sundays in her bed, moaning about her head aching. Or so Becky Clarkson tells me."

Snowflakes sped past as they reached the stable. The head groom, a wiry man clothed in a red tartan, came out to greet them. "Yer here about that valet that's gone missin'."

Finally, a face that Hector recognized. "We are, Coggins. Do you remember me, Hector Evans? I left eight years ago for London."

"I 'member ye. Didn't expect ye to be gone so long." He jerked his chin up, as if pointing at the house. "Chalmsley needed a man with yer sense, specially the last few years. Mebbe ye can talk some sense into this here valet." He'd led them into the stable, redolent with horse and straw, and through to the tack room where the grooms kept warm beside a little iron stove, its pipe venting through the wall.

And there sat the valet Dowding. He looked dapper in a camel flannel jacket and quilted blue weskit, with pressed handkerchief and artfully arranged blue ascot. The grooms around him wore dun-colored coats and flannel shirts with greyed plaids. His polished town shoes shone beside their scuffed workboots.

"I'm not going back," he declared as soon as he saw Hector. "You can't make me go back to that house. There's been murder done there. It's not safe."

Hector came up to the circle around the stove, more men than he expected until he realized the guests' coachmen and post-boys would wait at the stable until they were needed. Bee hung back, he checked, within the room but only a few steps. She stood against the wall rather than standing in the passage and in the draft from the wind squeezing into the room.

He nodded around the circle, noting more new faces among these men. He gave extra nods to the weathered men that he recognized. *Just how many new grooms did Chalmsley now employ?* he wondered.

Half of the men ignored him. They were looking at Bee, still swaddled to her ears in the cloak and shawl, and clearly wondering what reason had brought her to the stables.

"Do you know who I am?" and he reckoned that was as good a beginning as any. All eyes came back to him, then most of them turned on the valet, who folded his arms and jutted his narrow chin.

An older groom spat onto the straw. "Yer Constable Evans. Used to be here."

"You're Hicks, aren't you?" When the man nodded, Hector said, "I spent almost ten years here at Chalmsley."

"Almost ten years away," Hicks retorted.

Coggins came up beside him. "He's been in Lunnon, working with the Runners."

"Then he'll know 'bout murder." An unknown groom gave a decided nod. "They's got a murder on the street ev'ry day and night up in Lunnon. Sometimes more. There's evil crimes done up in Lunnon."

"It true what he said?" Another older groom, with an accent slightly different from Coggins, spoke up: Another of the guest's coachmen, Hector thought. The man jerked a thumb at the valet. "Murder up at the manor? His master?"

"Mr. Kennington, Dowding's employer, was killed last night. Lord Chalmsley sent for me to solve the murder."

"It's luck you'll need," the third man said. "He's saying his master's throat got slit open."

That piece of evidence had likely made the rounds four or five times since morning, with a couple of those rounds increasing the size of the wound, the number of wounds, and the amount of blood. Hector had more reasons to correct the rumor than to hide the truth. "His throat was not slit open. A narrow-bladed knife was thrust into his throat, deep enough to sever the major veins and kill him."

"I'm not going back to that house," Dowding vowed. "You can't make me. I'll be killed next. I know I will."

"I don't need you at the house," Hector said, surprising the man. "You can stay here, if Coggins sees no difficulties with it." He glanced at the head groom as he gave the offer. Coggins's mouth twisted, but he nodded agreement. "But, Dowding, I do need you to remain here at Chalmsley until I have found the murderer."

"I didn't kill him!"

"I don't believe you did." He knew better than to pull out his notebook before this group of men, most of them unlettered. They depended on their memories. To keep their trust, he also needed to resort to his memory. "Whoever visited him during the night killed him."

Several of the grooms elbowed those beside them, and several affirming nods revealed what the conversation had covered between the arrival of the valet and Hector.

He decided to avoid the usual question of who came to Kennington's door. "Can you tell me the reason that you believe you would be killed next if you were at the house?"

"I'm his valet. I might have seen her go to his room. Or leave it. Won't matter that I didn't see her. What matters is that she'll think I might have. She'll come for me next. I'm not staying and taking the risk."

"You think the murderer was a woman?" He considered options. A vindictive woman. Or a desperate one, which made her just as dangerous.

The man looked sly. "Master Kennington wouldn't be letting a man into his room that late at night. He usually went off to see the women, but not here. And not every night. That was another difference. Here, she came to him."

He was getting snippets, but he didn't know which were important and which he should let fall. *She* meant one woman. Someone who didn't come every night. Someone who wasn't watched every night, just some nights. How did he ask that question of the ladies of the house? "Do you have an idea with which woman he was having an *affaire*?"

"No idea. He wanted me gone long before she were expected. I wasn't to return until sunrise. He was very specific. I only knew that she'd been with him from the bedsheets in the morning. I do know that it weren't that Scottish girl."

Hector interpreted *from the bedsheets* as Kennington's seed spilled on the bed. So, the man hadn't wanted to risk the woman becoming pregnant. That helped him very little: Both married and unmarried women would not want an unexplained pregnancy, although a married woman had a better chance of hiding the unintended result of an *affaire*. "How do you know that the woman wasn't—" he hesitated, gave a look around the circle and spotted a white-whiskered man scowling harder than the others. He decided not to name any of the ladies. "that the woman wasn't his fiancée?"

"He complained that his fiancée was a virgin who had vowed to keep herself pure till the wedding. He weren't helped by her chamber being side by side with her parents and on the other wing. That did irk him when we arrived, then he said 'twas to his advantage."

"Then which woman came to his room? One of the married ladies? One of the other young ladies?"

Bee coughed, drawing eyes, and the men shifted uncomfortably as they connected her with the questions being asked. When she saw the battery of eyes, she murmured something and left the room. Hector wanted to follow her, to tell her to keep inside the stable, but he didn't want to leave his interrogation. Coggins went, though, and he hoped the man had sense enough to keep her indoors, even if it was just in the aisle of horse stalls.

He turned back to Dowding. "Do you have any idea which lady came to his room?"

Dowding leaned back. An odd smirk played on his mouth. "For all I know, it was a different woman each time. Mr. Kennington liked the ladies, and they liked him."

A younger groom snorted. "And the last one on his string killed him."

"That's why I won't come back to the house. I don't know which one it was. I don't care. When you tell me I can take his body back to Kennington Close, I'll go and gladly. Till then, I'm here." And his weak chin jutted out again.

"Would Mr. Kennington have had letters? Did he keep a journal?"

Dowding shook his head with an exaggerated swing. "He never put anything like that to paper. Said it was asking for trouble."

"You packed his belongings. Did you notice if anything was missing?"

"Not a thing. Everything was there. Clothing, smalls, rings, tie pins, wrappings, shaving gear, salves and balms, journal—."

"You said he never wrote anything down. What did he write in a journal?"

"Dates. Initials. That's all."

"Do you have his journal?"

"It's packed amongst the rest of his belongings."

Dates and initials. Dates of encounters and the initials of the ladies? Could it be so easy? "Dowding, I want to see that journal."

"I'm not coming back to pull it out. You'll have to do it. It's in the small trunk, at the bottom."

He nodded. That would be his first task as soon as he returned to the house. "Two last questions, for now. I may have more later, Dowding, after I've read Mr. Kennington's journal. How did you discover the manner in which Mr. Kennington had been killed?"

"Saw the blood spilled all over the mattress, didn't I? All of it up there around his head. And I heard that maid talking. What's her name? Holly—Holyfield. She said the blood was all over his neck. Nothing could do that but a knife."

"Do you have an idea how a woman could overpower a man and stick a knife in his throat?"

"She'd have to make him feel safe, wouldn't she? And get him all relaxed. A bit of wine, a bit of—exercise, and Mr. Kennington would have been plenty relaxed."

Yes, that was Hector's own view of the crime. Not a fight between Kennington and his murderer, when a woman had little chance to overpower a man. Kennington had suspected nothing. Slipping into sleep, he would be easy prey. The only thing that would have restrained the woman would be her moral compass. That, obviously, she had lacked. "Thank you." He nodded around the circle again. "I suppose I've given you fodder for more hours of speculation."

"That ye have," Hicks said, "and we're eager to get to it. Beggin' yer pardon, sir, but come back tomorrow. We might have it solved for ye."

"I wish," he retorted.

.~.~.~.

Coggins waited with her. Silent as usual, the head groom had crossed his arms over his chest and stared down the long aisleway.

Cold air swept in through the open upper-half of the doors. She shivered. The head groom acted as if the cold wouldn't affect him even if icicles dripped from his pointed chin.

Bootsteps heralded Hector's appearance. Bee refused to turn toward him, not wishing to seem eager for his company. Coggins turned, but he wasn't fighting a revived attraction that threatened to overwhelm good sense.

"Ye get the information ye needed from Dowding?"

"I did. More than I expected. See that he remains here, Coggins. I may have more questions for him later."

"He'll be going home when his master does. No stopping him."

"Yes, but Lord Chalmsley will not release Kennington's body until I give the word. That should not be too much longer." He touched Bee's cloaked arm. "Shall we return to the house?"

They walked back through the deepening twilight, guided by the golden lights of the manor house. Neither Hector nor Bee spoke. She didn't know what to ask him. His questions had strayed in directions that no decent woman would inquire about. She had already disconcerted him by not swooning at Kennington's dead body. If she asked questions about the unknown woman involved in a salacious *affaire* with Kennington—Hector would be even more unsettled. So she tucked her face into her shawl and walked quickly, as if driven by the cold.

In the back hall, Mad Aunt Beth loomed out of the shadowy corridor. " 'O where ha'e ye been?'" she sang the old ballad. "'O where ha'e ye been, my handsome young man?' And pretty young lady," she added, fitting the words to the rhythm. "No poison for the two of you, though. No poison in the dish. No poison in the cup. Watch for poison in the cup. Did you go to the wild wood?"

"Only to the stables." Bee disentangled from the cloak and handed it to the waiting maid. "Aunt Beth, do you remember Hector Evans?"

"No blood on his sword, no curse on your fair head, little Bee," she said obscurely. "I saw him ride in. Carrion crow, out of the oaks, come to catch a murderer. Said I, didn't I? Constable Evans. Stepping stone then a bell then in Hell."

"Aunt Beth, what are you talking about?"

The woman flitted back into the shadows. Her singsong drifted back to them.

"'The Maid and the Palmer'," Hector said.

Bee gave him a scowl. "You are as confusing as she is. What are you talking about?"

"An old ballad. A maid who claims to have never had a lover but has buried six babies in the woods. The palmer sentences her to seven years as a stepping-stone, seven years as a bell clapper, and then seven years in Hell." Then he frowned. "I would say Aunt Beth is as mad as she ever was, only there's a crazy sort of sense to her words."

"Aunt Beth is only mildly deranged. I know 'Lord Randall', but I have never heard this 'Maid and Palmer' ballad. How do you know it?"

"I heard it in the pubs in London."

"Oh, London."

His frown vanished, and he gave an impish smile. "Yes, London. A den of iniquity, some of those grooms must think."

"As much as a den of iniquity as William Kennington's chamber must have been. Hector, what more did—?"

"There you are." Portia trotted along the passage from the entrance hall. "I've looked and looked. Papa insists that you join us for dinner." She tucked her hand in Hector's arm and looked up with a winning smile. "Papa's valet unpacked for you and gathered up what would be suitable for dinner. You are to confer with Correyton now. Should anything be lacking, he will have sufficient time to provide it." She tugged on his arm. "Now, Hector. Papa says."

His frown had returned. "Lord Chalmsley must be obeyed. I had hoped to speak with Miss Fraser and her parents before dinner."

Bee found herself trying to resolve the difficulty. "Would a half-hour be sufficient time for your interview? I will have them in the library by seven o'clock. We don't gather for dinner until half-past seven." At his quizzical look, she added, "London hours. We've become quite stylish."

"Would you do that, Bee? Thank you."

She watched him walked away with Portia.

Quite stylish, she castigated herself. *How inane can I be?*

Lord Chalmsley had clearly stated that she was best suited to apprise Hector of the guests and their connections to the family and each other. That order fell in with her own desire to help him. She had a faint hope that she might discover the reason he hadn't written. She had an even fainter hope that their attraction might be renewed.

That was a foolish hope. She was engaged to Edmund. They were to marry in June. Or July. After Cordelia and Portia married. Maybe she could delay the ceremony to August. Or later.

She only deceived herself in hoping Hector's love would be rekindled.

She dashed the tears from her eyes and went to locate Lord Fraser or his wife or even Moira, closeted in her chamber since this morning.

Then she would seek out Aunt Beth and get her to sing "The Maid and the Palmer". A mad song from a mad woman for a mad situation.

Chapter 6

Hector tugged at the starched collar that Correyton had forced upon him. Conversation flowed around him at the dining table. He had expected to be quizzed throughout the meal, but they were apparently keeping him for after-dinner entertainment.

He'd taken William Kennington's position at the table. With Moira Fraser keeping to her bedchamber, the numbers at table were off. Even with her chair opposite removed and the chairs on that side opened up a little, the board felt uneven. Lady Chalmsley had apologized twice. If Hector waited another ten minutes, he would hear her apologize again.

His feeling of intruding was only heightened when the young Miss Herrick, seated to his right, ignored him.

When the course changed, Mrs. Nashe on his left leaned closer. "Do not fash yourself about any of these young ladies, Constable Evans," she whispered. "They all have their eyes elsewhere. Except Miss Cordelia Seddars. She's arranging her silverware again. Poor girl. Now, where are you usually based? Not Chalmsley Village, I think."

As Hector answered, he tried to look at Cordelia without her noticing. She was aligning the forks on one side of her plate. She placed her hand in her lap, stared at the forks, then once again straightened them. He remembered her compulsions—her dolls in perfect rows, her dress ribbons of equal length, her penmanship with careful slant and loops. Successive governesses had to stop her from over-sharpening her pencils or checking the latch on the nursery door again and again.

If Bee called Mad Aunt Beth mildly deranged, what would she call Cordelia with her compulsive need for order?

The next course came. Miss Herrick ignored him.

He looked down table, toward Lady Chalmsley, then up table toward her husband. The entire assemblage wore silk and jewels, fine worsted and glittering gold. The men wore subdued dark colors. The women wore an array of peacock colors and debutante white. They all looked the same, acted the same, talked the same.

Even if his coat were superfine, his shirt of silk, with a diamond tie pin, he wouldn't fit in this company. He never had, not even before Lord Chalmsley freighted him off to London.

The clothing was only part of it, although the valet Correyton had tried. From his put-upon air as he reviewed Hector's attire, he had clearly felt called to a duty beneath him. He had deemed Hector's best collar too dingy for dinner. The valet had sniffed at his dark coat and knee breeches but found them passable. His shirt needed ironing, his shoes needed polishing. Correyton had born them off with an injunction to Hector not to leave his bedchamber until he returned.

He had grinned at the valet's belief that he could order Hector about. Kennington's journal had preyed on his mind the long minutes that he had dealt with Correyton. When the valet left, Hector had nipped down to Kennington's bedchamber.

The small trunk had not held Kennington's journal.

With only a single glance, Hector knew that someone had searched the room. Lord Chalmsley had asked that the room be kept locked, which had fit with Hector's own plans. After he finished his examination, he had locked it and rattled the doorknob to check it. He had kept the key in his watch-pocket. Then, while he was interviewing Holyfield and Dowding, someone had unlocked the door, searched the room, then re-locked it before they slipped away.

The search wasn't obvious, but Hector had a particular way of leaving drawers and small items on the dressing chest. And nothing was missing—except the journal that Dowding had piqued his interest with.

He had heard Correyton returning and hurried back to his own chamber where he cowed under the valet's censure for not obeying a simple request.

Mrs. Nashe had more questions for him when the course changed and allowed their conversation to resume. "I understand you were with the Bow Street Runners in London. That must have been exciting work." Her dark eyes fairly snapped with curiosity.

He answered those questions without having to consider his words, and he let his mind train over the ineffective interview with the Frasers.

A half-hour with the Frasers had given him no clues to the murder. Miss Fraser had had little to say. Her shock evident, she sat mute even when he directed questions to her. She had answered only at her mother's prompting.

Her parents had had little to tell him about their future son-in-law. William Kennington, of good family and good reputation, had had wealth to offset his lack of a title. Miss Fraser was their fourth daughter, and she had attracted Kennington's interest almost as soon as she arrived in London in the late autumn. They had good reports of him from their various connections in town, and he had acted the gentleman with their daughter. Their solicitor's quiet inquiries raised no concerns. When he proposed on Christmas Day, Moira had accepted him with alacrity.

And how did they know Lord and Lady Chalmsley? Their daughter knew Cordelia and Portia. They had attended the same parties in London over Christmas. When the Chalmsleys extended their invitation, they and Mr. Kennington had accepted.

Then they wanted to know when they could leave.

Hector could see no reason to suspect them of murdering Kennington, but he asked them to remain a few days longer.

He expected more requests to leave from the other guests, and he must deny them all, from Dowding to the Frasers to the exalted Westovers.

Back to his non-conversation with Miss Herrick, he watched the others at table. Dowding's comments had him studying each woman. Which one had involved herself with Kennington?

Hector could not see Kennington with the older ladies. Mrs. Nashe must be fifty. Lady Westover and Lady Osgood must be nearly that age. Mrs. Wilton—no. The man would never have a chance to kiss her, she talked so much. And surely he would have considered his future mother-in-law as beyond bounds.

Now Lady Paton, she was a decided option. A former beauty clinging to that past and dressed to draw men's eyes. Would she hate a man enough to kill him? Or would she just move to the next young man who wanted a conquest?

Lady Pierpont—no, he thought, watching her struggle through her conversation with Lord Osgood. She was attractive enough, but she had a sweetness that couldn't be faked. Hector could recognize sticky treacle. Lady Pierpont looked to be sweet and wholesome honey.

That left him with the younger ladies. Younger, less certain of themselves, less certain of the men they had attracted as their fiancés, and if not yet affianced, much less certain of capturing the lone men remaining.

Cordelia. She loved her neat little world. Would she have a messy *affaire* with Kennington? Would she stab the man and spill that much blood?

Portia. She welcomed everyone. She talked easily with everyone. The little girl he remembered had charmed her father and her governesses into getting what she wanted. But her tantrums were legendary. Loud, with thrown hat and stomped feet, but soon over. Her traps could be painful, but she always pled that she hadn't wanted anyone to be hurt. The young lady wouldn't have altered that pattern, would she? Had she charmed Kennington but lost him? *He was mine, you know*, she had said to Hector. Had she tried to win him back? Had her tantrums turned into murderous violence?

Bee?

She picked at her plate as she listened to the younger Mr. Wilton.

He didn't want to consider Bee as a murderess.

He'd known her only a little while, less than half a year. Long enough to fall in love. He didn't remember any quick, unreasonable anger, and if a young lady had a right to anger, she had. Ripped from the only home she knew, orphaned by a violent storm, thrust into a place she didn't know with cold people who refused to welcome her, she could have screamed until the rafters shook, and Hector would have understood. He'd come to Chalmsley Court in much the same circumstance. Yet Bee had controlled her anger and depression. She'd kept her spirits high.

After eight years of restraining her emotions, would she turn to murder? Would she involve herself with a stranger? Would she pick William Kennington for an *affaire* because she had agreed to a marriage that she discovered she didn't want?

Missy Wilton he dismissed. With the world at her feet, she wouldn't risk her future. That young lady was too practical.

But her sister: Christina Wilton's bitter streak ran deep. Would she involve herself with Kennington? Thinking that she could snare him for a husband? When he refused, had she killed him?

Daphne Herrick was a puzzle. She seemed friendly to everyone but him. Why? Did she fear him? Or did she just think him too base for her attention? She had not yet snared a fiancé. He thought she had her eyes on Clarence Wilton—although Wallace Osgood was not yet betrothed to Phaedra Dunham, another young lady who wouldn't look him in the eye. Afraid? Or only arrogant?

And Moira Fraser. Hector really shouldn't let her slip through his tightening circle of suspects. Had she discovered Kennington having *affaires* and decided to punish him as well as free herself from him?

Seven suspects. Eight, when he added Lady Paton. Nine, if he added sweet Lady Pierpont.

No man here would suspect any woman.

Sir Richard Ford had warned Hector, early in his training, that quiet people had hidden depths of evil.

Yes. Nine suspects.

And his list presupposed that a man hadn't silenced Kennington by killing him.

. ~ . ~ . ~ .

Bee shivered in the chill attic but dug deeper in the trunk. She hadn't seen her journal for eight years, but she clearly remembered shoving it to the bottom of her parents' trunk.

The first pages were childish outpourings. She had written rarely until her parents' deaths. Then the journal accepted her selfish cries of loss and abandonment, the torrents of true grief, and gradually, her first summer at Chalmsley Court and her growing feelings for Hector.

The latter pages she had filled with her misery when he left for London, her confusion when he didn't write, her anger at his obvious rejection, and—.

There. She felt the hard edges of a book, curled her fingers around it, and pulled it from the bottom of the trunk.

The chancy light danced over the leather-bound journal. Embossed on the front was a rose. The reddish stain that had tinted the rose had faded over time. Long before she hid away the journal, the rose-red had dwindled to a fainter color. The dye had disappeared entirely in the last eight years.

Bee backed up to a rickety chair stowed away many years ago and opened the journal.

Her round, school-room handwriting met her eyes. She skipped several pages, reached the erratic writing of the first days of her loss. She had barely filled a full page in those days. Loss had snatched away her whole world, not just her parents but her home, her friends, even her servants. The solicitor handled her parents' finances, the vicar handled the funeral without bodies to bury, the vicar's wife kept Bee moving from one day to the next.

She skimmed the pages, reading snatches of her refusal to believe her parents were gone, her anger at losing them and losing her easy world and losing her home. Her utter sadness. One day she had listed all the changes. The house and its furniture to be leased. Her father's writings to be sent to his old university for someone, someday, to review and revise and publish. Her mother's jewelry to be kept safely by the solicitor until her twenty-sixth birthday. The better silver and china and paintings to be stored, watched over by the solicitor. Herself to be packed and bundled off to her great-uncle, Lord Chalmsley.

Just listing the paintings she had loved had taken three pages of the journal.

Flickering candlelight jumped over the dates at the top of the journal's pages. From the night before she left her parents' home to the next night that she recorded a day's event, almost a week had skipped past. Her young self, so changed already, evidenced by a blocky script, wrote that she had arrived at Chalmsley Court, she had met her cousins, a maid had unpacked her trunks which were to be stored in the attic, and she sat in a little blue room, with night fallen and her hopes all fallen.

Then, the first day after her parents' death that she had laughed. Her mute questions of her journal: *How can I? Why had I? Will I ever again?* Hector entered her journal on that day.

Bee knew time passed, knew the hours crept deeper into the night, but she continued to read. Confused days, brighter days, happier days. The day Hector dragged her from the pond when she'd tried to save drowning kittens and nearly drowned herself. The day she laughed and felt no guilt after. The days of adventures in the summer sunshine and summer rains. The day she realized how highly she esteemed Hector. The day she announced to her journal that she loved him.

She found that page. Three stark words. *I love him.* She'd drawn a wedding bouquet underneath and ribbons around the margins.

More idyllic days.

Then a page with shaky handwriting. Lord Chalmsley had announced that Hector would journey to London. He would not return. She wrote of his promise to send her a letter a week. "Four years," he had claimed, "only four years." He'd made no promises, but those words had carried a wealth of meaning for a fourteen-year-old girl.

He left. By late October, she wrote of her bewilderment when no letters arrived for her. Then her sadness. Then her dejection. Hector didn't respond to her letters, written in care of Sir Richard Ford of Bow Street.

Heart sinking, Bee remembered the next page. Slowly she turned the page, the aged paper stiffly crackling. Great splotches where her tears had fallen had washed out the ink. *12 November 1805.* Eight years ago. She vowed not to cry for him. She resolved to forget his plans, to set plans for her own future in motion. The solicitor kept a close accounting of her invested monies. At twenty-six, she would have a tidy independence. Great-Uncle Hamilton talked of giving her a dowry when she married, but at heart-broken fourteen, Bee had vowed never to marry. And she also vowed to give up her journal. She had brought it up to the attic and shoved it deep into her parents' trunk.

She hadn't looked at it since the day she wholly gave up that blissful summer.

She studied that ink-washed page. *I didn't forget my vow. I want a family. I don't want to go to my grave alone, bitter because I isolated myself from life. I want to have a life and children and my own home. Edmund Tretheway offered that life.*

Even if she wanted a different man to give her that life.

Bee snapped the journal shut. The candle's flame danced about as she stared at the rose-embossed cover. Then she shuddered, stood, and walked to the trunk. Back the journal went to the very bottom. She tugged the cloth above it back into place then gradually added the other items she stored in the trunk. Treasured remnants from her old life, last letters from her parents, little mementos given over the years that she couldn't part with, not yet, although they served no purpose except as unhappy reminders.

Last of all, she refolded the white gown that she'd worn on her eighteenth birthday. She had held a fugitive hope on that day. After all, he'd said, "Four years." She folded the silk with the wine stain uppermost, tugged the torn hem so it clearly showed, then she closed the trunk and climbed to her knees.

Her hours in the attic had chilled her. Drawing close her wool cloak, she picked up the candle, burned nearly to the socket. She protected the wavering flame as she crept on slippered feet down the stairs.

The third floor was quiet. The old nursery wing no longer housed children, only Mad Aunt Beth and her nurse, and the servants had too early of a start to their day to linger before sleep.

On the flight to the second floor Bee smelled smoke. She stopped, sniffed, descended more steps, sniffed again. The smoke was stronger.

Guarding the candle-flame, she peered up and down the second-floor corridor.

Halfway to her room, light flickered on the carpet runner. It streamed from beneath a shut door.

A chill lifted the hairs on Bee's nape.

Cloak billowing behind her, Bee ran down the hall. A slipper flew off. She stopped only to kick off the other, then hastened bare foot to the flickering light. She stopped and watched the light flicker over her toes. Then she stared at the door.

William Kennington's door.

Memory of the last time she'd entered the room filled her.

The candle guttered. Bee inhaled. *You won't need a light in the room*, she chided herself. Setting the candle on a hall table, she reached again for the doorknob. Her hand shook, but she grasped the knob and turned it. For a second although it felt much longer, the room's brighter light blinded her. She blinked, and then she saw.

Flames leaped in the center of the bed.

Chapter 7

"Help," she cried along the hall. Then Bee rushed for the pitcher on the washstand near the window.

Empty. She swore and dashed back to the hall.

"Fire!" she cried this time. She banged on the chamber door opposite Kennington's then ran to the next chamber, then a third, using both fists to wake the occupants, calling "Fire!" as loudly as she could.

The first door opened. Bee pushed past the man in his nightshirt and grabbed his pitcher. "We need more water," she gasped as she raced into the hall. "Lots of water. Fire!"

He followed her.

She flung the water on the mattress. Papers flew away. The water dashed out half the fire, but flames still licked over the bed linens.

The bed curtains beside her were yanked down. She saw the man— Mr. Wilton, she thought, yanking at more of the bed curtains. Bee ran for more water.

Standing in her chamber door, Mrs. Wilton dragged at her wrapper. "Is it out?"

She ran to the next opened chamber door. "Water," she gasped to the man standing there.

The woman behind him shoved a pitcher into her hands, and Bee ran back to the fire.

Mr. Wilton used the curtains to beat at the fire engulfing the mattress.

A man pushed past her. He grabbed more curtains and started beating the fire from his side. The papers on the floor still burned. Bee grabbed another curtain and flung it over the papers before the little flames caught the carpet. She stamped the material then lifted it away. The papers were partially burnt but were out.

She dashed for more water, but a man passed her carrying his pitcher. Then another man with another pitcher. Heart in throat, she stood back as he passed and watched the men fight the flames.

It seemed to take forever, but it must have been only a few minutes. Light diminished then became a streaming shaft from the corridor. The men stood back from the bed. "Fire's out," one of them said. She thought that was Mr. Nashe.

Her heart still thumped madly. "Thank you." The smoke clogged her throat. She coughed, coughed again, couldn't stop coughing.

"Here," one of the men said. "You shouldn't be in here." He took her arm and propelled her back to the corridor, lit now by other candles besides her own. Mr. Dunham, she identified.

People packed the corridor. The clearer air gradually filled her lungs. When Bee's eyes stopped watering from her coughing fit, she looked around and gradually identified those standing near.

Including Richardson, a plaid robe wrapped around his girth, boots hiding his big feet.

"Richardson." She coughed again then swallowed drily. "Is my lord awake? Or Lady Chalmsley?"

"They have not ventured upstairs, Miss. What do you wish me to have done?"

"I think," she had to clear her throat. "I think the mattress and the rest of the bedding and all the curtains must be removed. This will ensure the fire will not re-start. And I believe we must have emptied every pitcher on this floor. Please ensure they are refilled before the servants return to their beds."

"I will see to it, Miss."

"Thank you. I believe everyone else," she glanced around her. "I thank you all for coming to help. I believe the fire is extinguished, as Mr. Nashe said. Richardson will ensure that the rest of our night is safe from fire. If your pitcher was emptied, please set it outside your door, and the maids will see it re-filled. I think our morning will start a little later, yes?"

Nods, voiced agreement, and gradually they eased away. A couple of the men complained loudly of the smoky smell to their nightshirts. Pitchers found their places beside doors. Doors began to close.

Bee's knees felt watery. She wanted to sit somewhere—or just lean against the wall, but too many people remained.

And Cordelia and Portia came to her.

"Did you suffer any harm?" Cordelia asked.

"No." She coughed and managed a smile as weak as her knees. "A throat full of smoke is all."

"We missed the excitement," Portia complained.

"I am glad we missed the excitement. How did the fire start?"

"I do not know, Cordelia."

"Obviously, someone wanted to mourn Will's death. A memorial fire."

"Which should have been outside," Bee snapped then felt guilty. Her youngest cousin had merely tried to apply logic.

Cordelia gathered the sides of Bee's cloak and tugged them around her shivering frame. "You are cold."

"Reaction. And hours in the attic."

Portia's blue eyes opened wide. "That's how you knew about the fire. Why were you in the attic?"

"Old memories haunting me." Then she saw Hector over Cordelia's shoulder.

He stood, legs braced, arms folded over his chest. Those light eyes, their color washed out in the remaining candlelight, merely watched her. His blonde hair was tousled from sleep. In his haste, he hadn't tucked in his shirt, and his trousers weren't tucked neatly in his boots.

Her heart ached with want. She should remember 12th November eight years ago and forget him. She wanted to forget him. As much as she wanted him.

That contradictory thought reminded Bee of Edmund. The shouts of "Fire" and "Water" hadn't roused him. His chamber was on the second floor, on the opposed south wing, yet even Cordelia and Portia had heard the commotion and come upstairs. And others, like the Pierponts and the elder Osgoods, came from the first floor. They slowly returned to their chambers, talking quietly as they descended one flight. Where was Edmund?

She knew how soundly her great-uncle slept. And Great-Aunt Lucille, who took laudanum on her doctor's orders. She sometimes suspected that her great-uncle also followed the doctor's advice. Perhaps her fiancé and Wallace Osgood and the others had slept through the uproar.

Or they couldn't be bothered to rouse unless they faced personal danger.

Cordelia had spoken. She patted Bee's shoulder then turned for the stairs. Portia looked as if she had something more to say. She stared at the still-open door to Kennington's chamber. Yawns splitting their faces, servants were going into the room while Holyfield carried a large pail from which Clarkson dipped water to refill the pitchers.

Portia gave a little twisted half-smile to Bee. "I'm glad you weren't hurt," she said then followed her sister.

And Bee stood still, staring at Hector.

Portia murmured something as she passed him. He responded, even though he didn't look away from Bee.

Richardson appeared. "Miss Seddars, the servants will finish clearing the debris. You should return to your chamber."

"I will. Thank you, Richardson."

"We all thank you, Miss. You're quick thinking saved us all."

She had no answer to that.

The butler went to oversee the last work in Kennington's chamber.

And Hector came toward her.

. ~ . ~ . ~ .

She looked as if a wind would blow her away.

As he reached her, she swayed. His hand shot out to grasp her arm and steady her. "Are you hurt?"

"No. No."

"What happened?"

Her mouth twisted. "Someone set fire to the mattress."

"No. Tell me what you saw. Tell me how you saw it. Tell me what awakened you."

Hector didn't realize how open her expression was until she shuttered it. Her eyes lost light. Her mouth tightened. The softness of her features hardened.

"Must we do this now, Hector? I am exhausted."

"Now is better than later. I want your immediate memory. You can add anything more in the morning."

Her hand moved in a cutting gesture, then she sighed. "I want to sit down."

"Your chamber—you said you have the end room?"

"You can't come into my chamber in the wee hours of the night."

He turned her and headed up the corridor. "We'll keep the door open. If you want, we'll have a servant stand chaperon."

She stopped lagging behind his grasp. "No, I will not take away another hour of their sleep. As it is, they'll drag about their duties tomorrow. The open door is acceptable."

Her bedchamber had few items besides the usual, which surprised him. A few drawings pinned to the wall: the parkland view from her window, trees bare of leaves, a circular maze of different-sized stones. Those were the most personal things in the room. He remembered that she collected interesting rocks, but he saw no signs of them except in the drawing of the maze. A closed book on the stand beside the bed. A desk at the window, everything tidied away except an inkwell and its quill. She seemed merely to inhabit the room as opposed to making it her own. Unless she kept her personal things tucked away.

Hector released her arm, and she immediately went to the bench before her vanity. She sat with her back to the mirror. The reflection revealed her hair slipping free of its braid. When Bee lifted her chin, she looked as if she faced an interrogation rather than a few questions. Her defiance was a little ruined by the soot smudges on her cheek and chin.

He thought about taking the cushioned chair, but he would have to drag it over from its place by the window. And the straight-backed chair at the desk looked uncomfortable. He stood, hands linked behind him, feet braced apart, wishing he didn't have to interview Bee. He would rather walk with her through the gardens and along the parkland path to the river.

"Ask your questions. I have lost enough sleep tonight. What do you want to know?"

"I think we'll start with my last question first. What awakened you?"

She winced. That question wasn't the one she had expected. She dragged the edges of the cloak around her, hiding her flannel nightrail. "I wasn't asleep," she admitted.

"Something this evening disturbed you?"

Her mouth firmed. "I have been *disturbed* since Mr. Kennington's body was discovered this morning. My *disturbance* tonight should not be considered unusual."

With a nod, he granted her that answer. "You were awake. Did you hear someone in the corridor?"

Bee's gaze dropped. "I wasn't in my chamber. I was in the attic, returning something to my parents' trunk. It's stored there."

He knew her well enough to know she hedged her answer. He wanted to know what she had found so necessary to take from a trunk and then return. He had to glue himself to his focus. "When did you realize a fire was burning?"

"I smelled smoke when I came down the stairs. It didn't smell like coal or wood smoke. An off smell, if you understand."

"What did it smell like?"

"I don't know. I don't want to guess. If I smell it again, I will tell you."

He nodded, allowing her that answer when he wanted to press for more information. Her shoulders had slumped. Her chin dipped, losing its rebellious tilt. She looked ghostly pale against the dark grey of her cloak. "You came down from the attic. You smelled smoke. You saw the fire?"

"I suspected fire," she corrected, not giving him an inch. "I saw a flickering light. Then I realized it came from Mr. Kennington's room. No one should have been there, not since—you did lock it back after you examined it?"

"I did."

"Then no one should have been in his chamber. How did they get a key?"

"They wouldn't necessarily need a key."

"More knowledge gained from your Bow Street days?"

"Yes. These locks are easy to open. A little jiggling of any key—."

"Wouldn't someone hear a key jiggling in the lock?"

"Not necessarily," he hedged. The sound *should* have carried. He would have to ask that question tomorrow, during his interviews of the other guests. Hector had hoped to avoid questioning all of Lord

Chalmsley's guests, but he had gathered very few clues that pointed to the murderer. "You had no trouble opening the door?"

"None. Once it opened, I saw the fire on the bed. I tried to put it out with water from the pitcher, but the pitcher was empty." Bee described her next actions and the people she remembered helping her. "I may have missed someone. I was not focused on them."

Hector nodded. "Did you notice anything particular about the fire?"

"Yes. Whoever started the fire burned a whole sheaf of papers. They were on the bed, scattered around. They blew off when I threw on the first pitcher of water."

"Fuel for the fire or letters being burned?"

"Both? I know handwriting covered several of the sheets, but I didn't even see the handwriting. The papers burned to ash."

"Which means you also have no idea what was written on those papers?"

"The next time I find papers burning on a mattress, I will stop to read a few before I put out the fire."

"I'm not castigating you, Bee. I find it unfortunate, nothing more."

She winced. "My apologies, Hector. I am weary. I am perturbed that someone wanted to burn papers in Mr. Kennington's chamber."

"On Kennington's bed," he pointed out. "Letters about their *affaire*?" Her eyes opened wide. "Letters burned on the very bed where they last had relations. Letters where he had sworn some kind of affection."

"You think the murderer is a woman?"

"The evidence points that way."

"The very bed where they last had relations?"

"There were signs on the sheets."

"Signs?" she asked, revealing her innocence. "Besides the blood?"

Hector merely nodded.

Bee winced. "I didn't realize. The bloody burned bed. Burned letters of false love. That sounds like one of Aunt Beth's ballads. Could a woman kill him? A woman against a man?"

"If he were relaxed."

"You mean *after*?" He nodded, and where once she had looked pale, color bloomed. "I am a fool," she whispered. "I didn't consider any of that. What more can I tell you?"

He quizzed her a little longer, but her answers were the same, no matter which direction his questions came from. Her shoulders drooped lower. Shadows formed beneath her eyes. When she stumbled over words, Hector knew he should delay more questions for the morning.

Including the question that he wanted answered most of all, that question he would never ask.

"Enough," he finally said. The earlier defiant Bee would have halted his questions. Why had his belief that the murderer was a woman deflated her antagonism? *Is she protecting someone*? "Get some sleep. I will have more questions in the morning."

Rather than protest, she yawned.

Bee followed him to the door. He turned and looked down at her. He wished—hundreds of things, but mostly that he had never left for London. The world had opened up for him. When he left Bow Street and returned to serve as Lord Chalmsley's constable, he had willingly closed his sphere back to a small circuit of miles.

When he accepted the employment, he hadn't known then that Bee would become engaged before he could re-connect with her. Too late.

"Good night, Hector," and Hector could only ensure that she shut her door before he trod back to his room.

He couldn't sleep. He undressed and resumed his bed only to climb from it when the clock struck the three o'clock hour. Without lighting a candle, he strode to the window, shoved back the curtain, and stared into the night.

Bee's whole attitude had changed when she realized his choice for murderer was a woman. Had she guessed the culprit? Was she protecting that person? Who would she protect? She had no special feelings for any of her relatives—except Mad Aunt Beth.

He could see the old woman burning a bed without thought for other people's safety. Yet old Mab had minders both day and night. And her derangement had only ever harmed herself.

This madness—if madness drove the murder and the arson—was directed outward, at Kennington. At what Kennington must have promised and then reneged on.

An unmarried woman, then. An unmarried woman who expected—what? Marriage?

Phaedra Dunham. Daphne Herrick. Christina Wilton. Those three young ladies were the only ones not yet betrothed.

But the murderess could still be betrothed. Desperate for Kennington's affections. Trapped in a loveless courtship. Angry that he was betrothed to Moira Fraser.

And Kennington suffered the consequences of his engagement.

Yet that didn't fit with what Hector knew of women. Too many times he'd broken up fights between two women over a man. The man had initiated the two-timing. He had broken his vows of devotion, yet his woman blamed the other woman, not him. Instead of attacking him, they attacked each other. While he went off and found a third woman.

Kennington had died. Not because *his* engagement made him unavailable. Not because of *her* engagement to someone else. A woman with whom he had a sexual relationship. The bed-burning confirmed that. A woman to whom he'd made certain promises only to betray those promises. The burning of the letters implied such a betrayal. What promise had he made then broken? Why had he broken the promise? What had changed in his circumstances? Something that he hadn't expected: a vow, an oath, an unforeseen honor, an unforeseen love. Why murder him now? Was he murdered at Chalmsley because of something elsewhere? Or had he broken his promise here?

That last question meant that Bee or Portia or Cordelia was the murderess.

God, he hoped not.

Hector prayed that no one else would be in danger now that Kennington was dead.

Chapter 8

Before the morning reached noon, Hector realized two things. One, Chalmsley Court had changed more than he realized. Second, he needed someone to explain the personalities here, the ones he thought he knew as well as the guests he'd never met.

Only one person could tell him that information.

He presented himself to Lord Chalmsley after lunch.

When he made his request, the baron sank back in his chair. When Hector merely waited, he shifted uncomfortably. "I am not certain that I heard you correctly. You say that you need Beatrice's assistance? How can she possibly assist you with your investigation?"

"Beatrice knows your guests. She can smooth over any questions that I might ask in the wrong manner. She also knows the servants. I've been away eight years, my lord. You have many, many new faces on staff."

"We have no trouble keeping servants."

"Yes, I know, my lord. I didn't not intend to imply that. I see many servants that I do know from eight years ago. My work here will go much more quickly if I have an assistant who can answer many questions and point me to people who can answer other questions. I believe Miss Beatrice Seddars is the only person who can serve in that capacity."

Chalmsley scowled. "You have no other motive?"

Hector had an answer prepared. "What motive could I have other than to solve this crime?"

"You're making no headway on this murder, are you?"

"A little headway, my lord. I can tell you that Mr. Kennington's body may be returned to his family, and his valet released to attend to him on that journey. I can tell you little more. I do believe Miss Seddars will help this investigation."

"I removed you from her presence years ago."

Many things suddenly dawned clearly for Hector, most especially that his fortunate position in London had occurred only because his lordship wanted him gone from Chalmsley Court. He bit back several retorts. He worked hard to keep his comment mild. "I understand that I am not worthy of her."

"Beatrice will inherit a tidy fortune in three years. I will not see it wasted on a man who has little substance of his own. Edmund Tretheway is an appropriate match for her. His name is one of long standing. His grandfather's an earl. Your father was nothing more than a barrister, and his father before him was little more than a shopkeeper. I helped your father to a position at the Inns of Court."

Hector didn't argue. It was useless to argue against gentrified prejudice. He merely pointed out, "I do not seek to court Miss Seddars, my lord, merely to use her mind to work more quickly to find Mr. Kennington's murderer. After last night's fire—."

"About that. You think the murderer set his room on fire? It wasn't that Fraser chit?"

Moira Fraser had displayed no erratic derangement that might lead Lord Chalmsley to suspect her of the arson. Why would his lordship expect her to be guilty of it? "The murderer burnt some papers on the bed, my lord. That speaks to a correspondence between Kennington and his murderer. I do not believe Miss Fraser guilty of any crime."

"Going to tell her that? Or her parents?"

"It would be remiss of me to do so until I have an arrest, my lord. I regret that I must ask that they remain at Chalmsley Court until I have more evidence that will point to the murderer or clear them of suspicion."

Chalmsley bent back to the ledgers opened on his desk. "If you seek only evidence, then Beatrice has my leave to assist you."

"Thank you, my lord," but he left the study with a growing anger, first for the enforced separation eight years before and second for the slight against him now.

Chalmsley had not wanted Hector and Beatrice to form an attachment. Bee, his newly orphaned niece, with an inheritance to manage, could not be removed from Chalmsley Court. The only person his lordship could remove from the situation was Hector, and he had quickly bundled him off to London. Dependent on Sir Richard Ford's good will and the quickly dwindling competency Lord Chalmsley had placed in the London bank, Hector was forced to remain in London and seek his own way in the world.

Had Lord Chalmsley interfered between Hector and Bee in other ways?

Bee had promised to write. Had she done so? Had Chalmsley intercepted those letters? Had he intercepted the letters that Hector wrote to her from London?

All correspondence to the Court went first to his lordship before being parceled out to the rightful recipients. It would be a simple matter for Chalmsley to pick up Hector's letters to Bee and burn them. And an even simpler matter for him to burn Bee's letters to Hector rather than frank them and send them on by post.

None of this mattered now, not after eight years. Bee would marry this summer. She had found a name with a rank attached to it. She deserved more than a no-name nobody with little substance.

With clenched fists, he went to locate his new assistant. After last night's antagonism, he wasn't certain how Bee would accept her new role with him.

.~.~.~.

When a man loomed close, Bee looked up from sorting her aunt's embroidery silks. Hector stood before her. *Constable Evans*, she reminded herself and wished her heart hadn't tripped faster.

"Lady Chalmsley, I have come to steal away your assistant."

She thought for a long moment that Great-Aunt Lucille would not acknowledge his intrusion, then she spoke firmly. "I need her. No one has Beatrice's eye for matching colors. Not that goldenrod, my dear, not with pink."

"Lord Chalmsley has agreed that she might provide to me several insights into your guests."

Although Bee gave a quick upward glance to him, she continued to offer the bright yellow skein to her aunt. "Have you ever noticed the yellow center of the pink roses?"

"I have." Her aunt took the skein then matched it to the pink already worked into the linen. "I would never think of putting those colors together. See, Hector, I do need Beatrice."

"My regrets, my lady. She will return as soon as she answers several questions for me."

That sounded ominous. Hiding a new apprehension, Bee dusted snippets of silk and thread from her skirt. When she stood, Hector led the way from the sitting room and into the entrance hall.

She slowed when he turned toward the conservatory. "You have more questions of me?"

He turned, and she was snared by his smiling eyes and the light gleaming on his blonde hair. "I need your assistance," he repeated.

"I am flattered you still trust my word. May I inquire what special assistance you need?"

"I want your honest opinions of the people here. The guests and the servants. The guests, primarily."

Quick-witted Bee picked up on his focus. "Then you don't believe a servant killed Mr. Kennington?"

He glanced around. "I don't believe so, but I won't rule it out completely."

"You are cautious."

"Without more evidence, I must be cautious. Will you help me,

Bee?"

When he asked that way, with a smile and a pleading tone, he reminded her of the youth who had enticed her away from her studies to go fishing at the river or climb trees to catch the summer's wind or lay on their backs and study cloud formations.

Those days were long gone.

"I will help you, Hector. Yet if it's an honest opinion that you want, we should not talk in here. Anywhere inside will be too public."

"I thought the conservatory—." He stopped as her point was proved by a maid passing through, carrying a coal hod.

Together, they went to the back entrance, with its pegs crowded with outerwear. Bee separated out her old coat while Hector shrugged into a large greatcoat, "big enough for Sampson," he laughed.

"Not by half," she countered with her own laugh. "Perhaps big enough for Daniel. He's almost as tall as his father and nearly as broad." She led him outside, through the knot garden. The path split, leading to the kitchen garden or Great-Aunt Lucille's roses or the terraced lawn with its path down to the river. Bee turned toward the river and hoped he wouldn't stop her from pursuing the longer walk.

Hector followed without commenting on her choice. "Where is Sampson?" he asked. "I expected to see him, and I haven't. Not a whisker. And Daniel? Are they still on the estate?"

"Of course. Sampson would never leave the Seddars and Chalmsley Court. He and his son are—they're with George."

Crows lifted from the lawn and flew to the trees. One remained, stalking over the snow-buried grass. It kept a beady eye on them while the others scattered to different trees then cawed back.

"I understand George is in Europe. Isn't that dangerous with Napoleon still rattling the saber, even after his disastrous invasion of Russia?"

"My great-uncle believed the importance of George's rest-cure out-weighed the threat. He is at a hospital in Vienna."

"He's ill?"

"Not ... ill. We had a tragic incident here at the Court. We keep this secret, Hector. George attacked one of the upstairs maids."

He stopped walking. "How badly did he beat her?"

Bee paused, checked to ensure he came with her, then began the long drop to the next terrace. "It wasn't that kind of assault."

Her high color helped Hector fit the pieces together. "Rape," he said, to have it clear.

"Yes. When she fell with child, he denied anything to do with her. I believe Great-Uncle Hamilton intended to give her a pension and remove her to a distant estate."

"That would not be acceptable to George, not when he denied

responsibility."

"You remember him well. He did learn patience, a horrible patience. When the girl delivered the baby, a little boy, George took him and drowned him." She choked as if the words damaged her throat.

"Drowned?" Hector expected violence from George, but the deliberate drowning of a helpless innocent appalled him. The shock unlocked the guard on his tongue. "Damn him. How did he escape a hanging?"

"The way he always did." Her bitterness was as caustic as acid. "The constable was old Sommersby, you remember? He refused to investigate. My great-uncle claimed George was riding with him all that day. How could George have stolen the child while the mother slept? He claimed the girl had no evidence. And she didn't. No one witnessed George take the child. No one witnessed——." She pressed her hand to her mouth.

"And Lord Chalmsley smoothed everything over by paying the girl off and sending her away? His modus operandi when I was a boy here," he explained. "I am surprised that he sent George to this sanitarium. Or is it an asylum?"

"An asylum," she admitted, "although my aunt and cousins will merely admit that it is a hospital."

"Sommersby's no longer in the district. I checked, last spring. Was he pensioned off as well, a reward for protecting the heir?"

"Constable Sommersby is dead. He had an apoplectic fit not long after the girl and her family left. And my great-uncle thought you would serve him well."

"I won't serve in Sommersby's manner. I won't cover up a crime, not for George or anyone. Was nothing else done except send away the girl and her family? No one protested? I know many here are creations of Chalmsley, but surely someone knew these actions were egregiously criminal."

"My great-uncle's riding accident followed hard on the baby's death. Once George left, afterwards, with Sampson and Daniel as his escorts——."

"As his guards, you mean?"

She nodded, although she didn't put her agreement into words. "Once George left for Vienna, no one agitated for anything more. I think everyone was just vastly relieved."

"We cannot blame George for Kennington's murder. He is far away in Vienna. Someone must have had a dire grudge against Kennington."

"I think you do not need my assistance to talk about George, did you? I thought you had a murder to solve." She took his offered hand to negotiate the icy steps of the lowest terrace. When she tried to loosen her grip, however, he kept her hand.

"Bee, I don't want—may we speak without last night's hostility?"

The question surprised her. "I wasn't hostile."

"I apologize. Hostile is the wrong word. I don't want to argue with you. I don't want us to be antagonists."

Somehow, his admission breached one of the walls around her heart. Its fall lightened her restraints. "Not even if I'm your murderess?" she teased then was appalled at her question.

He was still the Hector she had known her so well. "Are comments like that designed to set me off? Are you my murderer, Bee?"

"I am not," she said firmly, reining back any thought of teasing him.

"Will you once more be my friend?"

Oh, that was sneaky. He knew *her* too well. "I would like to be, Hector, truly, but I need to understand—." No. He didn't want her antagonism; he'd said so. Bee determined that she would not set conditions before him. Her heart was not so little. No matter how much the past hurt, she would be his friend. No matter what walls came up, friends supported each other. "I am your friend, Hector. Ask whatever you wish. What do you want to know?"

"The very thing we are taught not to speak. I need your honest impressions of the guests, Bee. Brutally honest, please. I am searching for a murderer."

When Hector had found his murderer, he would leave Chalmsley Court. She would marry Edmund Tretheway and remove to his home in the faraway fenlands. Bee would never see Hector again.

She swallowed. Tucking her hands into her sleeves, she headed down the sloping lawn. "Do you want my honest opinion of the men *and* women? Last night, you seemed to focus on a woman."

"I am. I have. Nine women, to be exact. But your impressions of the men can help me understand the women. I hope. Tell me what you thought of William Kennington."

She gave a huffing laugh. "Are you certain you want my opinion? You did say brutally honest, didn't you? William Kennington didn't like women."

Hector skidded on the snow-covered grass. "I beg your pardon? I understood that he flirted with several of the women here."

"Exactly. Mr. Kennington didn't care when he broke hearts. Not if, Hector, *when*. He charmed woman after woman, and he didn't care what results came of his casual charm. He flirted with Portia, so seriously that I thought he would propose. She flitted on to someone else, however, and he shifted his attentions as well. Even after that, they walked together on several occasions."

He trod beside her, his gaze on the river's glistening water. His scowl, though, revealed that his thoughts were not on the wintry scene. "Portia did mention that Kennington was hers. 'He was mine,' she said. I didn't know what she meant."

"They flirted madly for a fortnight."

"Then she turned her attention to Brougham Paton."

"The honorable Mr. Paton was not next in line. He was fifth or sixth. I stopped counting. But you asked for my reading of William Kennington. I will tell you that I believe he didn't care whose heart he broke."

They had reached the last terrace and had to use the steps to drop over six feet to the lower field that ran down to the river. Again Hector steadied her. "Your hands are cold."

"I forgot my gloves." Yet when she would have retrieved her hand, he tucked it under his arm, against his body.

"That only warms up one hand," she complained.

"I'll warm this one on the way down to the river, then the other on the way back. Now, give me an example of Kennington's behavior."

Bee didn't hesitate. "I can give you more than one. He would spend all evening focused on a young lady then ignore her at the next party. Even after he proposed to Moira Fraser, he flirted with other ladies. He spent one evening teasing me when he had no one better, poor man. I was definitely a means to stave off boredom."

He jogged her arm. "You shouldn't denigrate yourself. I have never found you boring."

"I thank you kindly, dear Hector. But Mr. Kennington's main conversation was gossip and fashion. He talked the latest styles so he could touch a young lady's hair. He talked fabric so he could touch her gown. He insisted that he knew the newest dances and would teach her the steps, lessons that entailed his hand on her waist or hip or neck as he turned her through the pattern."

Hector stopped and faced her. "Bee, did you fall victim to him?"

"Not I. I watched it happen, though, too many times. And poor Cordelia—the night he died, he had focused on her for a little while before playing up to Lady Paton."

"Moira Fraser, how did she react?"

She shifted her gaze away, remembering the evening, remembering her pity for both her cousin Cordelia and Moira Fraser and her growing loathing for William Kennington. "She tried to flirt with Mr. Nashe, but he has eyes for Missy Wilton, I think."

"You don't like Missy Wilton?"

Bee tried to remember the exact comment that had tarnished her view of the young debutante. "I've barely spoken to her," she admitted. "I dislike her sister, with whom I have labored through several conversations since we met them in London. As for Missy, that girl has the world wrapped around her finger. I envy her. She knew what she wanted, and she snared it."

"You are calling Alex Westover an 'it'."

"I did, didn't I?"

He chuffed. "Clever Bee. The lord's heir and little more, is he?"

She smiled sunnily. "Ask about another."

"Let's eliminate a few. Who do you like?"

"Are you operating on the belief that my esteem absolves that person of murder?"

His grin didn't diminish. "I do have to pare down my suspect list. Now tell me, who passes muster in Bee Seddars' eyes? John Nashe?"

"Except for his fascination with Missy Wilton."

"Wallace Osgood?"

"A prig. He wouldn't sully his hands with murder. He'd hire it done."

Hector snorted. "Brougham Paton?"

"Portia will lead him a merry chase."

"Barrington Pierpont?"

She paused. "I did not esteem him when Portia snared him."

"He is betrothed to Cordelia, isn't he?"

"He is. It's something else I held against him, the quickness with which he transferred his supposed affections to Cordelia. Yet he treats her so sweetly. He hasn't lost patience, not once, when she is stressed and has to line everything up with the edges of the table or the desk. He has honestly tried to learn how to manage the estate he will inherit. From a couple of conversations that I overheard—."

"Eavesdropped on."

"That I *overheard*. He has taken over the management from his father and actually turned a good profit for the past three years."

"Clarence Wilton?"

"That young man is following in his father's footsteps. He will marry a silly woman who will never realize that her husband is a narrow-minded dictator."

"Ouch." He paused then said, "Edmund Tretheway."

Bee paused. "A good man. Better than I deserve. I really do not wish to talk about my fiancé, please, Hector. He is a good man."

"Have I omitted anyone? No? Well, then, tell me about the other young ladies. I know your view of Missy and Christina Wilton. I think I can guess your view of Moira Fraser, a little gullible, out of her depth with Kennington. Phaedra Dunham?"

The abrupt change surprised her, but Bee was quick and didn't hesitate over her answer. "Not a *blanc mange*, but calm. Serene. That girl has poise. She will go far. Typical, that her father does not have a title or great wealth to promote her higher on the marriage mart. She has managed to snare the Osgoods' interest. I would not wish to see her married into the Osgoods. She deserves better than Wallace."

"Daphne Herrick?"

"She seems sweet. I really have no good reading of her personality, Hector. She follows where the others lead."

"I think she has a *tendre* for John Nashe."

"Splendid. That's a good match, if her parents can be brought to see the sense of it."

"You don't think she's guilty of murder?"

An adamant shake of her head, and Bee felt her chignon loosening. "I have seen no instance of strong emotion from her, and a murder requires an element of strong emotion, doesn't it? Hatred. Lust. Revenge. Ambition. Jealousy. I don't think Daphne Herrick is capable of those emotions."

"You believe the murder was motivated by one of those?"

They neared the riverbank. The current ran swiftly, evidence of the recent snowmelt that still swelled its banks. Bee clung to Hector's arm and watched the water sweeping bits of debris. "I have considered a motive since yesterday morning. I do not think it possible to divine the murderer from the air. A motive would help narrow the suspects. That is your difficulty, isn't it? You have very little evidence, and you have very little knowledge of the motive. I would think hatred must drive Kennington's death. Ambition and jealousy do not fit this particular crime, do they?"

"Do they not?"

She glanced at Hector. "I have cudgeled my brain, and I can see no evidence of those motives. Revenge? Yes. Lust? Only if it were lust for Moira Fraser, and no one has even attempted to coax her from her bedchamber. Her mother visits her, but no one else."

"That leaves us with hatred and revenge."

"A combination of the two, perhaps? A need for revenge that caused hatred? He certainly could have broken a young lady's heart, but I don't see the young ladies here acting on their desire to hurt him."

"We haven't talked about Cordelia or Portia."

"No. No, Hector. They're my cousins."

"Cordelia is more than a little eccentric, Bee. Admit it. I never connected her with Mad Aunt Beth, but she obviously has the same tendencies. In the two days that I've been here, I've seen her return time after time to her chamber to wash her hands, constantly line up the silverware on the table or the cups on the tea tray, and carefully fold her handkerchief or a napkin to align the corners."

"That's minor."

"Is going back upstairs then coming down again in order to reach some arbitrary number of steps minor? Is taking off her necklace in order to count the beads over and over minor?"

She frowned at him. Bee had seen those same behaviors. Inured by proximity, she had glossed over them, but Hector was right. In two days, Cordelia would not have normally exhibited so many of her compulsions to check things or align things.

"The murder—. She's under stress."

"We all are. But you haven't gone to your room three times in a half-hour or stood at the buffet straightening the flatware and turned the dishes just so. Have you?"

"No. But if you think Cordelia could have killed William Kennington, you might as well think that I did it. Cordelia has never hurt anyone or anything. Why, she tries to rescue lady bugs that find their way inside. Cordelia and Aunt Beth, their issues are mild, Hector. They don't hurt other people. I am more likely to hurt someone."

"If you had reason to, yes. But if Cordelia is acting under stress—."

"She wouldn't hurt anyone," Bee claimed stubbornly.

"Nor would you," he said flatly, "no matter what you think. I know you, Bee. You lack the necessary evil heart to commit murder."

"I could have changed. It's been eight years, Hector. I should have changed. You knew me for only a handful of months, when I was still shocked by my parents' death. A lot has happened to me since then."

"People don't change unless they've endured trauma. You are passionate, Bee. You aren't evil. I've seen evil. You will protect those you love, but you won't kill simply because you hate. Look at your defense of Cordelia. You've blinded yourself to her actual behavior. She can hate. You know it. You saw her fly at George when he decapitated her doll. You aren't capable of that behavior."

"She was a child then. She wouldn't do that now," but doubt crept into her voice. Hector made too much sense, and she *had blinded* herself to the reality around her. Too concerned with her own problems to see the problems of her cousins. "But the murder—that was premeditated, wasn't it? The murder weapon would have to be taken into the room then carried away. Cordelia wouldn't—she just wouldn't."

"I'll wait for my evidence before I accuse. I won't settle on any one person, not until I have that evidence. Every person here would be on their best behavior, the older couples because they are guests, the young ladies in hopes of snaring a fiancé, and the young men to ensure they made the wisest choices for their future brides. I am certain your fiancé is quite pleased with his choice of you." But his words dropped out like heavy rocks rather than sounding like a charming comment.

Bee glanced at him, but he kept his face in profile. She couldn't judge his mood. "Since I know you do not like the man, I cannot decide if you just complimented me upon my fiancé or condemned me for accepting his proposal."

"I compliment you, but I wish—no." He refused to continue. "You're shivering," and he used that excuse to return to the house.

As they climbed the terraces to the house, Bee wasn't certain if she had answered the questions Hector wanted answered. She had the sense that additional questions lurked between them. She didn't like his suspicions about Cordelia. Now that he had pointed out her behaviors, though, Bee herself could see the worrisome tendencies.

And his last comment—what had he refused to tell her? He seemed angry that she had accepted Edmund's proposal. Yet he hadn't contacted her, not even when he returned. He could have written to her anytime in the last eight years. Her address hadn't changed. He'd gone to London. His life had changed. Did he want her life to remain the same? Ever dangling for him?

She hadn't wanted to accept any proposal. Not even Hector's—*but that's a lie*, she admitted. Edmund's proposal, though, she wanted to explain that to Hector. Yet how could he understand the pressure on her? Over Christmas, she had the impression that Great-Uncle Hamilton wanted her gone from Chalmsley Court. With Hector returned to the district as constable, she also wanted a reason to leave. She had stared at her future and considered her options.

She would not gain her independence until age twenty-six. Three years. Too long.

Bee had considered writing to her solicitor, asking for permission to tap the capital in order to purchase a small cottage near her parents' old home. There, she would not be a complete stranger. Or one of the terraced houses in the Circus at Bath or Grosvenor Square or those contemplated for Regent's Park. Bath and London would be interesting places to reside, with the gardens and the theatre and museums. She could set up life on her own. Hire a companion. A small staff of servants. Surely her quarterly payments would stretch that far.

The quarterly amount that the solicitor had conservatively proposed in his last letter had popped her eyes large. She had written that she'd received an offer of marriage. He'd returned with information about the Tretheway family and a copy of the information that he had supplied to Lord Chalmsley for the marriage negotiations.

Was her well-managed inheritance one of the reasons that Edmund had sought her hand for marriage? Contrary to what Hector thought, bless him, in company Bee was little more than a *blanc mange*. Too reserved or too focused on Cordelia or too hampered by Great-Aunt Lucille's strictures and censures, she was surprised she had attracted any attention at Christmas.

What had led Edmund to her side, night after night, ball or soirée or party?

The same thing that led Great-Uncle Hamilton to pressure her to accept the proposal?

Would any man of name and rank have suited her great-uncle?

While Bee had wanted one man only, had thought him lost to her, and finally acquiesced to a proposal only to have the man she loved return.

Chapter 9

The footman took their coats away. Blown by the wind, Bee stood in the hall's center and re-braided her hair. Hector watched, fascinated by her ability to plait the silky flax without needing a mirror.

"Go on," she told him. "You're missing tea."

"I can be late for tea. My stomach's not yet sticking to my backbone." But she fiddled with her hair, and Hector had a strong impression that she did not want to enter the withdrawing room in his company. A cold chill swept over him. He obeyed her urging and walked alone into the room.

As Hector entered, Tretheway stood and looked past him. A deep crease between his thick brows, the man watched the door. Hector realized just how long he and Bee had walked this afternoon. Her fiancé must be more than a little perturbed that for two hours she'd been unchaperoned in another man's company. No wonder Bee had wanted to enter after him, her hair restored from wind-tousled to a sleek braid.

He accepted tea and a plate of pastries from Lady Chalmsley then drifted over to the pianoforte where John Nashe tried to coax Daphne Herrick into playing a country dance for tonight.

"I do not think it would be proper to do so, Mr. Nashe," the young lady demurred.

"We must have a break from melancholy," he countered. "Here, Constable Evans, do you believe it would be acceptable for us to have a little entertainment this evening? No games like charades or any dancing, but a little music would keep us from being so drear."

Hector wished he had drifted elsewhere. "You cannot take me for a dean of the *ton*, Mr. Nashe?"

"No, certainly not, but no one here was related to Mr. Kennington. We need not follow the rules of mourning."

"We must keep certain of them," Miss Herrick argued. "He died here."

Hector paid no heed to what she said next, for Bee had entered the room.

Tretheway stepped forward to greet her. Hector saw her cheeks and nose still reddened by the cold. He heard her say "walk to the river".

"In this cold? Come sit beside the fire."

Tretheway led her to an open seat to one side of the fire. Remembering her shivers as they returned to the house, Hector admitted her fiancé had scored more than a few points with his care of her. The man dragged another chair into place beside hers. Then he brought her tea and a filled plate.

Bee stared at the pastries then set the plate on a little side table. Cupping the thin china in both hands, she sipped. Over the cup's rim, her eyes roved the room. She hesitated when she reached Hector, then her gaze slid onward.

Leaning close, Tretheway whispered something. Bee nodded once. He spoke again. She shook her head, then shook it again at his next comment. He must have persisted, for Bee began to frown as fiercely as her fiancé had. "No," she said firmly, then "no" again.

The defender in Hector warred with the better sense that had been drilled into him. He wanted to pull her away from Tretheway. He needed to turn his back on their conversation and ignore them. Bee had accepted the man's proposal. As her husband, he would soon rule her, body and mind. Hector wanted more than anything to plant him a facer and drag Bee from the room and—.

He stopped his wayward thoughts there. Never could he give voice to his desires. Once spoken, they no longer were wishes. They became plans, and after voice came action. He couldn't risk destroying the future she had accepted.

Bee abruptly stood. Tretheway grabbed her hand. She took a step away, and he stood, towing her back. He said something, again in an undertone that only those closest would hear. A yard away, Lady Chalmsley pretended that nothing happened. She poured more tea, selected pastries to fill a plate, then set both aside, and picked up the silver teapot and another cup. To Bee's right, Lady Pierpont had obviously heard, but she turned her head as if listening to a conversation behind her.

Bee let her fiancé tug her back to her chair. He took the cup from her hand, placed it on a saucer, then extended it to Lady Chalmsley for refilling. Her ladyship obliged.

And Hector turned his back, trying to return to the conversation between Mr. Nashe and Miss Herrick. They had strayed far from the original topic, and he couldn't follow it. He would never be able to follow it since his attention remained focused behind him. He glanced to his right.

Missy Wilton once more centered a group, with her sister seated on an uncomfortable side chair while Portia and Cordelia were crowded on a walnut sofa with swept arms. The younger Miss Wilton listened to her fiancé and her brother discuss morning rides in Regency Park. Portia chattered to Mr. Pierpont, seated on a second uncomfortable chair. And Cordelia—.

Cordelia ignored their conversation. She fidgeted with the lacy cuff of her right sleeve. She tugged. She folded it under then pulled it out. She smoothed the thin fabric then tugged it again.

When she began jerking at the lace, Portia glanced at her then moved away. A hand extended to Mr. Pierpont drew him with her.

Cordelia didn't even look up when her sister rose. Her focus remained intent on the lace.

Hector set aside his tea and pastries. In a handful of long strides, he reached the sofa. He claimed Portia's seat. "Miss Seddars, I hoped to speak with you today."

She had found a loose thread and pulled it.

"Do you still enjoy watching swans? I remember the pair that used to glide across the pond. I haven't seen them since my return."

She didn't look. She didn't stop jerking the thread.

A sudden movement caught Hector's eye. He glanced away from Cordelia and saw Bee standing again. Tretheway once more had her hand and again tried to draw her back to the chair.

Cordelia clawed at the lace. Her nails raked her skin, leaving angry marks. She whimpered and jerked the lace.

Bee was suddenly before them. Hector stood, letting her have his seat. Bee, however, bent to her cousin. She covered Cordelia's hands, blocking the focus of her eyes and preventing her hand from its destruction.

Cordelia shuddered. She looked up at Bee. "Itches."

"I know, Cordy. I know."

"I *told* that dressmaker."

"I know. Your maid should replace the cuffs with something softer, don't you think?"

"Mama chose this dress."

"A matter of a few minutes will fix it, Cordy."

Tretheway had followed her. When she drew Cordelia up and turned to cross the room and leave, he blocked their way. "Leaving again, Beatrice? You haven't finished your tea."

She didn't look at him. Her gaze remained on Cordelia. "The tea was lovely, but I cannot eat so many pastries. I need to assist my cousin."

"Her maid can fix the problem. Isn't that what you said?"

She looked at him. If Hector had stood before her, he would felt incinerated by those deep blue eyes. No longer serene, they burned like the hottest part of visible flame. He hoped never to receive such a look from Bee. How had he ever thought she merely drifted, untouched and tranquil, aloof and cold?

"I wish to assist my cousin."

"Oh, Bee, sit down," Portia chided her. "Cordy is having one of her turns. Once the problem is removed, she'll settle. Won't you, Cordy? Go burn that dress so we all can finish our tea without worrying about your little quirks."

Cordelia looked blank, then she saw the battery of eyes watching. Her face flamed, an ugly purplish red. She glanced across the room to her fiancé. Hector looked too late to see his expression. Whatever it was, she shuddered. Her shoulders hunched and drew in. She jerked free of Bee's hold and stumbled past Tretheway. She ran to the door, wrenched it open, and fled the room.

Bee started to follow, but Tretheway grabbed her upper arm. "I wish you to stay, Beatrice. You spent the afternoon with that constable. You should spend a half-hour with your fiancé."

She stared at his hand. He didn't remove it. Hector wanted to knock the man back. He controlled his fists. He had no right to defend Bee, and he also agreed with the man. If he were Bee's fiancé, he would begrudge any time she spent away from him. And did she actually help Cordelia, standing between her and the world rather than letting her discover her own sturdy foundation?

Her gaze lifted to his. Then she looked around the room. Her face flushed, but she didn't yield. "I explained that Mr. Evans needed my assistance. I now wish to assist my cousin."

"A pointless endeavor, Beatrice." Lady Chalmsley had bothered to half-turn in her seat. "We should never have accepted the gown after Cordelia complained about the trimmings. Her maid will resolve the issue. Do sit down. You must finish your tea."

Her bright color faded. The passion left her eyes. As if her light was extinguished—while Hector wanted it to burn. "Yes, Great-Aunt Lucille."

Tretheway looked smug as he guided her back to her chair.

But Hector saw her leaning slightly away from her fiancé. Her gaze lifted to the mantle, not to the fire or the painting above the mantle.

He returned to his own tea, gone cold, and the pastries were cloyingly sweet in his mouth. He ate them, needing something to eat the time away before he could leave the drawing room without attracting attention. Because he was an arrant fool, he kept glancing at Bee, waiting for her life to re-kindle. And she looked again at the mantle.

The glance was so brief, he would have missed it if he hadn't been looking directly at her and if he hadn't seen her earlier look. He stared at the mantle then looked away before anyone noticed his attention. If anyone in this room would deign to notice a mere constable.

Very few objects dressed the mantle. Two candlesticks of highly polished brass. A Wedgwood vase. An orb of pink marble. And a box clock.

He glanced at the clock, glanced at Bee and saw her swift uplook before she glanced away and pretended to listen to her Great-Aunt.

Hector glanced again and marked the time. Then he tried to reckon the time since Cordelia had left the room. Bee had to be waiting a set time before she felt she could leave. He half-turned, keeping her in the corner of his eye, and engaged Mr. Dunham in conversation about steeplechases.

At the twenty-minute mark, Bee picked up her cup and plate, returned them to the table beside the tea service then seated herself beside Lady Pierpont. Their short conversation left the older lady nodding agreement, then Bee stood again.

The door opened. Cordelia stood before them in a grey gown with white collar and cuffs. Her hair was arranged in a coil at her nape, with bright red ribbons banded around her hair.

Bee crossed to her and led her back to Lady Pierpont. That lady patted the cushion beside her. Cordelia winced but took the seat. As Bee and Lady Pierpont and Mrs. Nashe discussed pearls and laces, satins and silks, tulle and organza, Cordelia's back gradually lost its stiffness, her fingers lost their clawed bend, and her face smoothed its lines. She chose organza as her preferred overlay and added that ribbons should trim bonnets, not fresh flowers.

Bee's gaze lifted from the other three and scanned the room. Her gaze skipped over her fiancé. It held no emotion as she studied her other cousin, chatting with Wallace Osgood about the maze her father had proposed for Chalmsley Court. Then she looked at Hector. She looked away immediately, but her gaze came back to him, as if lured.

He gave her a brief nod.

Her cheeks pinkened. She didn't look back at him. She excused herself from Cordelia and the other ladies and went to sort the music that Daphne Herrick and John Nashe had scattered over the pianoforte.

He waited until Tretheway left with Barrington Pierpont, arguing the rival merits of a banked billiards table with pockets and one without pockets.

When the door closed on them, Hector left the group around Miss Wilton. He idled over to the Lords Paton and Herrick, talking fertilizer. He listened without hearing, waited until more people left the drawing room. The great case clock in the entrance hall began striking the hour, so he moved to the grand pianoforte.

Bee didn't even look up from her sorting. "He is angry with me," she said without preamble. "I am not the young lady he thought I was."

He didn't question her comment. In a half-hour he had also learned that Bee wasn't the young lady he had thought she was. She was more, a greater mystery than he had thought. "He doesn't understand

Cordelia."

"Few do," she retorted. She set down the stack of music and turned to face him, leaning into the pianoforte's embrasure.

He shouldn't envy a pianoforte. Hector dragged his attention back to her problem, and he settled for honesty rather than a half-dozen platitudes that didn't solve anything. "I don't remember her quirks being so extreme."

"Although it appears that Kennington's death and last night's fire had little effect on the majority of our guests, they greatly unsettled Cordelia. No," she judged her own words, "that's an understatement. She seemed almost afraid today. I wonder."

"What?"

But she didn't share. Her mouth twisted instead, and she straightened away from the pianoforte. "A wild thought that isn't possible."

"Will Tretheway forbid your assisting me?"

The fire kindled in her eyes. "I am not his wife yet. Hector, would you demand that your wife not help her cousins?"

He had to be honest. He focused on his finger rubbing the top edge of the pianoforte, a small connection to where she leaned against the ebony wood. "I would make that demand if I didn't think her help was helping."

Her brow creased as she puzzled out his words, then that fire kindled against him. "How would my help to Cordelia not be helping her?"

He didn't flinch but met that heated gaze unwaveringly. "I've been here less than four days, Bee, and on several occasions you've stepped up to shield her from something. Do you intervene for her too often? If she worked out problems for herself, as in ordering her maid to take off those lace cuffs, she might feel more in control of her surroundings and thus her turns."

"Those aren't turns. They're not at all like the turns that Aunt Beth has, when she is bizarre one moment and completely lucid the next."

"I know, but if Cordelia began to work on her own solutions—."

"She doesn't know how, Hector." But she had listened to him, for she began to work through his opinion. "Perhaps we all do intervene too much. As if we empower her weakness rather than her strength. But I don't want her compulsion to increase. Especially not in front of Barrington Pierpont and his parents. Cordelia wants to marry and leave Chalmsley. I cannot blame her for wanting what I myself want. I cannot stop myself from helping her when she's in danger of destroying her dream. Can I just abandon her, right now, when a simple action on my part will prevent the destruction of what she wants so very much?"

"That's not a question to which we'll ever know the answer, I fear."

"I fear that, too. So I will help her. But I'll try to temper my help." Mischief twinkled in her eyes. "The same way I will temper my help to you, helping where you truly need the help, not helping where you do not need it."

"And how can you know the answer to that?" He wanted her with him. He didn't want her trying to find a middle ground between him and her fiancé's demands.

Bee shrugged. "I can't. We must just muddle along, the way poor Cordelia is doing now. She was so much better in London. It's as if returning to the Court—no."

He took her words and turned them around with the murder he had to solve. And the arson that was tied so closely to the murder but added no sensible evidence. "Have Cordelia's compulsions increased, then? More than what you usually see from her?"

"No, they're not at an extreme point. She was worse two years ago, then her quirks, if we may call them that, eased up."

He wanted to know what happened two years ago. "Around the time that Lord Chalmsley had his riding accident?"

She bit her lips. "Yes, around that time."

"So, only occasionally is she as mildly deranged as Mad Aunt Beth."

Bee frowned, but it was a frown of concentration, not anger. "Cordy is not even mildly deranged. Hers is more obvious than—." She stopped abruptly. "You've seen a wider array of deranged people in London. The ones who are dangerously insane, do you find that they do not appear so insane until they hurt others or themselves?"

"Dangerously insane?" The question echoed with an old memory, something he should know but had long ago forgotten, something he needed to remember. "What are you saying, Bee? Who is dangerously insane?"

"Bee," Portia called from the doorway, "come with me."

She winced. "Duty calls." And she left Hector with more questions than she had answered during their walk.

Chapter 10

Smothered.

Bee woke, trying desperately to breathe.

"Sh-h. Sh-h. Sh-h."

A hand covered her mouth. She twisted and tried to claw it away. Her eyes sprang open.

Flickering candlelight revealed Mad Aunt Beth. She held a single taper. "None of that, now. Sh-h." When Bee nodded, the older woman removed her hand. "'They dug him a grave an' they dug it sae deep',"she sang softly, "'An' covered it over with flow'rets sae sweet.' Poor man."

Bee sat up and rubbed her eyes. "Aunt Beth, why are you in my room singing 'The Forlorn Lover'?"

The woman slid off the bed. Before the bedcurtains closed, she whispered, "Come away with me, Bee."

She pushed back her bedcovers and then a curtain. Aunt Beth waited a couple of feet from the bed. The woman wore only a flannel nightgown, and her bare toes were curled against the cold floor. Her braided grey hair was tied with a pretty red ribbon. She must have lain down and pretended to sleep before getting up again—while Bee's hair curtained her shoulders, for it never stayed in a braid. Searching for her slippers, she reached for her flannel robe. "Where's Nurse Griggs?"

Aunt Beth gave an impish smile. "She sleeps, she sleeps."

She pulled her hair free of the robe and finally found her other slipper, half under the bed. Her feet were already freezing. "While you wander the halls. Is anyone else roaming about?"

The smile vanished. She retreated to the door, beckoning for Bee to follow. Bee obeyed, tying her robe and rubbing her arms against the cold air. She could almost see her breath. Almost. The candle's light wavered too much.

When she reached the corridor, Aunt Beth was halfway to the stairs. Her white nightgown billowed behind her, her bare feet pattered on the bare wood. At the stairs she paused, and Bee, hastening behind, wondered where the mad woman would lead her. *Mildly deranged*, she had told Hector, but the cold that affected her had little to do with the dropped temperatures in the house.

Before she came close, Aunt Beth hurried off again. She didn't descend the stairs. She continued across the landing to the other wing. And Bee's chill turned to a freeze.

The woman stopped far along the passage. Bee, who had assigned rooms for Lady Chalmsley when she had planned the party, knew Hector slept there. Her heart stopped.

Aunt Beth waited. Bee reached her, and still Aunt Beth waited. "What are we doing here, Aunt Beth?"

"Wake the carrion crow."

Wake him. He wasn't dead. Her heart started with a painful thud. "Wake Hector?"

"Carrion crow, out of the oaks, come to catch a murderer. Wake him. You need him."

Bee's heart still beat, but her freezing chill hadn't eased. "I need him? What's happened?"

The old woman looked over Bee's shoulder, then she reached out and opened the door.

It swung into darkness.

"Aunt Beth," Bee hissed. "He's sleeping."

"Carrion crow, out of the oaks, needs to catch a murderer."

"Who's dead?"

She didn't answer, just looked at Bee then into the unlit chamber.

"Will you stay here?"

"I will stay. Not long. She won't sleep long."

Bee swallowed then slipped into Hector's bedchamber.

The candle provided enough light to see furniture. She aimed for the bed. Mercifully, Hector must have been tidy, for she didn't trip over dropped clothes or boots. She whispered open one of the bedcurtains. Except for his blond head, he was a dark mound under dark covers. She touched what she hoped was a shoulder and gave a push.

He came awake instantly, sitting up. With metal flashing in his right hand, between him and her. "Who—? What is it?"

"You need to come with me. I think. I'm not certain." She backed up a step, the curtain swelling out behind her and admitting more candlelight. Not metal. A knife. He hadn't worn a nightshirt. And Bee's gaze fastened on his bared chest rather than the threatening knife.

"Bee? What's happened?"

"I don't know. Aunt Beth woke me and brought me to you. She said I need you."

His mouth twisted. "Mab? What turn has she taken?" Then his gaze went behind her, and Bee realized the light had increased. She took a sidestep and looked back. Aunt Beth stood behind her.

Her smile looked a little too wide. "Fairies' midwife, no. Much bigger than an agate stone. Over your nose, though."

Aunt Beth made a little too much sense for one of her turns. Bee looked back at Hector. "She quoted 'The Forlorn Lover' when she woke me."

" 'I once loved a lass and I loved her sae weel'," he quoted without Aunt Beth's singsong, "but 'she gaun to be wed till anither'."

"Yes. But later, when they've dug his grave."

"Wait in the hall," he asked. "I'll join you in a minute."

"Never thought Carrion Crow would know that ballad, did you?" Aunt Beth asked as Bee urged her into the hall and softly closed the door. "He lives it."

"Hush, Aunt Beth. We don't want to wake anyone else. Do we?"

"Only Carrion Crow. Sleeps with a knife, he does."

And what danger had Hector faced that he'd formed that habit?

He joined them, wearing a loose shirt and half-fastened trousers and boots, his hair still rumpled from sleep. He'd had the forethought to bring another candlestick, and he lit it from the old woman's. "Aunt Beth—."

"Queen Mab to you, Crow."

He didn't argue. "Queen Mab. Why do you need me?"

" 'Quickly to him would I make My smock, once for his body meet And wrap him in that winding-sheet'," she sang.

"Now we're on to 'Lady Bothwell's Lament'. What happened to 'The Forlorn Lover'?" Bee asked.

Hector didn't lose patience with the old woman. He only asked, "Who needs a shroud?"

And Bee's earlier ice returned.

" 'By some proud foe has struck the blow And laid the dear deceiver low'. Poor Cordelia will weep."

"Dear deceiver?" Then Bee slipped the two pieces into Aunt Beth's puzzle. "Cordelia's fiancé?" Already highly stressed by the earlier death and the arson, how would her cousin react to her fiancé's death?

As the older woman nodded, Hector asked Bee the question that was more important to him. "Who is our Queen Mab talking about?"

"Barrington Pierpont."

"Is he dead?"

For once she didn't sing the words, merely spoke them in a hushed voice. "Smothered in his wounds. Poor Cordelia. Find her, Crow."

"Find who? Cordelia?"

Aunt Beth shook her head. "She sleeps. All unknowing. Find *her*."

"The murder*ess*. Yes, I'll find her. Or him."

"Her," she said firmly. "*Her*. But first, Crow, tend to him."

"I will." He glanced at Bee. "Where does he sleep? On the first floor?" He started for the stairs almost before her "yes" was spoken, but he stopped when neither Bee nor Aunt Beth followed. "I'll need you, Bee. Queen Mab, you may return to your bed where it's much warmer,

I am certain. I will have questions for you tomorrow. Will you answer them for me?"

She nodded, bouncing on her toes a little.

And Hector smiled at her, looking nothing like the crow she called him. "Go on, Queen Mab. Get warm. Get sleep. You and I will talk tomorrow. In the afternoon, I think."

"Queen Mab," she giggled. She wanted to buss Bee's cheek. Bee obligingly bent enough, then Aunt Beth sped to the stairs.

When Bee joined Hector, he was watching the old woman climb to the third floor. She didn't stop at the top, just turned toward the nursery wing and the chamber she shared with her nurse.

"I thought she was watched," he whispered.

"She said her nurse was sleeping. I think she must roam the house every night. She said something earlier—."

"About Kennington's murder?" He touched Bee's arm and started her moving down the stairs.

"Not quite about the murder itself, but she did know he'd been stabbed with a steely pick."

"A steely pick. Like an ice pick? A heavy one made of silver," he mused, "for dining room use, not kitchen use. Yes, that would make such a wound. And she's convinced our murderer is a she. What else does she know? Is she our murderer?"

"Aunt Beth is no more guilty than I am," she snapped. Those questions made her reluctant to share what Aunt Beth had revealed in her singsong way. The family had ensured Bee never saw Hector whenever he'd come to the Court in the year since his return from London. And his letters—what had she said? *Wrote and wrote, never answered.*

The opportunity passed. Like so many opportunities, a window ajar then closed, a door opened then slammed shut. She shivered and rubbed her arms.

"Cold? I warrant you'll be colder before you can return to your bed." They reached the first floor corridor. "Which way?"

Bee turned to the guest wing.

Three rooms down the corridor, light spilled onto the carpet. Hector hadn't needed her guidance.

They reached the door. He put out an arm to block her then dropped it. "I would prefer that you stay out here, but you might see something significant, something I might miss."

Remembering Kennington's staring eyes and bloody neck, Bee would have preferred a post in the corridor, but she followed Hector in.

On one side of the bed, the curtains were again pushed back, revealing the man's unclothed body sprawled across the mattress. His eyes were shut, but he was just as bloody as Kennington had been. Bee averted her eyes but not before the image had etched into her mind.

"Hold this," and she took the candlestick so Hector could approach the bed.

Barrington Pierpont looked relaxed, like William Kennington taken unawares. The bedcovers were tangled at the foot of the bed. Sweat had beaded on his brow and wet his hair. He was not long dead. And remembering what Hector had said about Kennington's activities before his death, she knew the reason for his exertion.

"Still warm," Hector said, and Bee realized that he had touched the man's body.

"Aunt Beth must have seen ... ."

"Or come past the open door after the murderer left. How long between Aunt Beth waking you and your coming to me?"

"We came immediately."

"Come closer, Bee. I need a stronger light."

She didn't want to come closer. She didn't want more memories to haunt her. Her slippers shushed on the floor until she stood behind Hector. He reached back and pulled her forward, guiding her to hold her light near the bloody pillow. She shut her eyes to keep this view from burning into her eyes.

"Same wound in size and location."

Bee swallowed.

"Totally unexpected for him. What were they doing?"

Her face flamed.

"She must have stood exactly where you are. Here, give me the candlestick. Hold your hand out—."

Her eyes flashed open. "Hector," she protested.

"I want to see the angle of your hand to his wound."

"I shouldn't be here." And she closed her eyes with determination.

"Bee. Bee. All right, keep your eyes shut." He took her elbow and turned her, drew her closer until her knees touched the mattress. Then he pulled her right hand forward. He pulled harder until she had to bend over. "Can you put your knee on the mattress?"

She huffed, opened her eyes, kited up her nightgown and robe. Gripping his hand to steady herself, she hiked a knee onto the mattress and reached out. And she looked at Barrington Pierpont as she aimed an imaginary weapon at his neck.

Even in death he was handsome. A young man of good looks and good health. The color hadn't faded from his flesh. His full lips were partly open, as if he waited for a kiss. Perhaps *she* had kissed him. Kissed him then killed him.

Bee shuddered. She dropped her reaching hand and scrambled off. Tangling in her robe, she stumbled into Hector.

With one hand, he caught her, steadied her on her feet, then turned her away from the bed. "Easy, little Bee. I have you."

"You're mad. Absolutely mad."

"Mildly deranged."

As he must have hoped, the repetition of her words so very much earlier brought out a smile. She tried to extricate herself, but he refused to let her go. He lifted the candlestick again, and she watched him as he looked over the bed. Heat poured off him in waves. Bee curled her fingers in the soft linen of his shirt and closed her eyes.

A second murder. Richardson must be awakened first. Then Lord Chalmsley. Who would roar about being awakened and then would roar about another murdered guest. Did Hector have any clues to the murderer—the murder*ess*? What had Aunt Beth seen? Did she have a clue to the murderess? She'd been so certain that the woman was a murderer.

"Black widow."

"Because she kills the man after they have relations."

"Yes. That's cold. That's hate."

"Not revenge?"

"Hate motivated by revenge. That makes better sense. Mab called him a 'dear deceiver', remember?" Finally, finally, he drew her back to the corridor. He shut the door. He had somehow collected another candlestick, and he lit it from the first one before handing it to her.

She hated how the little flame shook and shuddered, revealing her trembling hands. "She also called him a forlorn lover. His love married another."

He steadied her hand then kept his hand on hers, imparting warmth and friendship, although she wished it were more. "His love married another after he deceived her with another."

That theory made better sense than all the ones she had spun. "Did you see anything significant that you didn't notice previously?"

"Nothing."

"Are you certain that none of the servants are involved?"

"Dear Bee, I'm certain of nothing at this point except that we have two murdered men and one murderess. A murderess who lacks any guilt for her crimes. A murderess who kills when her victim least expects it. Along with a mad woman who spouts ballads at me instead of straightforward evidence. And I have a clear expectation that my next round of interviews will definitely offend every one of Lord Chalmsley's guests. If I don't quickly find this murderess, Chalmsley Court will become known as a murder house."

"As long as the shades of Mr. Kennington and Mr. Pierpont do not haunt us, I care nothing at all for gossip about the house." The long case clock in the entrance hall began its chime. Bee studied Hector. He had called her *Dear Bee*. Of course, he then went on to talk about murder and ghosts. But *Dear Bee*. Surely that was significant. When the chime counted off to the fourth hour, she stirred herself to focus on their next tasks. "We cannot just stand outside this room until the house starts waking up. Do you want a guard to ensure the scene is not disturbed?"

"Volunteering to avoid being the one to wake Lord Chalmsley?"

"Yes."

He softly chuckled but shook his head. "I'll wake my lord. You wake Richardson. I think he will be our greatest asset in maintaining the scene. And after that, Bee, if you will dress and stand guard until a footman can be enlisted for that duty."

"My great-uncle will be difficult to wake, Hector. I believe he takes laudanum or a similar aid to sleep."

"I'll do my poor best. Now, go on with you, Bee. And check on Mab, will you? Right now, she's my best witness."

Bee nodded and hurried upstairs.

First, she checked on Aunt Beth. From the corridor she heard snoring. When she carefully opened the door, the snoring didn't cease. She crept into the room and over to the curtained bed. Before she reached it, Aunt Beth's head poked through the curtains.

Bee started. Aunt Beth grinned then disappeared inside the bedcurtains.

She drew the curtains back a little. The older woman had lain down. Her wide eyes watched Bee. "All quiet," she whispered.

"Stay asleep, Aunt Beth."

The woman shut her eyes. But her lips curved. She tugged her bedcovers under her chin. "Asleep until morning. Snug as a bug."

Bee crept just as quietly from the room and headed for the servants' wing.

No servant would be awake at this hour, not in the deeps of January's long winter nights, with four hours before dawn. Richardson had never failed his duty, though. She remembered his stoicism after Kennington's death.

The butler waked slowly. Her loud knocking roused other servants before Richardson reached his doorway. They stood, blinking and yawning as they stared at her. Far down the hall, where the candlelight barely reached, she spotted Holyfield and Clarkson. The two maids were whispering. Others were whispering. They had already guessed.

The door opened. Wrapped in flannel with a heavy cloth around his neck, the butler looked down his nose. The aroma of cloves wafted from him. "Another, Miss Seddars?"

"Unfortunately. Will you come?"

The whispers had increased. He cast a quelling glance down the hall and received silence. "Jameson, I believe you are needed. You may nap two hours in the afternoon to replace your lost sleep. Vickery, you are to go to Miss Seddars' room and wait there to attend her. White, if you will wake up Coggins and have him come to the kitchen, then you may return to your bed. I will send Coggins to the vicar, Miss. I believe the vicar should be brought early."

"That is a very good idea, Richardson. Thank you. We were a little delayed with that before, weren't we? And we will have more people quite upset by this circumstance."

He prepared to follow her, but he stopped abruptly. "May I inquire, Miss, as to the identity of the person?"

"Mr. Pierpont."

"And Constable Evans?"

"He is waking Lord Chalmsley."

Doors shut hurriedly.

Richardson asked nothing more, just followed her down to the murder scene.

Chapter 11

Waking Lord Chalmsley woke everyone on the hall. They emerged from their bedchambers. The daughters stood only a few feet away. Lady Chalmsley, whether from wisdom or incapacity, remained in her room. Cordelia and Portia held hands, a meager defense. Along the guest wing, several people milled in the corridor, gradually edging closer to hear. When Chalmsley jerked open his door and glared, Hector appreciated Bee's warning.

Bleary-eyed, the lord looked more hungover than drugged. "Demme, I'm sleeping. What could not wait?" He had started at a raised voice and ended with a roar.

"My lord, I have bad news."

"Constable." His shoulders dropped. In the candlelight, the pouches beneath his eyes looked shot through with blue veins. "Out with it."

"Another murder, my lord. Mr. Pierpont." He had added the name in a hushed voice, but the young ladies heard. Cordelia cried out. She sank to her knees and began sobbing. Portia tugged her hand free and crossed her arms.

"Have you spoken with Lord Pierpont?"

"No, my lord. I will inform them next."

"Demmed right you will. What time is it?"

"Just after four o'clock."

"Have my valet wake me at half-past seven." Then he slammed his door.

Hector turned to face everyone watching. Except Cordelia. Her cries had closed up to whimpers, and she rocked back and forth, back and forth.

"Did we hear you correctly? Barrington Pierpont is dead."

Portia's light voice, untouched by the tragedy, carried further than Hector's had, along the corridor and across the landing to the guest wing.

"No," a woman cried out. She broke from her doorway and ran to the door that Hector had shut firmly. She banged on the door. Her husband came up behind her, but he reached her too late. She flung open the door and darted into the room. Hector reached the landing. He winced, and then Lady Pierpont screamed.

By the time he reached the room, Lord Pierpont was guiding his sobbing wife from the room. Blood smeared her hands and had seeped into her nightrobe.

Her husband glared at Hector. "You should have locked the door. She didn't need to see that horror."

"My lord, my lady, I regret that I lacked a key."

"The key should have been in the chamber. You should have searched for it. Half the keys on this corridor would fit the lock."

"Again, my regrets, sir, but I thought my greatest duty was to notify Lord Chalmsley, magistrate of this district. Nor did I wish to paw through your son's belongings. I deeply regret that you and your wife witnessed that scene."

"Horror indeed," another lord said. Osgood, Hector marked. The man turned and ordered his wife to return to her chamber. "We are all better served if we retire for the remainder of the night and let the constable work."

Murmured agreements while most of the guests returned to their rooms although a few lingered.

Hector heard someone approaching and turned to see the butler. "Richardson, I am glad you are here." Beyond the man, Bee had joined her cousins. She knelt beside Cordelia and hugged her close while Portia held herself aloof.

"Constable, my apologies. I will have a footman guarding the door momentarily."

"My fault, Richardson. You had no way of knowing the circumstances here."

"Miss Seddars did say, sir, that Miss Cordelia will likely need a man's support to return to her room. Would you attend to that?"

Hector didn't see anything that he could possibly do, but he nodded and brushed past the older man.

Neither Bee nor Cordelia acknowledged his appearance. Portia looked at him and gave a decided nod. "Good. You can help. She's more upset than I considered she would be. I didn't think she actually liked Barr."

Cordelia, encased in Bee's arms, kept rocking. "He's gone," she whimpered. "He's gone. He is gone?"

"Yes, Cordy." Bee hugged her. Hector saw that she braced her cousin, controlling that rocking. "I am so very, very sorry. Richardson," she said over her shoulder. "We need whisky."

The butler followed Hector. He checked Barrington Pierpont's door and saw a young man in a ticking stripe robe standing duty outside the door.

"Lady Chalmsley's maid keeps laudanum in her cabinet," Richardson offered.

"Not laudanum. Whisky. I don't want to drug her, just relax her."

"Yes, Miss." The butler headed down the stairs, and Hector remembered that he kept the liquor locked up.

Cordelia hadn't reacted to Bee's conversation with the butler. Her rocking still swayed Bee. "He's gone. He was my escape. Mine."

"I know," Bee said. "I know, Cordy."

"How am I to escape now?"

"I don't know."

Her sister loomed, arms akimbo. "You don't have to escape, Cordy. Why would you want to escape?"

"I'll never escape," she moaned. "Never."

"You can't escape," Portia declared. "The family must stay together. George will return soon."

Rather than breaking the compulsive rocking, her sister's comments caused Cordelia to shudder and move more wildly.

Ice dug into Bee's bones. "George? How will he get here?"

"George?" Hector questioned. "He's coming back? When? Did he say when he would be back? How do you know this, Portia?"

"Silly. He wrote me, obviously. I don't receive prophetic messages, like that old bat Aunt Beth. George said he would return by spring. And we will all be together again. Even Bee."

Cordelia shrank. "I can't be here when he returns. I can't. I have to escape. But I can't," and the last words sounded like a banshee.

Portia knelt and awkwardly patted her sister's arm. "Don't cry, Cordy. When George comes back, everything will be wonderful again. The whole family will be together. We'll all stay together. He's the only one who understands me. I wish he were already here."

The last words lit a fire. "I can't! I can't be here! Don't you see?"

"Whyever not? He's your brother. He loves you."

Cordy swallowed. She yanked away from Bee, scrambled to her feet. Half-running, half-falling, she scurried to her room.

And Hector had a new question. "Did George hurt Cordelia?" He bent, grasped Bee's elbows, and hoisted her to her feet.

Portia gaped at him. "How could he hurt her? She's his sister." She refused his offer of support and climbed from the floor.

"He must have. I've never seen her—. She's terrified."

"Not of George. It must be something else. And escape. What could she want to escape?"

"This house. This life."

"The Court is a lovely place. I love being here. London is better, but this is home."

He thought of Cordelia's compulsions, increasing with her stress. She was twelve when he left, already eating like a bird, already compelled to keep her things exceptionally tidy, her stress caused by her siblings' malicious antics. As a child, she'd only straightened her dolls and primers, pared her pencil to a precise point, and insisted her dresses be folded neatly. "I want things just so," he remembered Cordy's explanation to Bee, when she'd welcomed the newcomer to the schoolroom.

Eight years had transformed an inclination into a habit that gradually mutated into a compulsion.

"Lovely for you," he said to Portia. "Not for her. Obviously not for her. May I read George's letter?" Hector held out his hand, as if he expected her to have it, even though she wore only a nightrobe and rail.

The young woman folded her arms, as if planning to refuse, then something flashed in her eyes. She nodded. "Of course. George will want you here, too. His parents, his sisters, his cousin, and the other boy from his childhood. All together as a family. Just as we once were." She dug into her robe pocket and produced a folded paper.

The postmarked side bore foreign marks as well as the British mail office. The broken seal was nondescript. Hector unfolded the letter. Bee craned to read as he scanned the lines. He flicked her a glance then began reading.

Dearest Portia,

Cold here. I miss the Court more and more. Nothing but madness here. And Sampson and Daniel. Always Sampson and Daniel, my faithful servants. They never leave. Not even when I go for my treatments, as Dr. Schroder calls them. Torture is what I call them. I can't think for days. They leave me weak, so weak. But my ever-faithful servants still watch over me. My guardian angels ... .

"I can't decipher the next words," Hector said. "I think it's something about family."

"Give it to me." Portia snatched the paper.

My guardian angels are with me always. They will be with me until I decide to return. That will be soon, dearest Portia, very soon. Never fret. I will return to Chalmsley by spring. I won't miss another spring. I cannot. We will all be together. We must all stay together. Promise me, Portia. Promise me that everyone stays together until I return.

"There." She smiled as she refolded the paper and tucked it away. "It's just a few words that are hard to understand, but they're the most important ones. They give us hope."

"When did you receive this letter?"

"It was waiting for me when we returned from London. That's when I knew we must stay together."

"Could George have returned already?" Bee asked, her faint voice hiding the dread she must feel.

Portia giggled. "Silly Bee. He's not hiding in the attics. George doesn't hide. He's brave. He has no need to hide."

"But if he didn't want anyone to know. If he wanted his return to be a surprise—."

"No. He would let me know." She waited, her gaze casting between Hector and Bee, as if she expected them to say or do something.

"Should you check on Cordy?" Bee suggested. "She was so distraught."

"Yes. That's strange, isn't it? Usually she's like Mama. Except when she has one of her turns. She doesn't cry, usually. Do you think I should show her George's letter? It might reassure her."

"No. His letter wouldn't reassure Cordy," and Hector murmured his agreement to Bee's certainty. He could guess the reason Cordy wanted to escape Chalmsley and George, but too many secrets hid behind strong locks.

"Just tell her to sleep," he advised. "She needs her sleep. She's agitated without it."

"You may wish to leave her a candle burning," Bee suggested.

But Portia hesitated longer. She eyed Hector, as if she saw someone new. "You infuriated Papa."

"It was necessary."

"Richardson would be shaking in his boots. Oh, here's Richardson."

The butler came with a decanter of amber liquid and a glass. He passed them without a glance and disappeared into Cordelia's room. He emerged quickly, still carrying the decanter, and half-closed the door. "Miss Portia, are you in need of anything?"

"I am perfectly fine."

Examining her, Hector realized that the night's news hadn't affected Portia. If anything, her eyes seemed brighter, her cheeks a little flushed. She almost seemed to bounce on her toes. He'd always known her self-absorption, but—could she really not understand the dark events that now cloaked Chalmsley Court?

"I don't know the reason Cordy was so unreasonable. She's not in danger." Portia sniffed. "If she were going to be upset, then she should have been so last evening. Instead, she just sat there like a—like a—a *galantine*, all stiff and stuffed in that flouncing gown she insisted upon, like a jellied aspic with only bits of good. She should have been slapping that Moira Fraser's face."

"Moira Fraser?"

"Didn't you see her flirt with Barr? She lost her fiancé, so she plops herself beside Barr and talks his head off. She wants to steal my sister's fiancé. Well, she can't have him."

No, Hector thought, *she can't have him because Pierpoint's dead.*

"Mr. Pierpont was merely being kind," Bee defended. "Miss Fraser spent the past two days in her room, crying about Mr. Kennington's death. I was pleased that she joined us for dinner. Very few people went out of their way to speak with her, as if she carried some infection. Murder is not an infection. She had nothing to do with his death, and Mr. Pierpoint was merely trying to lift her spirits."

"That's a Banbury story. He was flirting with her. He wanted to abandon my sister. Did you not see his reaction earlier, when she had one of her fits? And all about stupid cloth. After that episode, Barr wanted nothing to do with Cordelia. He told me so. I couldn't make him see reason."

"Lady Pierpont was most cordial to Cordelia. We talked with her after her return. She didn't hesitate to speak with Cordy. And I do not believe he will break their engagement. His parents would not allow him to—."

"Of course she was cordial, the old cow. They would not want my father to discover their plans. They have a reason to cry off that society would accept, what with Uncle Raymond's problem. They would merely have to hint that Cordy has the same problem. We can say nothing to stop that gossip. Besides, Barr's parents didn't want Cordelia from the beginning. I convinced Barr that she would be an amenable wife. She wouldn't interfere in his life, not one bit. We would still be able to—well. But yesterday morning he told me that he and I wouldn't be able—and then he flirted with that Moira Fraser. Oh! He enraged me!"

Mouth agape, Bee stared at her cousin. Hector didn't think she had caught all of Portia's meaning. He had. The pieces connected easily with the girl's earlier comment about her relationship with William Kennington: *He was mine. All of them were.* He hadn't understood the comment then; he did now. Good Lord, he realized, Portia and Barrington Pierpont had apparently had a fling. And had decided to continue their *affaire* after both married other people.

Portia must also have had an *affaire* with William Kennington. Had she visited Kennington on the night of his death? Had she visited Pierpont tonight?

Had she killed them?

Portia might be romantically involved with two men, or even more, but she had no strange quirks, not like her sister, not like her mother, and certainly not like Mad Aunt Beth. She seemed more amoral than insane.

Had someone killed William Kennington and now Barrington Pierpont because of their relationship with Portia?

Was he reading the crime scene incorrectly? With the men's position and the rumpled beds with their signs of sex, he'd thought the men were killed after. He'd thought the culprit had to be a woman who slept with both men. What if the men were killed because of the woman they had slept with?

Portia's fiancé was Brougham Paton. Had he discovered the *affaires*? Had he killed the two men?

Or was Cordelia trying to protect her little sister? Cordelia, with her mildly deranged mind? Had she killed Kennington in a mistaken attempt to protect her sister? Had she discovered her sister's *affaire* with Pierpont and killed him not only to protect Portia but also in revenge for betraying her?

Cordelia, then, had two motives. As for Brougham Paton—after seeing the first murder scene, Hector hadn't even considered a man. He would have to re-think everything.

He shouldn't forget Mad Aunt Beth, who wandered the corridors in the wee hours, without her minder, without anyone to see what she did, with a moral judgement warped by her derangement. Bee might think the woman mildly deranged, but given the correct pivot point, she could easily tilt into complete insanity. Had she seen Portia with Kennington and Pierpont? Had she seen them and decided to protect her beloved niece from what she might view as their exploitation of a naïve young lady, never knowing that Portia was not naïve?

With those insights blasting through him, Hector couldn't speak. Bee stood mute as well. Was she fighting the same insights? Or had something else silenced her? Had Portia herself, with her sparkling energy and glittering eyes, shocked rational words from Bee?

Portia had managed to keep her voice lowered enough not to carry beyond the three of them. She took a sly look at the guest wing then back at them. "Everyone's back to bed. I should go back to my bed, don't you think? Will you be up the rest of the night, constable, solving the murder?"

"I will look for evidence, yes."

"And you, Bee?"

"I think—I don't think I can sleep. Richardson may need to consult with me. I think I should remain awake."

"Nothing would ever keep me from my sleep. I'm like Papa in that regard. Good night," and she calmly pattered to her bedchamber, as if a bloody body were not only a few doors away.

"Bee, we need to talk," he murmured. "Now, not later."

Richardson gave the decanter to Bee's outstretched hand. After agreeing that Hector would need a master key and accepting the news that Lord Chalmsley wished to be awakened at half-past seven, the butler then excused himself.

Hector waited for Bee. He didn't know the reason he waited; he didn't question it; he just obeyed the inner sense that he needed to wait. Across in the guest wing, the corridor had finally emptied of all but the footman.

In the reduced candlelight, Bee looked drawn. Shadows lurked under her eyes and in her cheeks. She was another who looked bone-thin. When he had caught her, after she stumbled off Pierpont's bed, she'd felt so fragile. Cordelia lived on her nerves. Bee never had. What had pared her down?

Bee stared at the empty corridor before her gaze swiveled to Hector's look. She lifted the decanter, stared at it, then gave it a little shake. "If we're going to be up for hours, we should dress, I think. And then talk, as you suggest. Downstairs?"

The long case clock began its chiming. He couldn't believe an hour had passed. "Fifteen minutes? Then we meet in the library?"

Chapter 12

"Cor, Miss, anudder mudder."

Bee threw a paisley shawl around her shoulders, a bright color to lift her spirits. The drab brown wool gown certainly wouldn't. "Thank you for your assistance, Vickery. Back to bed with you now."

"Yes, Miss."

"Have no worries about this murder. Please tell everyone. Constable Evans will solve it, I am certain." She hoped Hector would solve it. Given Great-Uncle Hamilton's wrath, he must solve it and soon. Her great-uncle would not understand the need for carefully discovered evidence. He wanted a likely suspect that a jury would convict. Most jurors would call a person guilty simply because Lord Chalmsley as the magistrate stood the suspect in the prisoner's dock.

Vickery curtsied and hurried from the room. Bee hurried herself, knowing that Hector's attire would not be as involved as her own.

Yet something had delayed him. He met her at the second story landing. In the light cast by the three-taper candelabrum on the hall table, Bee saw that the scruff from his chin had vanished. He had shaved. His lichen-colored eyes looked lighter by candlelight. Damp from a quick wash and scrub dry, his blond hair looked darker, the waves tamed. Shirt tucked in, coat spruce, and boots buffed to a shine, he had turned out for the day, not just for a couple of hours before he retreated to his chamber.

Bee had also dressed for the day although she wished she had picked up a heavier ruanna instead of the woven shawl.

She handed the whisky decanter to Hector.

"We're surely not going to start our day with this?"

"After the past two hours, we should, but we won't. I intend to hand it off to Richardson when next I see him. It wouldn't be wise to leave it untended in my chamber."

"Holyfield."

"And others like her."

They crossed the first-floor landing and continued down the steps to the shadowed gloom of the entrance hall. Someone—Richardson or the footman he'd sent downstairs—had lit the candelabra on the gilt-decorated chests that faced each other across the marble floor.

"You are band-box fresh for a pre-dawn conference," he

commented. "Robin redbreast with touches of blue. I wouldn't have put a pale-haired girl like you in such a strong color, but it works."

At the surprising compliment, Bee faltered a little.

Hector's hand shot out to steady her. "No accidents, please. One death a night is enough."

She picked up her skirts to pretend they had caused her to trip. She didn't want him to know that his compliment had caused it. Bow Street officers were sometimes called Robin Redbreasts. Was Hector creating a link between them? Or was it simply a compliment? Either way, she hugged the words to her, a little glow warming her frozen heart.

He claimed one of the hall candelabra and led the way to the library. Once there, he handed the decanter back to her. She placed it on a kneehole desk then watched as he lit the fire.

Hector dragged two chairs close to the hearth. "Let's sit here. We'll be warmer."

Without comment, she claimed the chair that faced the door then stuck her feet toward the fire. "Portia probably thinks we are prowling around Mr. Pierpont's bedchamber, looking for clues."

"Richardson locked the door then gave me a key to use. I must return it as soon as I locate the correct key."

"You have his master key? He truly trusts you."

"He should. I am a constable."

"Your position would mean very little to him if he did not hold you in regard. Richardson is a good judge of people."

"While I am not," he admitted, then bent to add more wood.

"Yes, you are. You just do not know all the people involved. It is hard to judge strangers."

Hector used the poker to re-position a log then brushed off his hands and returned to his chair. "Lord Chalmsley will not be pleased if I do not produce a suspect."

"He will not expect to find you standing before his chamber door, suspect in your grasp, when he emerges at eight o'clock. My great-uncle may roar, and we all strive not to provoke that roar, but he is not an unreasonable man."

"One of the few in your family who are not unreasonable."

She stared at the fire. The addition of new wood had seemed to choke it, but the flames had gradually licked away until they caught the new wood and began burning over it. "'Not unreasonable.' What do you mean by that?"

"Chalmsley Court has its share of mild derangement."

"Just Aunt Beth and Cordelia."

"And Lady Chalmsley, although her disorder rarely lifts its head. It shows in her inability to connect with her own children and her refusal to interact with her guests. I remember George had unreasonable tantrums that would go on for hours. So did Portia."

"He stopped having those tantrums years ago. Portia's little rages, well, if you can redirect her, they will vanish. She doesn't scream and kick anyone who comes near, not anymore, not for years and years. You *are* eight years away, Hector. They did mature. We all matured."

"Eight years and sometimes it feels like yesterday."

Bee crossed her arms, keeping them warm under the shawl. "We are straying far afield. I thought we intended to talk about the murder. Both murders."

"We are, aren't we?"

"We're talking about the family."

"I believe the family is involved." He leaned forward to add more wood, crossing two sticks over the original wood, and the flames flared higher.

She swallowed. "Who do you think is involved? I will admit that Aunt Beth knows something. She may even have the key to solve this entire mess."

"She certainly knew about Pierpont's death before anyone else did. She responds to you, Bee. She doesn't really know me."

"She liked you naming her Queen Mab."

A corner of his mouth lifted up. "A bit of luck, that. She could very easily have become angry if she knew Mab stood for 'Mad Aunt Beth'. We'll keep that between us, I hope. And I want you with me when I question her. Please, Bee."

"Of course. Anything I can do to help you, Hector. You have only to ask." Then she realized that her fiancé would be unhappy that she spent additional time with Hector. *He will have to be unhappy*, she decided. *Solving the murders is more important than anything else.* Besides, why had Edmund not emerged from his bedchamber when the murder was discovered? Where was he? Everyone out in the corridor except for him. He had emerged only briefly then retreated. Why hadn't he come out with everyone else to discover what had the house in an uproar?

"What has taken you miles and miles away?"

She turned her gaze outward, banishing her hidden worry. "Only a half-mile, not more. So, we will question Aunt Beth. Ghosting along the hallways, she might have seen something. Hector, she could be in danger."

"All the more reason to question her as early as we can. She may give me answers that will point me in the right direction."

"Are you stumbling around with a list of suspects?"

His mouth twisted, and she wished she could hand those answers to him, so he could solve the murders before her great-uncle deemed him useless and sent him off. Yet solving the murders would also take him away from her. Job done, he would have no reason to return to Chalmsley Court. Bee stared at the steadily burning fire and wished— she wished—that life had taken different turns than the ones that had led her to this point, with its sharp pivot that tilted him away from her, no matter which direction he went.

"My list of suspects increases instead of decreases. For example, Mab herself could be guilty of the murders."

"Not Aunt Beth."

"She is deranged, Bee. Mildly, you claim, and I will accept that. However, the right trigger could tip her into the abyss."

"The right trigger can tip anyone into the abyss, Hector. They do not need to be slightly deranged to kill someone. With the right motive, even the representative of the law, Constable Hector Evans, might kill someone. Just as I might do so."

He smiled a little, as if her vehemence pleased him instead of offended him. "Ouch, little Bee. You need not sting so hard. I bow to your truth. Thank you for increasing my suspect list."

"I did not mean—."

His lifted hand stopped her apology. "Let's speak honestly, Bee. A half-hour ago I was thinking that Cordelia could have killed Pierpont. Then I considered Portia. I've even considered Brougham Paton, angry that his fiancée was having *affaires* with Pierpont and Kennington."

"Oh. You took that meaning, too. I thought I must have been mistaken. Surely, surely Portia would not have considered an *affaire* with her sister's fiancée?"

"'He was mine. They all were'," he quoted as a reminder. "When they initiated their relationship, he and Cordelia may not have been engaged. After all, Portia did say that she urged him to offer for Cordelia. She convinced him that Cordelia would be an *amenable* wife. Amenable to what? To letting her husband pursue the life he wanted? Tonight, she very nearly revealed that she and Pierpont had planned to continue their relationship, even though he would be married to her sister."

Bee remembered his earlier comments about motives for murder. Yet she shook her head, refusing to believe his theory. "But Pierpoint cried off. She implied that, didn't she? When he told her that they 'wouldn't be able to'. She had to mean that they wouldn't be able to continue their *affaire*, not after he married Cordelia. I am glad," she said caustically, "that he found a bit of honor before he died."

"Another sting. Careful, Bee. Sweet little bees lose their stingers and die."

She screwed up her nose. "I am not a sweet little bee."

"Nor is Portia. Pierpont's decision enraged her. You heard her say that. Rage, Bee. Hatred and revenge. Hatred for ending their *affaire* and for planning to break his engagement to Cordelia to marry another. And revenge."

"It doesn't make sense."

"It does, in a mad, illogical way. You kill my hopes; I'll kill you. It's a violent insanity, not a mild derangement."

"I heard Portia, as clearly as you did, but I can't believe that decision would drive her to kill Cordelia's fiancé. And look at Kennington's murder. Why would she kill him? It can't be Portia. And it can't be Cordelia, even though I know you want to blame her."

"Then you would have Mr. Pierpont murdered simply because last evening he chose to flirt with Moira Fraser?" Bee gave a decided shake to her head. "That certainly doesn't make sense. And why wasn't Miss Fraser murdered? She does tie to the two men together, engaged to Mr. Kennington and flirting with Mr. Pierpont. Shouldn't we look at her motives and her movements?"

"I don't believe Moira Fraser is guilty."

"Why ever not? She has just as much reason as Portia or Cordelia does."

"For one, she's too obvious."

"Is the obvious suspect never the true suspect? That can't be a rule by which Bow Street abides."

He grinned. "It's not. Our rules don't govern who we are to consider as suspects."

"Well then. You should look more closely at Moira Fraser, not Cordelia or Portia."

"Or Aunt Beth."

"Exactly." She plopped back against her seat, not realizing until that moment her vehemence had leant her forward.

"I could believe," Hector started slowly, "that letter of Portia's. I would believe George committed these murders if he were here."

Bee hissed. "If he had, the scenes would be much bloodier."

He leaned forward, propping his elbows on his knees. "What secrets are you keeping from me, Bee?"

"I promised not to speak of it to anyone outside the family."

"We have two men dead. Surely that warrants your telling me what you know of George?"

"I promised my great-uncle. I owe him. He took me in. He gave me a home. He does his best for me. Besides, do you seriously think George is lurking in the attics? He would trumpet whatever he did. He wouldn't hide."

"This is different. If he has killed these two men—."

"*If*, a gigantic *if*. He's in Vienna. And what is his motivation? To keep the family together? To prevent Cordelia leaving when she married Pierpont? Then why would he kill Mr. Kennington? He wasn't connected to Cordelia or Portia or—or anyone. He was betrothed to Moira Fraser. The murderer is not George, Hector. Don't chase shadows, please."

"If we see him, if we have even one hint that he's here—."

"Do you truly believe he would hide? George would announce that he had returned home. 'The heir has returned to his ancestral home.' He would demand a triumphant parade."

"I don't believe George thinks clearly. What kind of treatments is he undergoing? Why were Sampson and Daniel sent with him? He doesn't mention his valet. Surely that man would be with him rather than two rough field workers."

Yet Bee merely shook her head, maintaining the secret. "We have a greater problem, Hector. You do realize, if the sequence holds true, Pierpont's bed will be burned tomorrow night. I mean tonight."

"Yes, I've considered that. Followed by another murder tomorrow night. I'll keep watch to ensure neither happens. And catch my murderess in the process."

"If the murderess is also the arsonist."

He grimaced then got up to add more wood to the fire. "I didn't need to hear that," he said when he turned back. "I very much fear that I will have to catch my murderess in the very act in order to convince Lord Chalmsley and a jury that a gently born lady could murder anyone, let alone two men."

"You need evidence."

"There is no evidence. I might manage to find the murder weapon, but I can't even trust that the person who has it is the one who wielded it or a convenient scapegoat."

"You mean, the murderer might plant the weapon in someone else's possessions."

"It's happened before. Someone that I didn't think could have possibly committed a robbery winds up in possession of the swag. It's only after a lot of questioning and more evidence and picking apart alibis that I was able to prove who did the robbery. I firmly believe that robber had other people convicted of his crime and transported. Innocent victims. He's transported himself now and off my patch. Bee, it must be six o'clock. What say you to coffee and an early breakfast in the kitchen?"

"With the servants? Servants who will answer your carefully asked questions. Of course."

Richardson met them in the entrance hall. He had changed to his dark suit that he wore like livery. He looked as stoic as ever, although the aroma of clove lingered. "Miss Seddars, I was not quite certain of your location."

"We've been in the library. Constable Evans would like to ask a few questions of the servants, if now would be an appropriate time."

"They gather in the kitchen for breakfast, Miss, at six o'clock."

The clock began chiming. "Well-timed," Hector said. "May we also have a bite to eat while we speak with them?"

"That decision is up to Mrs. Shelton, sir," but he led them to the kitchen.

Chatter echoed along the service hallways, yet when Bee and Hector entered the kitchen, the servants fell silent. Nor could they be drawn to answer his questions with more than monosyllables. Bee wasn't certain what drove their reticence? Apprehension of the constable in their midst? Or fear caused by the second murder in the overnight? She herself might be the cause, a family member that they knew, who must report to Lady Chalmsley if this visit became known. Whatever the reason, Hector didn't receive any answers that led to clear evidence or clearer motives.

They soon found themselves using the narrow servants' stair to the third floor.

Aunt Beth's caretaker looked scarcely awake. With teacup still in her hand, she gaped while Hector made his request. "She's still asleep," she finally said.

"I am not," Mab rebutted. "Come away. 'Come away, come away, come to the fair, In your holiday gear Trim and dainty appear, Come away, come away to the fair'."

"That's a nice greeting," Hector said and pushed past the nurse into the room.

Aunt Beth sat on the edge of the mattress, her bare feet dangling a foot from the floor. She clung to the bedcurtains. As soon as she saw Hector, she called, "It's Carrion Crow!"

"Good morning, Queen Mab." He swept a low bow, extended with a flourish as if he wore a feathered tricorn hat. Behind him, Bee gave a deep curtsey, worthy of royalty.

The old woman giggled. "One for sorrow. But now I have two for joy."

"And you are very well met, Aunt Beth," Bee said, advancing past Hector.

"No, no, Queen Mab to you. The fairies' midwife, remember?"

"Indeed I do. Did you sleep well, your majesty?" She winked.

The older woman winked back. "I slept very well, although a snoring kept me awake."

"Miss Seddars, if you're to be here for a bit, I'll just nip down to the kitchen and back."

"Of course, Nurse. I am happy to extend my visit with Queen Mab."

"Where did she get that nonsense? She woke up with it this

morning."

Hector and Bee exchanged a look while Aunt Beth giggled again.

When the nurse left, Aunt Beth slid from the bed and went to stand in front of the hearth. "It's cold. Brrr. I should stay in my bed."

"We hope you can answer some questions, your majesty."

"Shall I be the clever lass?"

"If you will." He indicated the chair before the fire. "Will you sit down?"

She hopped onto the chair then extended her feet to the fire. "Ask away, ask away, then off to the fair we'll go."

Bee came to stand beside Hector. "Stop it, Aunt Beth. You are not mad. I know you like your songs and you like being mysterious, but this is not the time to confuse Hector with riddling snippets of song. Just give him honest answers."

The woman frowned. "Honest answers? In this house? In this room?"

"Yes, please. You *know* things, almost before anyone else does. Two days ago, you knew that a woman had killed William Kennington."

"Who?"

"The first man who died. You said '*she* killed him'."

She squinted her eyes. "When did I say that?"

"We were outside, Aunt Beth."

"Ah. In the cold, cold garden." Childlike, she swung her feet back and forth.

"Yes. We saw Constable Evans riding to the house—."

"Carrion Crow, out of the oaks, come to catch a murderer."

"Yes, you said exactly that. Then you said 'she killed him'. Who is *she*?"

"I thought the questions were from the crow."

"I want to know that answer," Hector promptly declared. "Who is *she*?"

"I don't know."

"Then how did you know that a woman killed William Kennington?"

Her shoulders hunched. "I just knew. I'm hungry."

"Your nurse will return in a few minutes," Bee soothed. "Please pay attention, Aunt Beth. We want to know who killed William Kennington, and we need to know who *she* is."

"I don't know."

When Bee gave a frustrated sigh, Hector laid a soothing hand on her arm. Then he dragged a second chair close to Aunt Beth's. He sat down, gave her a smile, then propped his elbows on his knees and leaned toward her. "What do you see at night, Queen Mab, when you are ghosting through the corridors?"

"I like you. You don't pester me." She frowned at Bee. Then she gave her impish grin. "I see things. Servants drinking wine. Guests going to rooms they don't belong in. Other people going to rooms they don't belong him. Not many. Not often. Sometimes not at all. I see, though, and they don't see me."

"Did you see anything last night?"

"A woman, drifting along the corridor. She climbed the stairs then disappeared into darkness. That's a pretty shawl."

Bee took it off and draped it around the old woman's shoulders. "Here. It will keep you warmer, I think. What did you see that made you come to my room, Aunt Beth?"

"Blood," she said immediately. Then shuddered. "Blood and blood." She held out her hands and studied the palms. "I didn't get it on me. Grimly ghost I'd be. I ran then. Bee would help me. Bee did help me." She smiled at the younger woman.

"Why did you sing about 'The Forlorn Lover'? Then you sang 'Lady Bothwell's Lament'. Why did you pick those songs, Queen Mab?"

She looked back at Hector. Stretching out her hand, her fingers inches from his face, she said, "A man deceived by the maid he deceived, a maid who bore a bastard child. Poor man. 'Over his white bones, when they are bare, The wind will blow forevermore'." Tears dripped from her eyes. "Poor Bee. Wrote and wrote, never answered. Most wanted, least expected, Carrion Crow. Don't break her heart."

"'Twa Corbies'," Hector and Bee said together.

Aunt Beth dropped her hand and twined it into the shawl. "Two crows making a moan. 'Where shall we go and dine today?' Will your dinner be sweet?" she asked them. "You're feasting on two newly slain knights, not one. There'll be three before she's done. Thatch your nest with his golden hair while his lady takes another man."

"There," Bee whispered. "That's her prophecy. She does that a lot. Here we are, both of us, wanting to know about the murders of two men. But why does she say there will 'be three before she's done'? Three men? What does she know?"

"Can you tell us anymore, sweet Queen Mab?"

Her eyes flashed open. "Not sweet, me. Angry. Devilish."

Hector leaned close to the older woman. "Who is the maid who bore a bastard child?"

Her eyes narrowed, her lips closed and curved, giving her the look of an imp. She locked her lips and tossed the imaginary key over her left shoulder.

He leaned back. "Will you not answer any more questions, Queen Mab? Even though we desperately need your answers?"

Clutching the shawl to her thin breasts, she shook her head. Her grey hair spilled out of her braid and over her shoulders.

"We do need your answers. You know things, I think, that would help us stop this murderer before she kills again."

Again she shook her head.

"I need your help. Carrion Crow that I am, I didn't see the murders. Only the bodies, afterward. I didn't find either one. Only afterward do I see the death. Only afterward can I act. I would like to prevent the next death. I cannot do that without your help."

Aunt Beth slid from the chair. She walked to Bee. For a moment she stared up at the younger woman. She rubbed her hand over the shawl. Then she turned away and returned to her bed, climbing onto the mattress and pulling the bedcovers up before she leaned back against the pillows.

Hector stood. "No answers, Queen Mab?"

Again she locked her lips and tossed the key. Her eyes slid to the door.

Her caretaker stood there, her gaze darting from one to the next. When she saw them spot her, she came into the room. "Queen Mab? Are you the one that started that, then, Constable Evans?"

"I am."

"Did you get your questions answered?"

He ignored the woman and turned to Aunt Beth. Again he bowed deeply. "I take my leave, your majesty. May I see you later? I do hope so."

She smiled but touched a finger to her lips.

Bee curtsied again, then followed Hector out of the room.

He shut the door then drew Bee to the third-floor landing. "She doesn't want to talk when that nurse might hear."

"I can understand that. Lady Chalmsley is forever asking the woman what Aunt Beth has been doing and saying."

"That's interesting."

"How so?"

He shook his head. "It just is. Does anyone else ever want to know what Mab says?"

"Not that I know of."

He started her down the stairs. "Why did she tell me not to break your heart?"

Bee stopped. He turned and met her eyes. On the higher step, she had a couple of inches on him. Standing so close, she could see the radiant lines in his pale green eyes. Her reflection filled his pupils. Tiny reflections of a pale-haired girl who didn't look as scared as she felt.

"She said you wrote and wrote, but never answered. I suppose she means that you wrote letters to me that I never answered. I never received any letters, Bee. Did you receive mine?"

"You wrote to me? No, I didn't receive any letter from you."

"I didn't think so. Not after Lord Chalmsley removed me from your presence. He told me that, you know, those very words, on the day I asked for your assistance with my investigation. I think he was afraid that I would contaminate you. He reminded me that you had an inheritance, making you a jewel to which a mere barrister's son should not aspire. You are better suited to a man of rank and name like Edmund Tretheway."

"My great-uncle said that?"

"Not those exact words, but that was his meaning. I believe he intercepted our letters and burned them."

"My great-uncle?"

"You don't believe me?"

She met his gaze, as unwavering as her own. "Oh, I believe you. Poor man, having to intercept the mail for months and months. You wrote to me?"

"Writing you was all that kept me sane those first weeks in London. A country boy in a soot-filled city, surrounded by strangers. Yes, I wrote to you. I poured my heart out to you."

"Hector—." Before she could form any words, he caught her close and kissed her.

Bee had dreamed of his arms around her, his kiss unlocking her heart. He'd never been a hesitant young man. His kiss was like him. His lips pressed to hers. Then his tongue touched the seam of her lips. When she opened her lips, he swept in to taste her mouth.

For a few frozen seconds she didn't know what to think. Edmund had kissed her this way. She hadn't liked the thrust of his tongue into her mouth.

Hector's kiss was different. He didn't overwhelm her. His tongue touched hers, played with the tip, invited her into the kiss. Her heart thudded in her chest. The feel of him, the heat of him, the taste of him overwhelmed her. He insisted on her participation. When she returned his touch with her own, his whole body trembles. His arms tightened. His heart pounded in rhythm with hers.

He broke the kiss to skate his lips over her chin, down her neck. "Bee, my little Bee," he whispered. His mouth tracked to the hollow of her neck. His tongue touched her there, tasting her, marking her. Then his mouth returned to hers, and the sweet pleasure started over again.

She was drowning in it, willingly succumbing to the sensuality of his kiss, when Hector lifted his head. Her fingers knuckled in his hair, Bee wanted to pull him back to her, but he resisted. When her eyes fluttered open, she saw that he looked down the steps. Hands on her ribcage, he held her back from him, keeping inches between them.

"Hector," she whispered and arched toward him.

He frowned. Not at her but at whatever had yanked him from the pleasure of their kisses. "Bee, my Bee, we can't. Listen."

Men talking. A young woman's laugh. The world had crashed back into her dream.

She tried to pry his hands away. "We can't be caught. If my great-uncle finds out—."

"Are you afraid of him, Bee?"

"No." She stilled. Her trembling fingers touched his cheek. She remembered how Aunt Beth had stretched out to touch him. But the old woman hadn't let herself connect with the carrion crow. She'd been too afraid. Yet Bee couldn't deny herself, not any longer. "I'm afraid *for* you. Hector, my great-uncle will forbid me to work with you. He won't let me break my engagement. He will dismiss you. He will send you far, far from Chalmsley Court. I'll never see you again."

He looked back. A fire had greened his eyes, giving them more life. He wrapped his hand around her cold one and touched his lips to her fingertips. "His lordship won't stop me this time, Bee. I'll no longer be 'most wanted, least expected'. Not now that I know."

"Know what?"

"I know that you love me." Color burned in her face. He chuckled. "Did you think I wouldn't know?" He set her back but only to take her arm and tug her down to the step beside him. "Come. These two corbies have two murders to solve before there's a third slain knight."

"We have no evidence."

"Then we have a trap to set."

Chapter 13

Yet setting a trap for the murderess waited on the night, and the night waited on the long hours of the day, and the long hours of the day were filled with troubles.

The first came when Hector realized that the carriages of the Frasers and the Pierponts waited in the forecourt.

He watched the butler direct two footmen carrying a trunk from the first floor. When he opened the great door for them, Hector saw a carriage with impatient horses and post-boys milling about.

"Richardson, what's toward? Whose coach is that?"

"The Pierponts, sir. If you would step to the right, sir."

He obeyed, and a page rushed out with a bandbox.

"The Pierponts are leaving?" Even as he asked it, he saw the second carriage through the windows of the first. "Who else?"

"The Frasers, sir."

"I did not give permission for anyone to leave. My investigation is far from concluded."

"Lord Chalmsley allowed them, Mr. Evans."

He controlled the curse that wanted to roll out. "Richardson, where will I find his lordship at this moment?"

"In his study, sir."

"Has anyone else been given permission to leave?"

As the butler shook his head, Hector turned for the study on the back connecting hall.

Three sharp raps on the study door elicited a "Come." Hector opened the door and shut it with restrained violence.

Lord Chalmsley continued writing.

"My lord," Hector said, refusing to wait when witnesses might slip away.

Those deep blue eyes, so like Bee's, so like his younger daughter's, lifted briefly then returned to the ledger before him.

"My lord. You are allowing the Pierponts and the Frasers to leave."

Chalmsley continued writing. "The Pierponts just lost their son. I will not delay them in returning to their home." His eyes lifted then again dropped. "Not when they must bury him as soon as they arrive there."

"And the Frasers?"

"I see no reason for them to remain when they are grief-stricken about Mr. Kennington's murder."

"My lord, I have not finished my investigation. I may have additional questions for them."

Chalmsley set down his quill. He lifted his head and frowned at Hector. "What more do you need to know? Surely you do not believe that the Pierponts murdered their own son. Surely you do not believe that the Frasers murdered Mr. Kennington. In three months he would have become their son-in-law."

"I have not finished my investigation."

"Your investigation needs to move more rapidly as well."

"How am I to complete my investigation when five witnesses are leaving?"

The lord slammed the ledger shut. Then he controlled his anger. Pushing back his chair, he slowly rose. He rested his fingertips on the desk, inches from the ledger. "Constable Evans, I expected you to use that mind you should have inherited from your father. He was clever. Do you not understand that the Frasers and the Pierponts had nothing to do with these deaths? If you had properly concluded your investigation, Barrington Pierpont would still be alive. Instead, you go here and there, asking questions but not making an arrest. Do you have any idea who this murderer is? Any idea at all? I know that you have questioned my guests. They have complained enough about your interrogations. Have you questioned the servants? Can you determine nothing about these murders?"

Hector refused to let those rapid questions intimidate him. He crossed his arms over his chest. Knowing that he skirted close to insubordination of the district magistrate and a peer of the realm, he still scowled. "I have questioned the servants. They are not involved in this case. They knew neither man. I also do not believe a heartless killer is on your staff. I do believe that the same person is perpetrating these murders. Yet I can hardly make an arrest, my lord, when I have no evidence to point directly to that person."

"No evidence? I would hope you have an idea who held a grudge against William Kennington and Barrington Pierpont."

"I do have an idea. However, evidence will hold the case together through the inquests and the trial. I have theories, not proof. Theories will not convince juries, my lord. I should not make an arrest with tangible evidence."

"Sir Richard Ford did not teach you that."

"Begging your pardon, my lord, Sir Richard very carefully instructed me on that very point. He drills into all of his officers that suspicion is not sufficient for conviction. Proof is needed."

"Have you even looked for proof? Or are you too busy flirting with my niece?"

Hector produced his little notebook, brimming with his notes on the case. He snapped it across his palm. "I am constantly looking for proof, my lord. I have conducted interviews, as you yourself know. I have checked alibis. But when the murderer walks off with the weapon, when I am prevented from searching the bedchambers for that weapon, when no person can serve as witness to the crime, then I must build my case on circumstantial evidence. As of this moment," he jabbed his forefinger at the floor, "I have too many potential suspects. And you have given leave for five people who might be witnesses if I had time to speak with them when they are not emotionally charged with grief."

Chalmsley leaned over his desk. "Are you taking me to task, Constable? I'll have you remember that I am magistrate here, not you."

A tentative knock came on the door.

Chalmsley straightened and tugged down his waistcoat and then his coat. "Come."

The door swung open. Richardson, looking stern. "Mr. Jonas Henning, my lord, from Bow Street." Then he stepped side.

A man in blue coat and a robin-red waistcoat entered. The Bow Street Runner didn't glance at Hector, just walked up beside him then bowed to Lord Chalmsley. "My lord. Forgive the delay, but Sir Richard would not release me until yesterday morning."

"I do not forgive it, and I will inform Sir Richard of my dissatisfaction with this delay. Had you arrived yesterday, then Barrington Pierpont would be alive, and I would not have my own constable taking me to task for his lack of *evidence*." He reached a roar with the last words.

The door shut as the butler strategically retreated.

"My lord? Barrington Pierpont?" the Runner questioned the name. "I understood that Mr. William Kennington was the victim."

Chalmsley huffed and flopped down his chair.

"Kennington was murdered first," Hector supplied. "Pierpont was murdered last night. And Lord Chalmsley has seen fit to allow five people to leave this morning."

"The carriages that just left the forecourt?"

"Tell him who is leaving, eh, Constable?" the lord snapped. "Tell him the reason I allow them to leave. And then he questions my authority," he muttered. "I'm the magistrate here."

"Mr. Kennington's fiancée and her parents are leaving as well as Mr. Pierponts' parents."

"People who would not commit these murders. Do you not agree with that, Constable Evans?"

"I do, my lord, but I also remind you that evidence is needed for a conviction. They are potential witnesses who may be able to attest to motive or circumstance."

"They saw the crimes?" the new arrival asked.

"No." Hector glanced at him. From his years working with the Bow Street Runners, he didn't remember a Henning. He didn't recognize this man, all drab blue and brown except for the waistcoat typical of the London officers. Yet Henning could have entered the force after Hector left London. "No, and they are emotionally stricken by them. However, they would have offered perspectives on the people who remain here, perspectives that might help narrow my list of suspects."

"I see. What determination have you made?"

"The same person committed the murders. From the state of the crime scene, from the relaxed nature of the bodies and the wound, I believe the murders happened after the victim had fallen asleep. We also have signs that the victim had sexual relations with the murderer. Both men were unsuspecting when they were killed. The wounds were made by a similar weapon, easily wielded by the perpetrator. The size of the wound fits an ice pick, a heavy one such is used in the dining room as opposed to a kitchen pick."

"You believe the murderer is a woman?"

Hector's view of this crime-catcher improved. He nodded while Chalmsley breathed through his teeth. "A woman?" his lordship questioned. "A woman killed two men? After she had consensual relations with them? Not possible!"

"It happens, my lord." Henning's support sounded calm. He'd undoubtedly faced his share of women who committed heinous crimes. "How many people do you suspect?"

"Nine."

The officer's eyes opened wide. "Good lord."

"Exactly."

"Nine suspects," Chalmsley ground. Red suffused his face. "Nine! Have you no way to narrow that list even by half? Have you even tried? Are have you been wasting my time, letting Pierpont be killed, while trying to winkle back into my niece's affections?"

Hector faced the peer. He tried to keep his voice bland, his expression blank, but he felt the color heating his own face at Chalmsley's two accusations. The first suggested that Hector didn't know how to do his job. The second also slighted his work, implying that he was unprofessional in his service. "My lord." He pressed his lips together and started again. "My lord, I have narrowed the list. I believe our murderess is one of two people. Perhaps one of three. I do not like to fasten upon any one person, however, without more substantial proof than guesswork. Once I name a single person, the wheels of justice will begin rolling, and she will likely hang. I would rather be certain than name the wrong woman. Justice can be swift. I do not want to find out I am wrong after she is hanged and in the clay-cold ground."

Only as he said the last words did he recognize the quotation from an old ballad. Queen Mab's derangement was infecting him.

"Who? Which two?" Chalmsley insisted. "Tell me. Who is the murderess in my house?"

"I do not like to say without evidence, my lord."

"Who?" he roared.

Hector waited until the walls no longer shook. "Your own daughter, my lord. Either Cordelia or Portia. I do not believe they are working in tandem. I cannot determine which one is the culprit."

"No. No, no, no," he started as soon as Hector completed his first sentence, and he didn't stop denying it until Hector finished. Then he swore long and hard, growling the curses, and ending with "Demmed fool. Not my daughters. Neither one of them," he shouted. Then he turned to Henning. "You see what I must contend with? Fool!"

Henning had rocked back a step. He didn't change position, just turned his head to look at Hector. "Have you reasonable suspicions, Constable Evans? Or is this merely a guess?"

"I have reason for my suspicions, yes. I would not have revealed my suspicions to Lord Chalmsley had he not demanded them."

"My lord." Henning waited until the peer swiveled his glaring eyes in his direction. "I will review the constable's case notes—you have been keeping them?"

Hector produced his notebook.

"Good. I will review these case notes with Constable Evans. Should I come to the same conclusion, we must act. Two deaths in three days, that is dangerous, my lord. A murderer does not usually kill so quickly."

"Not my daughters. Not either one of them," Chalmsley insisted. He jabbed a finger at Hector. "He's worthless, you hear me? Worse than worthless. You, Henning, you find out who he's protecting. You find it out. I won't have my jewel and my poppet accused, not outside this room, not without evidence. I place you in charge."

"My lord, Constable Evans is the local authority."

"Not when he names my daughters. You are in charge, Henning. Now leave me, both of you. Review your case notes. When you find out who he's protecting, arrest her. Not my daughters. Demmed fool."

When they were in the hall, with the closed door between them and Lord Chalmsley, Hector said bitterly, "He won't listen to sense unless we give him incontrovertible evidence."

"I see your difficulty. You have not collected the evidence you need."

"I have not," he agreed. "Unless I can find the murder weapon in her hand or catch her before the next person is killed, I may not get the evidence I must have for his lordship to accept his daughter is murdering these men."

"Shall we get to it, then? Where may we work without interruption?"

"The conservatory."

.~.~.~.

Bee didn't know the reason she glanced at William Kennington's door as she passed on the way to her room. A sound, perhaps something else. Richardson had locked the door, or so she thought, but she remembered Hector saying that any key would open it, with a little jiggling and rattling in the lock.

When she touched the door, it swung open.

The fire-ravaged bed caught her eyes first. As she entered the room, movement to her left made her jump.

The curtain remaining on the front-facing window had belled out.

"Who's there? Is anyone there?"

A hand reached from behind the curtain, then a woman stepped out, her hair a golden halo. The sunlight created a glare that left her face in shadow, but only one person had such beautiful hair. "Portia? What are you doing in here?"

Her cousin laughed. "I could say the same of you, Bee."

"I saw the door—." She stopped. She hadn't actually seen anything. "Why are you here?"

The young woman placed her hand on a charred bedpost. "Why am I here? Did you know that Will and I were seeing each other? In London. He liked to tease me. Oh, and he could kiss. He swore that he loved me, but he forgot all about me. He shouldn't have done that, Bee, should he? He proposed to that Moira Fraser and forgot all about me."

"If I remember correctly, you accepted Brougham Paton's offer before Mr. Kennington offered for Miss Fraser."

"That means nothing. He knew Brougham was merely going to be my husband. Brougham wasn't going to interfere in my life. Will knew that. He knew we could still have our fun." She sighed. "And he was such fun. You never kissed him, Bee. You should have. Will gave the best kisses." Then she saw Bee's widened eyes and laughed. "Don't be so shocked, Bee. Will wasn't my first lover. None of them were. They were all mine, you know."

She *was* shocked—her cousin was apparently involved with several men—but she tried to hide that jolt by asking about Portia's previous statement. "What do you mean when you say Brougham wasn't going to interfere in your life? He will be your husband."

"Brougham knows I like to have my fun." She glanced at her cousin then caroled a laugh. "You are so strait-laced, Bee. Or perhaps you like to pretend to be. I saw you on the stairs, kissing Hector. You stayed up with him, didn't you? How well does he kiss?"

"Better than Edmund," she retorted. Then she registered everything that Portia was saying. Hector needed evidence. Would Portia's statements to her count as evidence in court? "Were you angry at Will?"

"Yes. He wasn't supposed to forget about me. He swore that he wouldn't. And then, once he came here, he lied to me. He said that he hadn't forgotten me. I wanted to believe him." She released the bedpost. "Goodness, I've dirtied my hand. May I wash it in your room, Bee?"

"Of course. Did you use a key?" Portia stared at her. "I will need to lock the door. I thought Richardson had locked it."

"He did, but virtually any key will open the doors, Bee. Didn't you know what? How silly of you. You've been running this house for years, and you didn't know that."

She ushered her cousin out. Portia seemed more concerned with getting the soot off her hand than her presence in Kennington's bedchamber when the room should have been locked.

The butler had the appropriate horror. "Miss Portia entered there? She should not have. I did not think, after she was in—."

Bee caught his cut-off words. "Richardson, tell me."

"I should not, Miss Seddars. His lordship is very upset this morning. Something that Constable Evans told him, I am not certain of the specifics, but it concerns Miss Portia and Miss Cordelia."

Did Hector share his suspicions with my great-uncle? That hadn't been wise, not without evidence. "Where is Constable Evans this morning? I haven't seen him since breakfast."

"He is currently closeted with the Bow Street officer who arrived this morning, Miss. They are in the conservatory, I believe. Should he be informed of Miss Portia's activities?"

"A Bow Street officer. Who arrived this morning."

"Yes, Miss."

"No. No, don't interrupt them. I will tell him later. Now, tell me what you thought better of saying."

He bit his lips, rolling them, then nodded to himself. "Miss Portia was in Mr. Pierpont's room, Miss. This was after Lord Pierpont had his body transported to the wagon and sent back to their home. When Lord and Lady Pierpont left the house, I went to ensure the room remained untouched until Constable Evans and the officer—his name is Henning—until they examined the room. I believe they intend to do so. When I opened the room with my key, Miss Portia was already there."

"What was she doing?"

"I could not say, Miss Seddars. When I saw her, she was merely staring at the bed."

"Why? Why was she there?"

Knowing the question wasn't for him, Richardson remained stoic.

"Could it be—? No. I won't speculate. We need evidence."

"Constable Evans will find evidence, I am certain of it."

Bee blinked. "You have great faith in him?"

"We all do, Miss. All the servants, you understand. We have known Mr. Evans since he was a boy. He has grown to be a good man, an honorable man, a gentleman. He will make some woman a fine husband." With those last two sentences, he gave her a direct look then bowed and strode away.

Blushing, Bee wondered how many people had seen her kissing Hector on the stairs early this morning.

What was the butler hinting, telling her that Hector would make some woman a fine husband?

Chapter 14

Tea was a disaster.

Cordelia came in with her hair cut short, chopped so close in places that her scalp showed whitely. Black lace draped her shoulders. The stark color emphasized her pallor. Red scratches covered her hands. Her appearance silenced everyone.

"Cordelia! What have you done?" her mother cried. Portia reached for her hands to examine the scratches, but she sidestepped her sister. She picked up her cup and saucer, chose a sweet pastry, and went to sit beside the fire.

"Good lord," John Nashe said and removed himself to another seat.

Mindful of Hector's injunction to let Cordelia learn to cope, Bee remained in her seat. She tried to keep her gaze away from her cousin, but it kept returning. Everyone's gaze fastened on Cordelia.

"Why?" Portia asked. "Why have you cut your hair? It was so long and beautiful. I loved it. Why did you cut it? No, you hacked it off."

"I used scissors."

"It's not even cut evenly. You just chopped at it."

"My penance."

"What did she say?"

"Her penance. What can she possibly mean?"

"Did she kill him? Did she kill them both?"

Over the murmured questions, Portia asked again, "When did you cut your hair? How?"

"Silly, Portia. I told you. I used scissors. This afternoon."

"But—why?" she asked again.

"My penance."

"Don't keep saying that. You have done nothing that needs punishment. You're good."

She looked at her sister as if she were simple. "Poor Portia. Do you not know? We are all evil. We all must be punished. This is the first part of my penance. The second part, the worst part, is that I will never escape. I know that now. Never, never escape. I will never marry. I will never leave the Court. Like a nun, married to this house."

"O, woe is thee," Portia mocked.

Cordelia's eyes never blinked. She just turned her teacup handle to align with her thumb holding the saucer. "Woe is me, sister dear? This is your fault."

"How is your chopped-off hair my fault? Say it—if you dare."

She opened her mouth, then faltered and looked away. "I should not have left my chamber. I should not have."

"Better to live there than out in the world," Portia snapped. "Especially if you are to do such stupid things as cutting off your hair."

"Did she kill him?" a woman whispered.

Bee could no longer be quiet. She jumped up. "She didn't kill anyone. Cordelia would never hurt anyone. Can't you see? She turns everything inside, on herself. Gods, Cordy."

She tried to take her cousin's tea from her, but Cordelia snatched it back. "I want my tea."

Bee sank onto her chair and watched Cordy determinedly eat her pastry and drink her tea. Then she set aside the china, wrapped her arms around herself as if she were cold, and rocked back and forth, back and forth.

.~.~.~.

The review of Hector's case notes quickly became a disaster.

Henning opened by asking, "You have a gaol to house this murderess once we arrest her?"

"It's dank and filthy. Fit only for drunks coming off a bender and local farm boys after fighting at the end of Market Day."

He nodded. "We'll be using it, though, won't we? We should have our murderess in irons before afternoon tea."

"If we come to a conclusion later than that, Lord Chalmsley has a storage room in the cellary that we can press into duty."

"Good, good." Henning started his review, asking for Hector's suspicions of Portia and Cordelia. He listened without comment to the explanation, the background, the motives.

Then Henning ignored everything Hector had said.

He flipped back to the first page in the little notebook. "I've heard this before: *Smiles disguise knives; innocence is a cloak easily shed.* Where have I heard that?"

"Sir Richard used to say it. I start every case writing those words. They remind me to look closely at every person involved in the crime."

"But you haven't, have you? You've blinded yourself, Evans. Who found the first body?"

"The maid Holyfield."

"Who did she report this to? Miss Beatrice Seddars. Not the butler. Not the housekeeper. Would they not be the appropriate persons for a maid to report her discovery to? And here, you've written that *B*— Beatrice Seddars, I presume?" When Hector nodded, the officer continued, "*B examined the body first, before anyone else. She directed the maid to stand outside while she herself was in the room alone.*"

"Yes, but Holyfield said——." He dragged his gaze from the bright blue sky above the frozen landscape, with frost that the sun's rays hadn't managed to melt. Henning's question had a trap in it, although Hector couldn't see it. "I have a note on the next page or so, I believe," he directed and waited until the officer turned the pages. "The maid notified Miss Seddars because she would know what to do."

"Miss Seddars controls the household?"

"No, I wouldn't say that. It's more that she manages it for Lady Chalmsley, who won't manage it."

"That's interesting. Her ladyship is remiss in her duties."

"Neglectful rather than remiss," he corrected, not wanting anything misunderstood. If Henning was going to pick at every little detail, then Hector would ensure each detail was accurate. "When a difficulty arises, the servants turn to Miss Seddars."

The man turned a page, turned the next, scanned the block print, then flipped back to the original page. Eyes still on the page, he asked, "Who set up your first interviews? With the chambermaid and the valet?"

"The butler, through Miss Seddars' direction."

"Did she speak with them before you did? Did she perhaps provide them with ideas about what they should say in answer to your questions?"

"Bee—Miss Seddars wouldn't do that. Besides, she was here all the morning. She had ample opportunity long before my arrival to speak with Dowding and Holyfield. My understanding, however, is that she was busy following Lord Chalmsley's instructions about removing Mr. Kennington's body to the chapel and closing off the room prior to my arrival. Then the Frasers had to be dealt with. Miss Fraser was distraught. She didn't come down from her room until that evening."

"The Frasers. That's Miss Fraser, his fiancée, and her parents. Among those who just left in their carriage. After your arrival, when it became obvious that a full investigation into the murder would occur? Did Miss Seddars speak with this Dowding and Holyfield then?"

"Not with Dowding. By noon he was out of the house." He leaned back, one booted foot crossed over his knee, his hand resting negligently on his ankle, seemingly at ease, while every sense stayed alert for sneaking snares. "With the maid, Miss Seddars may have discussed the events that I would question."

"What is this note about curtains?"

"Miss Seddars opened the curtains in order to see Mr. Kennington more closely."

"You've also written *before sunrise.*"

"That was a discrepancy." He hadn't remembered that one. Now, though, Hector recalled that jarring note when Bee had confessed she had forgotten how early it was. That wasn't like her. "She said she opened the curtains to have a steadier light by which to see the wound, but the sun was not yet up."

"That doesn't make sense."

"No. In her defense, she'd recently been awakened, and she'd been shocked by Mr. Kennington's body."

Those brown eyes rested steadily on Hector. "She said this to you."

"No. I surmised it."

"I see. Why did she have the maid wait in the hallway while she alone examined the room? Did this Holyfield see what Miss Seddars did?" When Hector shook his head, Henning drew a finger across the page. "Did you also surmise that Miss Seddars ordered the maid to remain in the hallway so she would have opportunity to alter evidence before anyone else viewed the body?"

"I didn't write that."

"But you acknowledge the possibility?"

"I would be blind if I didn't acknowledge it, but Miss Seddars wouldn't alter anything. You don't know her, Henning. She wouldn't do that. If she murdered Kennington, she would have the wit to clear up any evidence before anyone found his body."

"You are saying she would be a clever murderess."

Hector very carefully corrected the officer. "I am saying Bee— Beatrice Seddars is clever, not that she's a murderess. The maid said that she didn't want to look back into the room. Miss Seddars asked her to wait in the hall. She didn't order her to wait there. She then sent Holyfield to wake the butler Mr. Richardson and the housekeeper Miss Lovell."

"You have written the word *coached*." He displayed the note page with the word in capitals.

And Hector understood how witnesses felt during his interrogations. The cold landscape was nothing to the freezing temperature in the conservatory where they sat. He expected icicles to drip off the ferns, ice to glaze the flagstones. "Something I noticed during the interview. Holyfield kept looking to Miss Seddars for her approval."

"You think Miss Seddars anticipated your questions and guided the maid's answers?"

"I wondered that," he admitted. "I am suspicious by nature. The job teaches us to be, and I was in the job for over seven years."

"Yes, I am aware of your reputation before you left Bow Street. Even though I came after your exit, the name Hector Evans was renown for solving the trickiest of cases. You never lost a case, I hear, even when your perpetrator was wealthy. I understood you never hesitated to lay a case against merchants and gentry."

Henning sounded grudging. Hector tried not to sound arrogant. "The Crown prosecutor made good use of the evidence I found. Only one man that I brought to justice never admitted to his crime. He refused. Highway robbery was a hanging offense. He went to his grave claiming his innocence."

"Do you perhaps still wonder if he was innocent? Is that the reason you refuse to move forward without clear evidence?"

"I refuse to move forward because I have no evidence, only speculation. And that man was guilty. I had two eyewitnesses, men who didn't know each other in any way that I could find. He also kept a journal. That wasn't reading for the weak of mind. He carefully selected his victims, people he held a grudge against. In one case, he regretted that he hadn't shot the man."

Henning nodded. "Your notes are not reading for the weak of mind. I find it difficult to read your scrawl." He offered a smile, which Hector didn't return. "Yet you say this case has stumped you."

"I've only been on the estate three days. I expected a few more days before Lord Chalmsley grew impatient."

He didn't pursue that comment. "These notes, *removal from estate* and *control of property*, what are they about?"

Hector nearly sighed. He'd put too much into the notebook. When he'd written it, he hadn't truly understood Bee or her decisions or her situation. Writing the words helped him slow down his thought process enough to work out what she had experienced. "Miss Seddars had stated that she was late for sleep because she'd been writing a letter to her man-of-business. His name's Cosgrove. He's in London. He currently manages her inheritance while Lord Chalmsley serves as a trustee. She wished that her fiancé not have control of her inheritance upon their marriage, that Mr. Cosgrove retain all control."

"It is curious that she would accept a man's proposal when she didn't trust him. It is Mr. Edmund Tretheway to whom she is betrothed, is that correct?"

He wondered where and when Henning had received his information about the guests at Chalmsley. "Tretheway's her fiancé," he confirmed with a nod. "She said something later, I can't remember the exact words, that had me wondering if she'd received pressure to accept his proposal. I had the impression that she would not remain at Chalmsley Court if she didn't accept him."

"You thought Lord Chalmsley would want Miss Seddars removed from the estate? He wanted her removed from any association with his family if she did not accept Tretheway's proposal? Is he so desperate to have her gone from the estate? Does he wish she did not have so much control of his servants and the house?"

"I don't think Lord Chalmsley views Bee as a threat. He's tight-fisted, and he cannot access any monies from her inheritance, only a percentage of her quarterly payment and stipends to reimburse her board and living. He may be weary of the yearly outlay of funds for a woman's presentation during the Season without any anticipation of a return. Marriage to Tretheway would not only remove her as a financial drain on the estate but also create strong ties to the Tretheway family. Edmund Tretheway is related to an earl. His family is of excellent reputation although the fortune's a little weak. Tretheway probably needs Bee's funds more than he wants a wife. Chalmsley promoted the match. She acquiesced. I wouldn't have expected her to do otherwise."

Henning leaned back in his chair. "That's a long explanation when I expected a simple 'yea' or 'nay'."

"We should be accurate."

He lifted an eyebrow. "Indeed." Yet he scanned Hector, as if expecting to see—what? Signs of love? Signs that he was under Bee's influence? Signs that Lord Chalmsley had burned the last friendly bridge to Hector? Signs that Hector would leave his lordship's employ once this case ended? He didn't know half those answers himself until this very moment. How could Henning see them?

The Bow Street officer—and Hector knew the job he wanted when this case ended—returned to the notebook. He squinted. "*B claimed that she looked for the weapon after she examined the wound closely.* You underlined *claimed* and *closely*. Why would Miss Seddars do these two things? Examine the wound and then look for the weapon?"

"She thought he had committed suicide. She hoped he had."

"She hoped for suicide?" He put down the notebook and folded his hands over his trim belly. "Miss Seddars seems remarkably cold-blooded. She enters a room where murder has occurred, a bloody scene if I read your notes correctly. The gentleman is naked, covered in gore, and she closely examines his wound. Then she searches for a weapon. Is that the reaction you would expect of a gently reared young lady?"

"Not the normal reaction. Not the one I would have expected eight years ago. Miss Seddars is the same, yet she is different."

"That's correct. You were here several years before going to London to join us?"

"My time here and her time only coincided for a few months. She was recently orphaned. Her normal behavior was considerably dampened by grief. Yet I saw her iron will even then, tamped down as she struggled to fit in here."

"An iron will. You admired her then." Hector nodded once. Henning tapped his chin. "Even so, you must have been on guard from the moment you realized you had a murder to solve."

"On guard with everyone, Henning, not just one or two people. For example, I noticed quite a number of new servants. I found it odd. A small change-over that brings in new servants is to be expected, but over half the staff are new additions. This is not the Chalmsley Court I once knew."

While the man nodded, he picked up the notebook and flipped back and forth a couple of times. "I see that you have no conclusion to your interview of Miss Seddars. You shift to a Dowding next."

"Kennington's valet."

"Why did you not conclude your interview?"

"Dowding had left the house. As soon as he was located, we went to interview him."

"Miss Seddars accompanied you?" He shook his head. If he'd been an old woman, he would have tsked, tsked. "I begin to doubt your ability to conduct an objective investigation, Evans. Lord Chalmsley must have noticed your difficulties on that first day, for he sent for me—." He flicked back to the first page. "Yes, I received his letter the day after you arrived. He would have had to reach his conclusion that very evening to send a messenger post-haste to London the next morning."

"I cannot read minds. I do not know the reason Lord Chalmsley decided to request a Bow Street officer to assist his constable. A handful of days is hardly time to locate a murder weapon when the murderer is intent on keeping it hidden. I have no witnesses. Or I may have one, but a court wouldn't accept her evidence. No Crown prosecutor and jury will rely on my opinion alone to send someone to the gallows. Or would you have your murderess already locked up, waiting for inquest and trial and hangman's noose?"

Henning didn't answer that question. "You have your murderess but no evidence."

"I hoped our afternoon would point out something that I have missed."

"It has. I would have arrested this Beatrice Seddars on the first evening."

"No." He felt hollow. Halfway through, the dread had built. He'd known—but he'd ignored the foreboding. He'd trusted his training. He shouldn't have trusted that Henning had the same training. "She didn't kill these men."

"And you know this how?"

Only through the weakest and flimsiest of evidence: love. Henning would laugh him from the room. "Just keep looking at my notes. You haven't read yesterday's notes, not a page of them."

The officer obliged him, but only by looking at the valet's interview, not by turning to Hector's notations yesterday. "Dowding refused to return to the house. He thought the murderess would fear he'd seen her. Had he seen her?"

"No, he had not, although Kennington must have had a night-time visit more than once during his time here. You'll have to trust my notes, though. Lord Chalmsley allowed the valet to return home today."

"I am not concerned about the valet. You have another notation here: *not Moira Fraser.*"

Hector explained Dowding's recitations of his master's dissatisfaction with his virginal fiancée.

Henning, though, had continued to read. "Kennington kept a journal?"

"So Dowding said. Dates with initials beside them. I never found it. I suspect the journal was burned that very night."

"On Kennington's bed, destroying the murder scene." He skimmed the next pages of Hector's notebook. "Who discovered the arson and called for help? I notice that alert was too late to save the papers from burning. You need not answer. Miss Beatrice Seddars. An exciting evening, Evans, followed by another one, with Mr. Pierpont killed. Only this time, Miss Seddars awakened you to go with her to examine the body."

"Aunt Beth awakened her. They both awakened me."

The officer shrugged. "You have an interesting list here. *Christina Wilton, not her sister. Daphne Herrick. Phaedra Dunham. Moira Fraser.* I thought you had ruled her out?"

"I have no evidence for a conviction. Nor do I have evidence to clear anyone's name. Read the rest of my list."

"*Lady Paton.* I am surprised you included her. All the rest are young unmarried ladies."

"When you meet Lady Paton, you'll understand. I believe the young men call her Lady Bountiful. I also included Lady Pierpont. And Portia, Cordelia, and Beatrice."

Henning closed the notebook and returned it to Hector who tucked it inside his waistcoat. The officer leaned back. Resting his elbows on the chair-arms, he templed his fingers and touched the points to his chin. "Evidence would help your case. From what I can divine, you have circumstances and hearsay, neither of which will hold in court against a wily barrister. What I find most interesting, however, is that at the end of your first day, every idea you had seemed to point to Beatrice Seddars, but today you accuse Portia and Cordelia Seddars to their father. What brought about that change?"

"As you say, circumstance and hearsay."

"I've heard your circumstance. Tell me the reasons you believe Portia is killing these men."

"It's a long tale." Henning merely motioned for Hector to continue.

Where to start? Portia's obsessive claim that the men were hers, all hers? Mad Aunt Beth and Cordelia? Or the first deadly violence? "Two years ago, Lord Chalmsley—."

The officer frowned. "Two years is a long way back."

"I think it may be the start."

"Go on, then. What happened two years ago?"

"Lord Chalmsley fell from his horse. His lordship is an excellent rider. The girth strap broke. He was lucky that he wasn't jumping the horse at the time. He suffered only broken bones. Coggins, the head groom, is reticent to discuss Lord Chalmsley's riding accident. He keeps the tack in excellent repair. Since Coggins inspects the riding tack every morning and the groom who saddled the horse wasn't dismissed, I can surmise that something happened to the strap after it was placed on the horse."

"More speculation."

Hector shrugged. "If you can get the man to tell you what he thinks happened, it won't be just my speculation. That event pointed me to problems in the family. I thought the chief problem was George, but he's been—."

"Who is George?"

"The heir. He's been abroad for the past two years. A vicious young man. Physically abusive to the servants and to animals. Here's evidence for you. When I was just a boy here, I stopped George from torturing a puppy he received for his birthday. Every morning the gardeners searched for snares and freed any rabbits or other animals that were captured. George set the snares. Talk to some of the old gardeners, if they're still here. Quite a number of the former servants have left. Anyway, from a few comments dropped by his sisters as well as a couple of the servants, I know that George became more irrational and more violent when he reached his majority."

"Where is this George?"

"Vienna. Far enough away that he cannot be the person committing these murders."

"Austria? Lord Chalmsley sent his heir to Austria when Napoleon controls much of Europe?"

"My very thought." Beyond the conservatory's glazing the day had darkened. They had talked the afternoon away and had more talking to do.

A deer came out of the trees. A doe. She looked around then warily stepped onto the lawn. Dipping her head to the grass, she grazed. Another deer came behind her. Gentle creatures, easily scared. Hector didn't remember deer coming so close to the manor house when he'd lived at the Court.

"And this George, he is violent enough to kill people?"

"That is the understanding I have reached. Again, I have no evidence, only speculation. As a Bow Street officer, you might have weight enough to get the servants to talk."

"You have no notes about George."

"No. I only began considering the Quenton derangement early this morning."

"Who are the Quenton's? I didn't see their names in your list of guests."

"Lady Chalmsley is a Quenton. The woman we call Mad Aunt Beth is her relative. Aunt Beth is definitely deranged. When you interact with Lady Chalmsley, you will see a mild form of the derangement."

"And you began considering insanity as the cause of these murders only now? After Pierpont is murdered?"

The deer lifted their heads. They looked toward the stables then dashed into the trees, leaping over bushes and disappearing into the darkness that already blanketing the woods.

"The Quenton derangement." Henning had propped his elbows on his knees. He stared at the flagstones under his boots. "Why do you call it that?"

"The family has streaks of bad blood. Years ago, I heard Lord Chalmsley railing about the Quentons. If they're not mad, they're dangerous. He roared it. You've heard him roar when he's angry. I was a boy. I had no idea what he might be talking about. After my years in London, I now know what he meant."

"You're connecting separate ideas and separate time frames."

"With good reason. When you look at the Quentons, with George and Mab, we have two types of derangement, violent and self-directed. George is obsessed with torturing animals, hurting them. He moved to hurting people or worse. Aunt Beth is what Bee calls 'mildly deranged'. She has a nurse who keeps watch over her, day and night, mainly to keep her from hurting herself. She can be lucid. She often chooses not to be. It can be difficult to have a coherent conversation with her."

"This Mab is the one who came with Beatrice Seddars to awaken you? How was it that she was away from her nurse?"

"She apparently slips away from the woman every night and roams the corridors."

"I do wish to speak with her."

"I wish you luck," Hector said grimly, remembering his failed interview. If Aunt Beth had answered his questions, he might not be sitting here now, arguing with a Bow Street officer who said he knew Hector's reputation but still doubted his word. *Because Lord Chalmsley doubts my word,* he admitted. "Call her Queen Mab, and you may get more than riddles and old songs. She won't tell me what she knows."

"She may be the murderer."

He shook his head. "No, not Mab. I did consider it, but she has no reason to hold a grudge against these men. She didn't know them. Beyond the method of their murder, we have no pattern that would tie them together."

"Except their association with Miss Portia."

"Except that."

"She could be protecting her niece."

"She could be," Hector agreed, "but I don't believe she is. We have a violent death committed in a devious way, when the men are asleep. Like Mab, Cordelia and her mother have mild compulsions, most often revealed when they are stressed. It stands to reason that Portia, who shows no compulsions or slight derangement, would take after her brother rather than her sister."

Henning shook his head. "I hear your argument, but I have difficulty accepting it. George is violent. Mab is deranged. Cordelia and her mother are compulsive. Portia, who shows no signs of any madness, must be the one committing these crime? Evans, surely you see the lack of connection?"

"Which is the reason I'm waiting for evidence. That is the only way that Lord Chalmsley will admit that the murderess is one of his daughters."

He straightened then jabbed a finger at Hector, one jab for each problem with Hector's argument. "You believe. You surmise. You think. You've speculated. You've guessed. You're blinding yourself, Evans. Go back to your first day, before you became blinded. You have your murderess there."

"Henning, you're focused on Beatrice Seddars because Lord Chalmsley won't accept that one of his daughters—that Portia, specifically—is guilty."

The Runner held out his hand. "May I see your notebook again?" Hector obliged. The officer flipped through several pages, flipped back, then riffled through a couple of pages. Then he looked from under his brow. "Here, she says 'I'm guilty'."

Hector remembered that notation. "No. What she said was 'Aunt Beth is no more guilty than I'm guilty'."

"Did the words 'I'm guilty' come out of her mouth?"

"You sound like a Crown prosecutor."

"That's the question they will ask. Or the defense counsel will ask it. Did Beatrice Seddars say those words?" he insisted.

"Twisting her words is not the way to build a case."

"Evans, you need to understand something very important. Lord Chalmsley is not the only person who wrote to the Bow Street magistrate, asking for an officer to lead the investigation. Lord

Westover wants a quick resolution. Do you know the position he once held in the government? Lord Chalmsley does not want his family involved."

Ice climbed his spine. He was going to lose this argument, primarily because Henning was thinking politics rather than evidence. He should have entered the Bow Street force when Sir Richard Ford served as magistrate. "His family is involved. His younger daughter committed these murders."

"This Beatrice is not his daughter, but——."

"But nothing. She's not a Quenton, with more than three generations of insanity raging through them. She's a Seddars. Chalmsley's niece. She holds this house together. She probably has since she arrived. She's the only rational person in the whole family. Chalmsley is blinded, not me."

"Look at your own notes, Evans. Page after page you've noted comments that she made."

Hector knew the reason. From the beginning, he'd focused on Bee. He could little remember others people's remarks when he'd been engaged with her. He hadn't recorded Portia's earliest comments. He hadn't recorded examples of Cordelia's compulsions.

Henning would distrust his defense of Bee even more if he knew Hector loved her. Had always loved her.

"We have to arrest her. I have orders from my director, who has orders from Lord Westover."

"No."

Henning brushed aside that flat denial. "You are no longer in charge here, Constable. You heard Lord Chalmsley. I'm in charge. Your own notebook is my guide. This B—Beatrice Seddars—is the murderess. Either you put the irons on her, or I will. Trust me, you will not appreciate the way I will handle her."

Chapter 15

A hand touched Bee's shoulder. She woke to candlelight and Aunt Beth leaning over her, and dread surged through her, leaving a trembling current.

She sat up, and Aunt Beth backed away from the bed. "Another one?"

The older woman beckoned.

"Hector—Constable Evans, the Carrion Crow, is not in his room, your majesty. He's on the first floor, in Mr. Pierpont's room. He and Mr. Henning are there."

"Come with me, Bee. Come away, come away." She flitted to the door. The candlelight jumped around the room. Then the mad woman dashed into the corridor.

Bee gathered her robe, shoving her arms into the sleeves and tying it as she hurried after.

Aunt Beth had reached the landing. She paused there, waiting for Bee. Save for her candle, the long corridor that traversed both wings was dark. Her candle guttered in a draft. Macabre shadows danced along the paneled walls and closed doors, along the ceiling, up and down the stairs. The older woman waited for Bee to near her before she crossed to the other wing.

Fear clenched around Bee's heart as Mab neared Hector's door. He'd said that he would be watching below, but what if he and the Bow Street officer had decided to take their watch in turns? What if he had returned to his room and the murderess had lurked there, waiting for sleep to overtake him? What if—? *Not Hector*, Bee prayed. *Please God. I've just found him again.*

Aunt Beth dashed past Hector's door. She passed several more. And then Bee saw a door standing ajar. Edmund Tretheway's door.

"No," Bee gasped. "No, no, no."

Aunt Beth stopped. She held a finger to her lips then pushed the door wider.

Bee stumbled to the doorway.

Aunt Beth stood near the bed. Like the other murder scenes, the tester curtains were pushed back, the covers tangled at the foot of the bed. Edmund lay sprawled, naked. Blood covered his neck and shoulders, seeped onto the mattress, staining the white linens.

Dread in her heart, Bee approached the inert form. She imagined blood gushed from the wound with each pulse of her heart.

Then his eyes opened.

Shock froze her. Fear spurred her forward. "He's alive. Aunt Beth, he's alive!" Bee scrambled onto the bloody mattress. That stream of blood must be stopped. Blood soaked her knees as she knelt beside him. She pressed her hand over the wound. Blood made his skin slick, but she pushed against the damage and prayed she stemmed the flow.

A flare of light reminded her of Aunt Beth. Bee looked around to see the older woman lighting another candle on the four-drawer chest near the bed. "Get Hector, Aunt Beth. Please, get Hector."

"Hector?"

"The Carrion Crow. He's in Pierpont's room. Where you took us last night. Go now!"

The woman fled, and Bee could only hope that she had gone for Hector.

Edmund's gaze never left hers. His mouth opened, formed words. No sound emerged.

"They're coming," she told him. "We'll get the blood stopped."

His eyelids fluttered.

"Edmund? Edmund! Stay with me."

His breath was only a shallow rasp.

Bee looked at him and wished she had loved him. She had barely tolerated his touch. He had betrayed their troth, for here he lay, naked, obviously killed after he fornicated with the murderess.

Was that the reason this woman killed? Because the men betrayed their fiancées? They had sworn preliminary vows, similar to the wedding vows of 'plight thee my troth'. And Edmund had broken his vows to her.

If she cared for him, she might care that he had broken his troth. She didn't care, though. She could only think what a horrible waste. No one should die without being loved. She opened her mouth to utter the lie that he would be fine, that help was coming, that all would be well.

Then his breath rattled in his throat. His eyelids stopped fluttering. His muscles went limp. His chest dropped and didn't rise again.

"I'm sorry," Bee told him. "So sorry, Edmund. God go with you."

. ~ . ~ . ~ .

When Hector and Henning arrive, Bee still knelt on bed. Her hand still pressed to his neck. Tears dripped off her face. She stared down into her fiance's face and didn't look up as they approached the bed.

"Ye gods," Henning swore.

Hector leaned a hand on the mattress. "Bee. Beatrice."

With a great in-drawn breath, she lifted her head and looked around. Her blue eyes had darkened, deep as a lake, limitless as grief.

"You can let go."

"It's Edmund."

"Yes, I know. You can let go. He's gone."

She looked down. Another deep breath, then she lifted her bloody hand away and sank back on her heels.

"Let's get you off there." Hector gripped her elbow. He helped her slide back, guided her bare feet off the mattress, steadied her when she tried to stand and her knees wobbled.

"What happened?"

She shuddered. "He was alive when I reached him. Bleeding so much. But I had scarcely touched him when he died."

"That don't make sense." Henning folded his arms, his very stance evidence of his suspicions. "Why did you keep pressure on his wound if you knew he were dead?"

Bee stared at the man, as if his words were nonsense. Then she lifted her stained hand and stared at the blood. "I tried—. Aunt Beth, she found you quickly."

"She woke you?"

She nodded. Her gaze shifted to the bed. Hector turned her, putting her back to the bloody scene.

"I sent her for you. I didn't want to leave him. I hoped—. It was a foolish hope. I suppose no one tried to set fire to Pierpont's bed."

"Not even a spark."

"She didn't follow the pattern."

"Definitely not. There's a logic to the madness then."

"She's killing fiancés who break their vows, either with her or with someone else."

"She?" Henning asked. "Who? This Aunt Beth?"

"No, not Aunt Beth. She's not violent."

"Not that we know of," Hector corrected, and Bee looked at him as if he'd betrayed her.

"It's convenient," Henning added. "Convenient that he died before we came in. He could have told us who stabbed him."

"He couldn't talk," Bee whispered. She stared at her bloody hand. "He tried to tell me something. I couldn't read his lips."

"Was he trying to say a name?"

"I don't know."

"George," Hector suggested, drawing a confused look from the Bow Street officer.

Bee wasn't confused. "Not George. The same reasons still hold. He's not here. He's far from here." If she hadn't been so shocky, her denial might have held heat. "George isn't hiding somewhere, ashamed of his violence. George was never ashamed. He only hid until he needed to accomplish his sorry deed, then he brazened it out."

"Who is George? Is this the son who's in Vienna?" Henning asked while Hector agreed with Bee's assessment.

"His murders would be more violent," he added. "These are just the killing wound and then walking away while the men bleed out."

Bee scrubbed her hand down her nightrobe. "I suppose I must prepare for the day. Where did Aunt Beth go?"

"Back to her chamber, I would think. Did she say anything to you?"

"Nothing. I think she was as shocked as I was. We didn't—I don't think anyone expected another murder."

"Then we better start expecting them, or we'll have a fourth and a fifth. Go on. Will you notify Richardson again?" he asked. "I depended on him a great deal yesterday morning. You're hesitating. Are you afraid? Should I escort you to your room?"

She winced. "I don't think I have anything to fear from whoever this murderer is. She—or he—is killing the fiancés, Hector. You do realize that? First Moira Fraser's, then Cordelia's, now mine."

"That leaves who? Brougham Paton. Alex Westover. Anyone else?"

"No. The other young men aren't officially engaged. Will you—?" She stopped, pressed her lips together, an age-old sign of hers that said she'd thought better of the words that had escaped. Her shocked distress about Tretheway had worn off, helped by his question about George.

"We'll need guards set on Paton's and Westover's doors as well as Pierpont's and now Tretheway's. Richardson will help there. Go on," he told her. "I depend on you, Bee, to bring Richardson to me and to keep the house running."

She nodded and hurried into the dark corridor. Hector didn't even try to stop his worry over her. He walked to the door and watched her disappear into the shadows of the other wing. He waited, barely daring to breathe, listening for the sound of her chamber door. When he heard it open and shut, when he saw light flare along the bottom edge of her door, he stepped back into the chamber and turned to face Henning.

"You depend on her." The man scowled. "Sshe likely killed this man here and the other two."

"No. Would she have tried to save him if she dealt him that wound?"

"By her own admission, she knew she couldn't do anything to save him."

"That's not what she said. If you're going to twist her words, at least get her words correct."

Henning walked over to the bed and stared at the corpse. "We only got her word that he didn't say nothing before he died."

"Look at that wound. Look how deep it must be. It must have damaged his throat. How could he speak?"

"Convenient," he said again.

"You can accuse Mab as easily as you accuse Beatrice."

"While you make it easy for both of them to go scot-free. Listen to that Beatrice Seddars. She knows the reason these men are murdered. Killing fiancés who break their vows. Only fiancés haven't said any vows yet. They won't until they reach the altar. That's a warped way of looking at life. It takes a warped thought process to kill someone what's done you no wrong. You need to arrest her, Evans."

"She didn't kill these men."

"Arrest her," Henning ordered. "If you had done your duty when I ordered you to, this man would be alive. His death's not only on your conscience now, but also mine. I let you talk me out of arresting her tonight."

"She didn't kill him," Hector insisted. "Bee wouldn't kill her own fiancé. She's not capable of that."

"It's been what? Seven years since you knew her? Six? That's a long time away from somebody to keep claiming you know what she would do and not do. You don't know what she's capable of, Evans. You can't know that. Too much water's passed under that bridge. You don't know how she's changed. You don't know what's driven her through all those years. You don't know what's driving her now. What we do know is that three men are dead. Arrest her, Evans, or I will."

Hector stiffened. "She is not guilty of any of these crimes."

"Almost thou persuades me," he quoted, "but will you be the one to tell Lord Chalmsley that? He won't believe you. He's had daily contact with her for all those years. We need evidence at this point, one way or the other. Either you arrest her, or I will. Your choice. But we arrest her now, before she can damage any more evidence or kill any more men."

Henning looked determined. And Hector mutely admitted that Bee could be construed to be the murderer.

He remembered the officer's earlier claim when he had twisted Bee's words. *Did the words 'I'm guilty' come out of her mouth?* Hector had heard similar questions from both Crown prosecutors and defending barristers. They both twisted any evidence in order to win their side of a case. The truth didn't matter to them. Just facts that could line up neatly and win over twelve jurors.

Facts, looked at coldly, would convict Bee. Tonight, with her blood-covered hands, with her testimony that she'd been here while Tretheway died, those two facts alone would hang her.

If he didn't arrest her, Henning would.

He tried one last effort. "And the murder weapon? Don't you find it odd that we haven't found it yet?"

"She had time to hide it, just like before. How are we going to find it? Search the house? It would take months. No, she hid it. We won't find it unless we get lucky."

"She didn't want Tretheway to die. She was holding his wound when we came in."

"A nice play actress, that. She wounds him, hides the weapon somewhere we'll never find it, goes back to her chamber, waits for that old mad lady to find her. Imagine her surprise when he's still alive. She sends the old lady for us, and then acts all shocked innocence when we arrive. No, Evans. I won't in good conscience let her run free without some evidence to prove she didn't murder this man."

"I won't arrest her."

"It's a narrow bridge then, across a flooding river? Which of us is going to drown in the cold water?"

"Neither. We'll compromise, Henning. I'll detain her, yes, but this is not an arrest."

He told himself that detention wasn't an arrest. Then he rapped on Bee's door and explained detention to her. Her widened eyes filled with tears. And he admitted that arrest and detention amounted to the same thing.

She had washed the blood from her hands and removed her stained clothing for a drab grey gown, but she hadn't had time for more than that, not even shoes. Her bare toes peeked from under the hem of her gown.

Bee's gaze flicked behind him, to where Henning waited, ready to do the chore if Hector backed out. "Are you to arrest me then? Hector, I didn't kill Edmund. I didn't kill any of them."

"I know, but if I don't detain you, he will. He won't be gentle, Bee. I'm doing this so he has no opportunity to touch you."

Bee's breath shuddered out. Then she held out her wrists. Her hands looked raw where she had scrubbed off the blood. "Do it then. Put the irons on me, Hector. Then find the evidence to prove I'm innocent."

"I refuse to put irons on you." That was one part of the argument he had won.

With Henning on their heels, Hector marched Bee all the way down to the cellar. Once she asked, "Where are you taking me? I thought you would lock me in my chamber?"

"Not likely," the officer growled from behind them.

She said nothing more, not even when he steered her through the servant's hall. The boy there lifted his head from his arms and gaped as they passed, a parade of three, Bee pattering barefoot behind Hector with the tall Bow Street officer behind them.

When he opened the door to the stairs that led below ground floor, she gasped and balked. "It's cold down there," she protested. "I need shoes. I need a cloak."

She was right. He regretted not letting her collect those simple things that would keep her from freezing. Behind him, though, Henning spoke with relish in his voice. "Not happening. Go on down."

As they descended the steep stairs, Hector wondered at Henning's glee. What did the man have against Bee?

Or did he merely want to fulfill his obligation to Lord Chalmsley? Bow Street officers sometimes hired out to people outside of London. Was that what drove his push for a resolution to this case? Was that the reason Henning hadn't balked at taking the case from Hector? A quick resolution to these murders, money in his pocket, and a return to London all within a week. Before he was counted missing from his regular beat.

In the cellars, the candlelight glanced off the lime-washed vaults, the support structure for the entire house. The wooden walls between the pillars looked dark, stained by age and damp. Arched doors gave access to the storage. Brick pavers created the floor, uneven and occasionally plastered.

Hector stopped at the third door along, the one that the butler had pointed out to him. He fished the key from his coat pocket. The heavy lock was unwieldy. It turned only with force. The door swung back, and the candlelight streamed in, revealing racks and gleaming dark bottles. Chalmsley's wine cellar, one of them.

"In you go," Henning said.

She went without being pushed. Just past the door she turned. "May I have a light?"

"No," Henning said, but Hector removed one of the tapers from the candelabra and held it out. Bee thanked him with her eyes.

"How long?"

"Sunrise," he gave her. As if to reinforce his words, the chiming from the long case clock sounded, muffled by distance and wood and brick but still clear. Four o'clock. She would be down here four more hours, at least. "Try to sleep."

Bee rolled her eyes. "Find the evidence, Hector. Or they will hang me."

"I'll do it. I promise. Today."

"Here now," Henning protested. "Lock her in."

"You're safer locked in," he told her. "Only Richardson and I can unlock this door."

She huffed. "Safer?" She looked at the wine racks with their dusty bottles. "Maybe so, if I weren't locked in. I can always throw bottles at you when you return."

.~.~.~.

Brave words, Bee thought when Hector shut the door and locked it. Brave words she didn't believe. The vaulted pillars were cold brick. The floor was cold brick. She put her back to a wine rack and was grateful that the closed door and lack of windows offered no draft. She tucked her freezing toes under her skirt and petticoat.

The candle wouldn't last the four hours she had remaining.

She wasn't certain she would last that long. The air felt close, musty with damp, heavy with staleness. The ceiling pressed down, a smothering weight. Dozens of wine racks filled the space between the door and the wall.

She wanted a window. She wanted a better light.

She dripped wax on the floor and created a little well for the candle to nestle into. It worked, somewhat, although the candle leaned, and the lean meant the flame licked at the wax and burned the wick all the faster.

Hector would get her out. She had to trust that. She had to trust that he would free her. She had to trust that he would magically find non-existent evidence and save her from the gallows.

Should he fail, Henning would take her to trial. The Crown prosecutor would convince twelve honorable men that she had murdered three men, including her fiancé, and her pretty neck would be stretched by the hangman's noose.

Bee tucked her hands under her legs and watched the candle flame until it flickered out.

Chapter 16

By nine o'clock, it became obvious that the whole house knew about Edmund Tretheway's death. The servants scurried about their duties, quicker and quieter than usual. The guests—.

Hector watched another guest leave the breakfast room after requesting their coach be brought round within the hour.

Lord Chalmsley, pleased with Henning's report that the suspected murderess was in custody, saw no problem with his guests leaving.

He neglected to ask who the suspected murderess was.

Hector chose to enlighten him. Expecting a roar, he was appalled when Chalmsley merely shrugged away any worries about his niece. "You have evidence?" was his only question.

Henning gave a careful answer. "We found her in the murdered man's room."

"She was trying to keep him from bleeding out," Hector supplied. "Do not think she is under arrest, my lord. She did not commit these murders. We have merely detained her until evidence arises."

"She didn't commit these murders? Demmit, who did? Why have you detained her?"

Henning glared at Hector. "We felt justified in doing so, based on the circumstances last night—."

"However," Hector interrupted smoothly, "on reflection, we must admit that numerous discrepancies prevent us from building a case."

"Discrepancies." The old man smoothed the blotting papers before him. He kept his gaze downcast rather than look at his constable and the Bow Street officer he'd called in. "What discrepancies?"

"We still have no murder weapon, your lordship. We came on Miss Seddars before she had time to hide any weapon. We've searched that room and found nothing. It's a discrepancy that should be removed before any trial."

Henning had finally stepped up. Should a few more planks be laid across the circumstances that they had, Hector thought he would have the man not only convinced but committed to pursuing the correct suspect. He moved quickly, though, to the main point. "With your permission, my lord, we would like to ask a few more questions of your guests before they leave the Court."

Permission granted, the two law officers stationed themselves in the entrance hall. Trunks were carried past them to waiting carriages. Footmen carried out food hampers to nourish the guests on their journey. Lord Chalmsley wouldn't have thought to order the hampers; his morning's temper was more at his guests' rapid departure and the spreading reputation that stained the family and the estate with red, red, blood. If Lady Chalmsley had thought of the kindness, she wouldn't bother to order it. The Chalmsley staff must be trying to maintain the manor's reputation.

Richardson came down and stationed himself beside the entrance, ready to bow and offer "good journey" to the guests as they left. Hector guessed that Beatrice, if she were about her normal duties, would stand beside the aging butler. Chalmsley's niece and staff cared more than the family themselves did.

The Osgoods rebuffed any attempt to speak with them. With a scant word for the butler, they swept from the house, with her ladyship's maid and the two valets hurrying after.

While his wife, his son, and Missy Wilton continued to their carriage, Lord Westover paused long enough to inquire who had been arrested.

Hector quickly corrected the White Hall lord. "Not arrested, my lord. Merely detained. Miss Beatrice Seddars."

"Not arrested." He scowled along his Roman nose. "That's a mistake."

"Last evening we found her covered in Edmund Tretheway's blood," Henning ventured.

"I'd expect an explanation for that."

"She said—," Hector started.

"Claimed," the Bow Street officer inserted.

"She *said* that she'd found Mr. Tretheway wounded and tried to staunch the blood flow."

Westover turned his scowl on Henning. "Miss Beatrice Seddars is the last person I would expect you to *detain*. I would believe that she bloodied herself trying to help that man before I would believe that she'd murdered him. Have you paid no heed to family background, man?" He bent toward Hector. "I thought you were well acquainted with the family."

"I am, my lord." He didn't toss Henning in the drink, much as he wanted to. "We discussed the family issue. That is the reason Miss Beatrice is merely detained."

"You should rethink your murderess. Miss Seddars doesn't fit the crimes. Look at Chalmsley's oldest gel. And the heir, where is he?" He gave an abrupt nod, as if his word were law, then stepped away. He paused at the door, exchanging words with the butler, then he stalked out, his greatcoat swinging behind him.

Henning folded his arms. "He's not like Lord Chalmsley."

"No. He won't accept an easy scapegoat. That surprised me."

"Didn't surprise us enough, though, did he? He didn't stay to see the case to its rightful end."

Loud chattering heralded the Wilton family. Mother and remaining daughter talked as they descended. They completely ignored the two officers standing in the entrance hall. Clarence Wilton paused, though, which drew his father to a stop as well. They, too, had heard of an arrest. They, too, were surprised that Beatrice Seddars was in custody. The younger man rashly added, "Now I would have thought it'd be Miss Cordelia or Miss Portia."

Henning sprang on the comment. He squared up before the men, blocking their easy exit from the house. "You'd blame one of the daughters before Miss Beatrice Seddars?"

They exchanged a look. While his son nodded, the older Wilton stepped a fraction closer and lowered his voice. "Have you seen Miss Cordelia?"

"Portia's obsessed," Clarence shot in quickly. Then he looked upwards, as if expecting to see the young woman lurking at the top of the stairs.

His claim gave Hector hope. If other people had noticed Portia's sane insanity, then it shouldn't be so hard to prove to twelve jurors, even if they were oppressed by Lord Chalmsley's scowling visage as his youngest daughter stood in the dock. "Obsessed?" Hector asked. "Why do you say that, Mr. Wilton?"

"Once she's got her claws into you, she doesn't let go. She never got them into me, but poor Kennington had his hands full of her, long after he cried off and started courting Moira Fraser. She's got a name, if you understand me."

"Clarence," his father warned.

The son merely lowered his voice. "Wild, I hear. Even with Pierpont, and he was engaged to her sister."

"And Edmund Tretheway?"

"Now there, I heard nothing. I wouldn't put it past Tretheway. Libertine, there. The old man didn't know it, or he did and still decided to get his niece from underfoot." The terminology sounded more like an older man than the young Clarence, and Hector saw Mr. Wilton wince at his son's words. "If Portia were offering anything, Tretheway would take her up on it. I was glad he never turned his attentions toward Missy."

Those few words confirmed that Edmund Tretheway's behavior as a husband would have kept Bee in tears.

Mr. Dunham didn't respond to their attempts to speak with them. Miss Dunham had to wait for the maid to bring her gloves. "Not

Beatrice!" she cried when she heard the news. "I would never think Beatrice."

"You would think someone else before her?" Hector asked to draw more out.

She shook her head, her dark curls dancing. "Oh, not me. I have no mind for figuring out such puzzles. But not Beatrice, that I know. She's too kind. She would be in trouble more for trying to help someone than for hurting them."

When the heavy door shut behind her and the maid, Henning looked at Hector. "I admit we were wrong. Satisfied?"

"Not until Beatrice is out of the cellar."

"His lordship won't be pleased if we release her before we have someone to put in her place."

"That someone may be one of his own daughters. You heard his reaction earlier. He won't accept any arrest unless we have hard evidence. And hard evidence we won't get."

The other guests were equally reticent to speak, even when both Henning and Hector tried to engage them in conversation.

Last to leave were the Patons, with the son heading the departure.

"Mr. Paton, I am surprised you are abandoning your fiancé while her family copes with these murders."

Barely pausing, he glanced along his nose at Hector. He didn't deign to acknowledge Henning. "Do you suggest that I remain and be the next victim?"

Lady Paton stopped behind her son. "I am not losing my Brougham the way Lydia lost her Barr."

"But your fiancé needs your support."

The young man gave a decided shake of his head. "My fiancé does not care for my support or anyone's. Portia informed me this morning that my presence in her life is no longer necessary. I cannot say that I regret the dissolution."

"Carry on, Brougham," his father said.

"My lord," Hector tried again to slow their departure. "Have you anything to impart before you leave?"

Paton drew himself taller. "Chalmsley should take charge of this fool investigation. Three men dead. House nearly burned down. His niece arrested by idiots. How's that for information to impart?" Then he stalked out, without even acknowledging the butler.

"Don't say it," Henning warned. "Lead on to the cellar."

Hector held out a staying hand. He had caught movement at the top of the stairs.

Cordelia, her back stiff, moving like a marionette, slowly descended. In the morning sunlight coming through the windows above the door, her chopped hair revealed the jagged cutting and the gaps where she had sheared nearly to her scalp. With her white gown and pale skin and her aimless walk, she looked ghost-like. Her shawl trailed her, and she didn't seem to notice that it had slipped off her shoulders.

Richardson spotted her as she reached the last step and tried to intercept her. "Miss Cordelia, you should retire. You have suffered a great trauma."

She ignored him and walked to Hector. She didn't notice the butler drop her shawl around her shoulders. Wrapping her arms around her bone-thin frame, she searched for words.

"What is it, Miss Cordelia?"

Her eyes searched his. "I had something—. I can't remember. It was about Bee."

"Bee? Do you want to know where she is?"

"Aunt Beth says the cellar."

Henning shifted position, drawing her gaze. "That's correct. You don't need to fear her. She's locked up in the cellar."

Her brow furrowed in confusion, and Hector realized her mind had turned. She had suffered a great trauma, as Richardson had said. Barrington Pierpont's death had affected her much more than he realized. Or his death had compounded some fear that broke the fragile shield around her mind. He remembered her cries. *He was my escape, mine. How am I to escape now?*

"Fear her?" Cordelia looked blank. "Fear Bee? Whyever would I?"

"Why do you think she's in the cellar, Miss Cordelia?"

"I don't know. She helps me, you know. When I can't manage." She looked down at her buttoned mutton sleeves. "Hawkins had to help me this morning. Bee helps. She doesn't hurt. She never hurts. I like Bee. Why is she in the cellar?"

"Three men have died."

Her wandering gaze sharpened and fixed on Hector. "Three men. Three? Yes. My Mr. Pierpont. And Mr. Kennington. And someone else. Someone—. Aunt Beth said he was important to Bee. I thought she meant you."

"No," Hector said, even as he wanted to take her last comment and puzzle through it. "Edmund Tretheway is the one who died. The one who was important to Bee."

"Edmund. I didn't like him. Bee didn't either, not really. Not the way she should have. Not the way Papa said she had to. Not the way she likes you. I remember those days. Endless days of sunshine. I was happy then."

"Days long ago, Cordy. Days better forgotten."

"I haven't forgotten. Bee never forgot. Portia wanted us to. George," she shuddered, "George wanted us to forget. Why didn't you come back?"

"I'm back now."

"Miss Cordelia," Richardson said, trying to get her attention. "Aren't you chilled, standing here? You need your shawl. You need to sit before a hot fire and drink tea. Wouldn't you like some tea?"

"Yes. Not now. I need to tell Hector something." Her eyes narrowed, shifted from the butler to Henning. She frowned at the officer, as if something didn't fit. Her hand lifted and touched her hair, then it fell to her side. The shawl slipped again. She ignored it. "Hector, I remember. I remember what Aunt Beth said. I remember what I need to tell you."

"What's that, Cordy?"

"*You* know. Aunt Beth calls you Carrion Crow. *Carrion Crow, out of the oaks, come to catch a murderer.* She sings it." She frowned then touched his arm. Her gaze had again sharpened. "Don't betray her, Hector, not this time. Don't betray Bee."

"And how would I do that?"

"Beatrice did not kill those three men. I know she didn't. I know *things*."

Even as Hector wondered what she meant, Henning pounced. "What things do you know, Miss Seddars?" When she bit her cheek, he grabbed her elbow. "If you are withholding evidence, you can be charged as an accessory."

She stared at his gripping hand then gave him a perplexed look. "Let me go."

"Let her go, Henning. She doesn't know what you think she does." He glared at the London officer until the man released her.

As soon as his hand dropped away, Cordelia said, "I do know things. Aunt Beth said to tell you. She said it might be important."

"Tell me. Tell Carrion Crow."

Her grin brightened. "That's what Aunt Beth said. Here, I know three things. Mama did not choose who came to visit us. Portia did. Portia wished for specific people to be here. Mama granted her wish. Portia wanted them here, the Pierponts and Mr. Tretheway and the Patons and the Frasers. I didn't, not really. The Pierponts had to come, but I didn't want them to. I didn't—. Mama invited them. Papa didn't want her to. But Portia wanted them here. I didn't understand why she wanted them here. I understand it now."

Although she had rambled through it, Henning gaped at her. "Damme, she knows about the murders. Miss Cordelia, what do you know about these murders? You need to tell us."

"Murders? No." She gazed at Henning, still trying to figure out who he was.

"Let me take her upstairs, Constable," Richardson offered. "She'll catch her death. She doesn't know what she's saying."

"She knows something," Henning growled. "We need to get it out of her. Tell us what you know, Miss Cordelia. Tell us now. What do you know about these murders? Did you see them? Did you hear something? What do you know?"

Cordelia backed away to dodge his hand. "You're no Carrion Crow. I don't know anything. I don't. I saw nothing. I heard nothing. I cannot help you." She backed several more steps, shaking her head.

"You don't like George. I got that much."

Her eyes widened. "He's evil," she hissed. Her shoulders hunched. She looked behind her, up the stairs, then whispered, "*A crafty, cunning elf, despis'd his friends, ruin's his self. The devil tempts him night and day.*"

"Sirs, let me take her upstairs. She's better off with her maid."

Henning looked like he would argue, but Hector forestalled him. "Do it, Richardson. And tell the maid to remain with her and keep her safe."

"Like Miss Quenton, sir. Yes, I'll see to it." He guided Cordelia by sweeping a hand before her and promising hot tea. She glanced at the two law officers. When she looked at Henning, she shrank away and turned quickly to follow the butler's lead.

"She can help us," Henning groused.

"It would be a mad sort of help, more riddles than answers. Like Aunt Beth."

"Is she that Miss Quenton the butler mentioned?"

"Yes. Mad Aunt Beth."

"Who calls you Carrion Crow. Feeding on victims, I suppose, in order to catch your murderer."

Hector shrugged.

"What was that mess she was so intent we hear about? Portia invited them all. Lady Chalmsley granted her wish, against Lord Chalmsley's direct order, I gather. What does any of that matter?"

"If we knew that, we might have the evidence we're after. She obviously thinks it was important."

"I don't see it." Henning directed a frown at the stairs. Cordelia and Richardson had long disappeared from view. "Then she turns around and says she saw nothing and heard nothing. One of three monkeys, Miss See No Evil. She's no help."

"She's afraid of George. Lord Westover thinks we should keep a watch for him."

"But he's in Vienna. That's what your Bee Seddars said. If we can believe her. Between your Bee Seddars and Miss Cordelia and all the others, I think there's some secrets we need answers to. And maybe a few hours in the cellar will have convinced your Bee to share those secrets."

For once, Hector agreed with Henning. Cordelia obviously had intended to share something. He didn't think it was the information about Lady Chalmsley's invitations being spurred by Portia. When he had arrived, he'd thought he knew these people. They had secrets, just like the roughest criminal on London streets. Shaming secrets, damning secrets. And if Hector didn't find them out, he feared they would never get the evidence they needed to free Bee.

Chapter 17

When she heard the key in the lock, Bee climbed to her frozen feet. She placed a frozen hand on the wall to steady herself. Hours and hours ago the candle had burnt to the nub. The wick drowned in the last of the wax. In the darkness, teeth chattering and body shivering, Bee had vowed to leave Chalmsley Court.

Her great-uncle, her only surviving blood, would let her freeze in his cellar rather than admit the truth.

What was the truth?

In the cold, cold dark, Bee came to that answer, a hard answer stinking of the grave.

One of her cousins had murdered three men. Not Aunt Beth. After Bee herself, the mad aunt would be the convenient scapegoat. Yet Aunt Beth was merely deranged, not violent, not obsessed.

No, the murderer had to be Portia or Cordelia.

Not Cordelia. She was too much like Aunt Beth and her mother. She had no violence in her, not against others. She would run and hide before she confronted anyone. Only dire necessity or fear would drive her to a confrontation. Even then—no. Not Cordelia.

That left Portia. Golden Portia who seemed to have no derangement. *Just as George seems to have no derangement,* Bee reminded herself. George would smile then grab a stick and beat a little terrier. He would tell a joke as he twisted the neck of a rabbit caught in a snare. He would tease a girl and promise treats then walk off with her baby and drown it.

Could Portia be that ruthless? That cruel?

Would she even recognize the murders as cruel? She certainly knew they were wrong. George didn't. He confessed to his crimes with never a blink of his blue, blue eyes. His golden hair and lovely features made him look like the angels in paintings, but he was no angel.

Portia appeared the same, all golden, all blue-eyed like the heavens, all beautiful. She had hidden her petty torments of Cordelia, though. She hid her flirtations from her parents, knowing Cordelia was too cowed to tattle and Bee preferred not to raise her relative's ire.

With cold seeping to her bones, Bee admitted the hard truth that no one else wanted to admit.

She must convince Hector and the officer Henning from London and her great-uncle. Or they would let her go to trial. She had sacrificed much over the years. She would not sacrifice her life. She would no longer sacrifice anything for them.

The door swung open. The first light blinded her. Bee shielded her eyes. "Hector?"

"Here," he said. He brought light with him.

She dropped her hand and gave him her fiercest glare. "I want out of here. Hector, I did not kill those men, and you know it. I don't want to hear that you have no evidence." She looked past him, at the sturdy body blocking the door. "Do you hear me, Mr. Henning? You know I had nothing to do with their deaths." Her teeth chattered on the last words, mocking them.

"Bee." Hector snared her hand. "You're ice. We need to warm you up."

"I want my cloak. I want shoes. I want hot tea."

"The kitchen, I think," Henning agreed and backed up.

She stumbled on her first steps. When Hector offered a supporting arm, she wished she could fling it off. Instead, she clung to him and limped her slow way out of the wine room. The footman who had apparently stood guard followed them. Their little procession traveled along the passage to the stairs, and then up and up, to the corridor that ran the length of the house and led to the kitchen.

Mrs. Lovell sprang to her feet when Hector led her in. "Miss Beatrice! Heavens, miss, you look a fright."

"I feel a fright. Is there tea?" she asked Mrs. Shelton the cook.

Cook quickly poured a cup. Hector lowered her into a chair as the woman set the tea before her. Bee's hands shook, but she lifted the cup and lowered her face to the steam.

"Not here," Henning said. "We need to talk with Miss Seddars. You're Mrs. Lovell, the housekeeper, aren't you? Is there a room, private?"

"My office is right down the hall. There's a little fire, miss, where you can get warm. I'll have your cloak fetched."

"If I must move, I'd rather move to my bedchamber."

"Miss!" The suggestion scandalized Mrs. Lovell, returning from commanding the footman to return upstairs. "Two men in your bedchamber! That's not to be done."

The housekeeper's opposition had Bee ready to stomp off to her room, but her prickling feet didn't want to walk the few steps to the little office.

She managed to walk, though, and released Hector's arm before they reached the little office. As she slid onto a chair, Bee noticed how shabby and stuffed the room was. She had visited Mrs. Lovell here more than once without realizing how the housekeeper needed a larger space. The desk was barely suitable for writing. Mrs. Lovell stored papers and ledgers in a crate. She had room for scarcely two chairs, one of which Hector dragged around to sit at an angle to Bee. And when he lifted her bare feet onto his knee and chafed them to restore circulation, she wanted both to cry gratitude and scream with anger.

Mrs. Shelton placed another cup of hot tea before her and offered a quick scramble, "to get some food in you, miss. That'll warm you right up."

She thanked the woman. When both Mrs. Lovell and Cook left, Bee leveled a glare at Hector. Warming her frozen feet was not apology enough. "That candle went out hours ago, Hector. I sat in the dark, freezing."

"We were conducting interviews, Miss Seddars."

She withered the London officer. "That's not adequate, sir. You know I am not guilty. What motive would I have had for killing Edmund Tretheway?"

"To break your engagement to him? Because your interest lies elsewhere." He nodded at Hector.

"That's a little extreme," Hector said, concentrating on her toes. "If Tretheway disgusted her, she could simply refuse to marry him."

"I thought the gentry class bound up the marriage settlements to prevent easy refusals by the bride or groom."

"They do. But that wouldn't stop me," Bee declared. "I'm a rare breed, an independent lady. My quarterly payments may go to Great-Uncle Hamilton at the moment, but Mr. Cosgrove will ensure that the funds come to me when I leave Chalmsley."

Hector stopped rubbing the little piggy on her right foot. "When you leave Chalmsley? You would leave here?"

"I've lived here eight years, and that's eight years too long. Have you not paid attention to these people? Lady Chalmsley is the sanest one, and she is not wholly sane. Even my great-uncle has his obsessions." She propped an elbow on Mrs. Lovell's desk. "Have neither of you seen what is happening under your very eyes?"

"I've seen Miss Cordelia. She seems to be deteriorating rapidly."

Bee huffed. "They've teased and tormented her for so long. I won't say that they started her mind on its downward spiral. I will say they made her much worse than she would have been. It's not Cordelia you need to be concerned with. They are."

The door opened. Cook bustled in with a tray, and Bee snatched her feet from Hector's lap. She had eyes only for Cook's steaming tray. A gleaming china plate held eggs and chopped bits of sausage. A smaller plate offered a yeast bun dripping with honey and butter. Another steaming teacup and a chopped apple completed the tray. Silverware and a carefully folded napkin were tucked at one side.

Cook waited for Hector to move then set the tray on the housekeeper's paper-covered desk. "Now then, you'll take a bite then up to your room with you. Mrs. Lovell's seeing your room warmed up and hot water brought in for you."

"Thank you, Cook. This looks wonderful."

"And you two." She rounded on the men. "You will let the miss eat without pestering her with questions, you hear."

"That we do," Hector agreed readily. He stood and shut the door behind the cook. He had the grace to let her get a few bites of egg and sausage into her, but Henning didn't.

"Who should we be concerned with, Miss Seddars? Who is they?"

Bee almost dropped her fork. "Do you truly know nothing about the Quenton family?"

"Enlighten us."

She forked up some egg, chewed and swallowed it before she responded. "I do not like you, Mr. Henning. I think you want me to accuse people so you can claim that I am a vindictive woman. I am not. I am far from being that." A bite of sausage gave her incentive to say, "I may have blinded myself, but I am no longer blind. Hours in that clay-cold cellar have changed my view of who is most important. I have to defend myself since it appears that no one else will defend me."

"Bee, I couldn't——."

"I'm not referring to you, Hector. My great-uncle is the one who let me down. I had thought better of him, but I should have expected he would be ruled by sentiment rather than sense. Mr. Henning, you will have to open your own eyes. I cannot help you see."

"Bee," Hector remonstrated, "we have nothing to work with. No murder weapon. Only you, covered in Edmund Tretheway's blood. Only you, with Mab, the first one to find Pierpont's body. Only you, first to find the fire in Kennington's bed. And only you, once Holyfield told you, first to raise the alarm on the night Kennington was murdered."

She sank back in her chair. "God help me. I didn't think of all that."

"You can help yourself, Bee. These three murders, all within a week, that is very like a murder spree I worked a few years back. Over several days, a man sought out and killed people he held grudges against. When we arrested him, he raved that he had more blood to spill."

Mouth agape, she stared at him. Henning had the same look. "I remember that case," he muttered. "They tried to keep it quiet."

"When I was a boy here at Chalmsley, there was talk about the Quenton blood taint, but I never quite discovered what that meant."

Both men bent their eyes on Bee. "You don't need me to tell you about George."

"I'll tell Henning what I know. But you have to tell us about the Quenton family, the secrets that I never learned."

Even though her stomach had tacked itself to her spine, the eggs and the bun had lost all flavor. She pushed back the tray and picked up the tea, cooled by the cool room. "You shouldn't ask me. Most of my knowledge of the family's history came in dribs and drabs. Tiny pieces that I had to fit together as best I could."

"We can't ask Lord Chalmsley. I doubt Lady Chalmsley would share information about her family with a constable and a Bow Street Runner. What secrets do you know, Bee?"

Hours locked in that freezing cellar broke any inhibition she might have had about keeping those family secrets. "The Quenton blood runs with insanity. Four generations that I personally know of, all the way back to a woman who poisoned three husbands. They hanged her when she poisoned the local minister of Parliament because he voted to behead the king."

"Wasn't there an aunt who committed suicide?"

"An aunt." Feeling cold again, Bee chafed her arms. "Great-Aunt Lucille's own sister, Ophelia. She committed suicide not long after she married. Great-Aunt Lucille told me about her a few years back."

"Ophelia? Like Shakespeare's Ophelia?"

"She didn't drown. She jumped from the roof."

"And Lady Chalmsley's brother? They used to laugh about his conversations with angels. What happened to him?"

"He's in Bedlam. He attacked his mother. He tried to strangle her. And that was after he had killed his valet. He used a cane to beat him to death."

"Good Lord. Violently insane," Henning said. "But this is all hearsay evidence."

"It's family knowledge."

Hector shook his head. "Family knowledge isn't good enough. They could refuse to testify and then lie. We can find a public record about an admission to Bedlam. A good parish register might give us more evidence. Those records would have to be located before we gave evidence in court."

"The locals might help you find those records. They must be tired of the Quenton legacy. Great-Aunt Lucille said something once, about the people near her family's manor. She said they refused to interact with the family. All because of these stories. Stories that the family doesn't talk about. Stories I couldn't believe, although Aunt Beth has confirm them."

"They're all insane?"

Mindful of eavesdroppers, Bee lowered her voice. "They might not look insane. It worsens as they age. It manifests either as sane and violently evil, or insane with self-directed harm. Like Cordelia and her chopped-off hair. And Mad Aunt Beth, with her cutting. They are not violent. It's the ones who look sane that are dangerous."

"And who looks sane?" Hector whispered, aiming his question at Henning. "Not Lady Chalmsley. Not Cordelia. Certainly not Aunt Beth."

"That only leaves Miss Portia, the one who looks like an angel."

"Her brother has those same angelic looks. Blond hair, blue eyes, beautiful smile. And a devilish disposition. He has killed helpless animals. He drowned an infant that a woman claimed was his."

"An infant? Surely he was prosecuted?"

"Lord Chalmsley is the magistrate. He paid good money to send the family away. He's covered over other crimes that his son committed. I do not know how many."

When Hector visibly shuddered, Bee guessed he had remembered a bloody pulp in the summer garden, a blight that lingered far past that singular day.

"Don't make the mistake of thinking Portia is an angel," Hector warned. "From my years here, I know that she tormented her sister. The tutors and governesses allowed those torments because Portia was distracted from playing her cruel pranks on them. Eventually, though, she bored with terrorizing Cordelia and turned on the governess or the tutor. They never stayed long after the first prank, usually reddened water poured into their bed or their clothes shredded with a kitchen knife. Lord Chalmsley would dismissed them with an extra month's pay."

"Tutors and governesses." Henning shook his head. "That is all long ago. Surely she has cast off her pranks, now that she is older. She is certainly not like her sister, with her compulsions to straighten things. Look at that one. She chopped off her hair. She's walking around with a beaded necklace, chanting prayers."

"Oh, Portia has her obsessions, Mr. Henning. She has learned, though, not to share them beyond the family. I have endured her tirades about things, however. Were you to hear one of those, you might believe me."

"Tell us about them."

Bee didn't trust the gleam in his eye. He might want to believe she herself was obsessed. No, he wouldn't trap her, the way he had trapped her in the cold cellar. In a hard voice that hid her aching heart, she charged him. "I have a better idea: You ask her. Ask Portia about her fiancé Brougham Paton. Ask her about Cordelia's fiancé and mine. Ask her about William Kennington. See what answers she gives. Or ask her about her brother George. You might get answers. I never did. I only had my suspicions."

"Oh God," Hector breathed, "babies buried in gardens?"f

He had remembered Aunt Beth's mad singsong ballads. Tears filled her eyes as Bee nodded. "Yes, that, too. Go to the garden. Talk to Peters, the head gardener. Ask him about the burned patch in the lower garden."

"Peters and a burned patch?" Henning asked.

"I don't know a Peters," Hector said.

"He's new. The last five years. Please inform him that I wish you to know about the burned patch."

"I'll ask him," Hector vowed.

"Good. I suppose I must stay locked in somewhere."

"I would prefer you in the cellar," Henning groused.

"May I have my cloak? And shoes. It's cold in there."

"No, you will not have your cloak," Hector declared, "for you're going to your own chamber. Where you have a fire. To please Henning and his lordship, we'll have to lock you in, but you will be warm there. And safe, Bee." He seized her hand then wrapped both of his around it, chilling her clay-cold flesh. "I need to know you're safe."

A whole list of arguments about locking her door arose, but Bee kept silent. She was free from the cellar. A small step, but an important one. Hector seemed to think her safety rather than her potential escape was the reason for the lock.

Her room had a window as well. A desperate means to escape if she needed it. The baroque decorations carved into the blocks that formed the façade might offer a way down. At the very least she had a balcony.

They appointed another footman to guard her door. Hector questioned how long the young man had worked at Chalmsley Court. He clearly did not like the answer of "only since last summer, sir."

Before Hector shut the door, Bee reminded him, "She hasn't burned Pierpont's bed yet. Now she must also burn Edmund's."

"She broke the pattern. She may not need to burn those beds."

"Burning them is part of her obsession. Obsessions can't be released, Hector. You can set a trap for her tonight."

"We will. You're safe behind this locked door, Bee. You will keep safe. Promise me."

"I have a cloak and warm clothes and shoes. Of course I'll keep safe."

She hoped she wasn't lying.

Chapter 18

As they turned from Bee's door, Henning asked, "What's important about this gardener named Peters being a new employee at Chalmsley Court?"

Hector gave them a few feet from the footman, another stranger on staff, before he answered. "New employees like Peters don't owe any loyalty to the family. He won't keep their secrets unless they ask. My guess is that no one has asked him to keep any secrets."

"So he'll answer your question."

"I would think so."

Halfway down the first stair flight, the Bow Street officer gave a huff. "I believe Miss Seddars thinks this Peters might owe loyalty to her. What did she say exactly? She needs him to tell you. That smacks of loyalty."

"Haven't you noticed, man? The servants look to her, not the family."

"She's family."

"She's a Seddars. She's not direct line, though. She wasn't born here, she wasn't raised here. Her father wasn't either. She visited, before she came to live here after her parents died. However, the loyalty they give her has nothing to do with being a Chalmsley."

Richardson waited for them at the base of the stairs. "Sirs, I have a message for you from Coggins. The head groom," he added for Henning's benefit.

"Coggins?"

"He requests that you come to the stable, forthwith, sir. He said nothing more."

"Forthwith. We were on our way to find Peters, the head gardener."

"You may find him at the stable as well, Mr. Evans. He often is there on cold days."

"Thank you, Richardson."

"Sir, is Miss Seddars returned to her room? Mrs. Lovell did mention that you had removed her from the cellar." When he confirmed it, Richardson looked determined and embarrassed and afraid, a strange mix that twisted his dour features. "When Staff met this morning, sir, the talk revolved around the events of the past week and most especially the events last evening. I am speaking particularly to your decision, sir, you and Mr. Hennings here, in that you chose to arrest Miss Beatrice Seddars."

"We didn't arrest her."

"Semantics, sir. You detained her behind a lock and placed a guard to watch so that no one unlocked the door, ensuring that she remained there. Could she have left? No. Do not quibble over words. Staff asked me to convey two particular items to the both of you. Firstly, sir, we do not like to interfere, but Miss Seddars has our trust. We would not like her to be wrongfully accused."

The butler's statement surprised Hector. Servants did not step out of their expected roles. They did their assigned duties as unobtrusively as possible. To comment without prompting and to state their personal opinion was unheard of. Henning looked as struck as Hector was.

"Thank you, Richardson."

"Very good, sir. As to the second point, sir, I am instructed, should you desire corroborating testimony about Miss Beatrice Seddars, that we will supply any witness that is needed."

"We only want the facts. What people saw, not what they wished they'd seen. Misrepresenting facts will only hurt Miss Seddars' case if she is brought to trial. However," he quickly added, since the footman standing stoically at the wall looked as if he wanted to tackle Hector, "she will not be brought to trial. Neither Henning nor I believe she is guilty of any of these murders. We would like to find the weapon used, if possible."

"The weapon, sir?"

"Long, slender, a rounded blade rather than a knife blade. Good steel because it cut cleanly with only a little push. I have reason to believe it is a silver ice pick, similar to one used in the dining room."

Richardson's eyebrows raised. "We will certainly look for such an item."

Walking across the garden to the stables, Henning took him to task. "Are you insane, asking servants to find the murder weapon?"

"Can we find it?"

"But—but—it's unorthodox. Surely we want to find the weapon in the murderer's possession?"

"Do you seriously think the murderer hasn't hidden it in a place not associated with her? If she fears that our attention is directed at her, she may plant the weapon among someone else's possessions. This murderer is lucky, but I think she has a mad sort of cleverness. The only way we will get the murderer together with her weapon is to catch her as she attacks her next victim."

"You think there will be a fourth victim? The guests have all left."

"Leaving her father, you and me. Which one of us do you think she will want to kill?"

. ~ . ~ . ~ .

Men had gathered around the little stove in the tack room. With the departion of the guests, the number had greatly dwindled from Hector's previous visit to the stables, but the place still seemed crowded. As soon as the law officers came in, Coggins rose from his chair and came to them. "Thank you for coming so timely, Constable Evans, sir."

"Richardson gave us your message. He hinted at some urgency."

"Yes, sir. The matter did not seem urgent until events last night." Coggins' comment had Hector wondering if the head groom had also attended the staff meeting this morning. "We had two lost sheep return to us late last night."

At his words, two men rose from the group. Giants of men who filled the tackroom's ceiling area. Each sported a beard. Grey liberally sprinkled one beard. The younger man, as broad as the father he so closely resembled, had an easy grin.

"Sampson." Hector thrust forward his hand to the older giant. A great maw encased his, shook once, then retreated. The son's handshake had a little more pressure to it, but he had also learned to be careful of his strength. "When I was here," he said to the younger man, obviously Daniel, "you were a tyke who looked to have no chance of meeting your father's height."

The grin increased. "Done passed him, though, ain't I?"

"That you have. You two arrived back last night?"

The grin faded. "Late. Walked it from the village after coming in on the mail coach. Took us long enough to get that far."

"And your charge?"

"You know about that, do you?"

"A little. We worried he had returned. Has Coggins told you what's happened here in this past week?"

"Told us that. Told us you arrested Miss Beatrice. That was a mistake."

Hector knew better than to argue what Richardson had called *semantics*. "One that we have corrected."

"Good. Else I might have to knock sense into you. And your London friend, there."

"I understood that you and your father were in Vienna with your charge. Yet here you stand. Where's your charge?"

Daniel looked uneasy. His father looked downright uncomfortable. He dropped back onto his seat. A stump, Hector saw, and realized that the rickety chairs the other men used would have given out if either giant settled his weight onto the frames. "We should tell his lordship first, in the right way of things."

"I don't have time for the right way of things. We have three murders, Daniel. I don't want another. You tell me if I need to be looking for George or not."

"Not." That was firm.

"He didn't slip away from you?"

"He couldn't." Once more, the young giant squirmed. "You know where we were?"

"A hospital in Vienna. I understood that George needed a rest-cure."

Daniel snorted. "Needed more than that. You know what he was like, better than me. You saw—. Well. They sent him to that hospital and no other because the doctor said his treatments could cure vicious deeds. Cured him all right. Cured him dead."

"What?" Only Hector and Henning looked shocked. The men around the stove just nodded and smoked their pipes. "He's dead?" Hector wanted it confirmed.

"Dead. We brought his body back with us. It's waiting, back at the village church, in a coffin. Vicar said it was right and proper to leave him at the church. He'll be buried there, after all. Traveling with that coffin's the reason it took so long to get back. That and having to avoid Napoleon's troops. I done seen me more of foreign parts than I ever want to see, and that's truth."

"Dead, then," Henning said, standing at Hector's shoulder. "He couldn't have committed these murders."

"Not possible," Daniel confirmed. "We've been steady traveling for weeks, way after dark, sometimes, trying to get back as fast as we could."

"How did he die?"

Daniel shrugged and looked back at his father. He fumbled inside his coat and produced a crumpled letter. His son handed it to Hector. "From the doctor to his lordship. Explaining, I'd think. Don't know if it says exactly how Master George died, though."

"What was the treatment for?"

"I told you. He were supposed to stop evil. Dr. Schroder said he were deranged. He never looked it. Looked like an angel. Covered in blood and smiling and asking why you were upset. You know his way. You had to deal with him more than anyone else did, before you left. He didn't change much after that. Just continued his ways. Didn't care who or what he hurt, people and little animals. Enjoyed hurtin' them."

"His horse," Sampson rumbled.

"Aye, his horse, once we got to Vienna and he realized he wasn't going nowhere else. That doctor locked him up in a proper little cell with no windows nor nothing. He tore up that room till he had nothin' but a pallet for sleepin' and gruel in a bowl. Couldn't trust him with anything else." Daniel glanced over at the head groom. "I will say this, Coggins. Master George done admitted lots he did, but he never did admit to cutting his lordship's saddle strap."

Coggins didn't look or sound surprised. "No, he wouldn't."

Mindful of Bee's comments and needing to clear her, Hector turned to the old groom. "Yet I heard that everyone believed George was responsible for Lord Chalmsley's riding accident."

Coggins spit on the straw-strewn floor. "Weren't no accident, sir."

"That's correct. It was attempted murder."

"Ya didna hear that from me."

"Cutting a girth strap and waiting for the strap to break," Hector pretended to muse, hoping to draw out the chief groom and get a witness statement that would finally persuade Henning. "That doesn't seem the kind of violence that George was capable of. I remember him drowning kittens and puppies, kicking his mother's terrier, trying to use a cane on that groom."

"Aye, those things Master George did," Daniel supported while Coggins merely nodded and puffed smoke. The head groom could be agreeing; he could be listening. A nod like that could be interpreted either way.

Careful not to look at Henning, Hector continued his assessment of the now-dead son and heir. "Direct violence. Immediate violence. Not waiting until later when he wasn't around. Not setting a trap that would cause pain he couldn't see. George never cared when people knew what he did. Would you agree, Coggins?"

He withdrew his pipe. After a long wait, long enough to worry Hector, the man nodded. "Aye, Mr. Evans, that I would. Master George weren't one for hiding what he did."

"Did you ever question the blame assigned to George for the attempt on his father's life?"

The question roused those around the stove. Coggins merely looked Hector eye to eye, as if he knew his plan. He might agree, but he wasn't going to overstep. He was Chalmsley through several generations, as would be his son and grandson, if they still remained on the estate. "Weren't my business to question it, sir. Nobody ast me."

"I'm asking you now. Here, in front of Mr. Henning. Do you believe that George caused the girth strap to break?"

"No, sir. Weren't Master George."

"Who do you think responsible?"

Coggins scowled.

"Not your place to speculate?"

"That'ld be right, sir."

Hector considered then re-worded his question. "Who was near Lord Chalmsley's horse after the groom saddled it?"

"The groom Hal. Not with us no more. Sister was Magsie, ya know."

"Magsie was the upstairs maid that George impregnated?"

"Aye, that's the one. Hal wouldn't mess with Lord Chalmsley's tack. And me, I were there. I held the reins when his lordship mounted up."

He considered another approach then drilled in. "Who from the family was also at the stable?"

Coggins stared. He chewed, then spat. "Miss Portia, sir."

Henning rocked back. "The angel. I begin to see."

See more, Hector wished on him. "Thank you, Coggins. We need facts like this, right now especially. We were told we would find the head gardener here?"

The head gardener proved to be a small, wiry man, dwarfed on one side by Sampson. He didn't move from his seat, forcing Hector and Henning to stand behind the circle of men to question him. He didn't look at them, just whittled a stick. Occasionally he grabbed up the shavings from the floor and tossed them into the stove.

After hinting around strange events in the garden then outright asking about a burned patch, Hector decided to use Bee's magic words. "Miss Seddars told me that she needs you to answer my questions."

That raised the man's brows. "Miss Seddars? Which one? Goldy? Or the bony one?"

"Miss Beatrice."

The eyebrows went down. The knife went into his boot. He tossed the whittled stick into the fire. "Ought to 've said so in the first place."

"You should have answered without havering around," one of the men said.

He didn't scowl, just picked up another piece of kindling and drew out his knife. "Aye, I know the burned patch she told you to ask about. Happens every year, five years running now. Same place. Same day. A little fire built. Flowers strewn around."

"Who sets the fire?"

His eyes opened wide, as if surprised Hector needed to ask the question. "Goldy one. Miss Portia."

"Have you ever spoken to her about this burned patch?"

"Just the first time. Asked her not to do it. She said it was a memorial for the little lost one."

"Dig it up," Hector ordered and shocked them all. "Do you remember the exact place, Peters? With the snow, will you have difficulty finding the spot?"

"No, sir. I know my garden."

"Then dig it up, man. And bring us what you find. My guess is, whatever it is, it will be small and it won't be deep."

"Babies buried in gardens," Hennings muttered, "damn it all. This case just gets worse and worse."

Chapter 19

Bee jiggled the long stickpin in the lock. The footman on guard had walked away a quarter-hour ago. If he'd returned quickly, she doubted that she would have even thought about unlocking the door.

Last night still steamed her. Warmed up by a good breakfast and hot tea, wool and leather keeping her feet warm, a fire merrily toasting her while she sat before it, she had dropped off for a short doze. She hadn't expected to wake up angrier than she'd been when Hector had opened the wine cellar to release her.

After washing her face, she paced until five steps one way and five steps back irritated more than it burned her seething energy. She ventured onto the balcony, into the freezing air, to stare at the snowy landscape. She studied the carved stone and planned her climb down— until the extreme cold drove her back into her chamber.

Was it only a few months ago that she had picked this very chamber? The view had drawn her, reminding her of a summer long ago, a summer that held both grief and happiness, the last summer that offered her hope. On this morning, though, the room held no happy distractions. Her few possessions were reminders of all the ones that had been broken or hidden. Her snowy view no longer looked beautiful; it looked smothering. This room had become a prison. The way her marriage to Edmund Tretheway would be a prison. The way her life here at Chalmsley Court was a prison. No longer could she trust Great-Uncle Hamilton to have her best interests in mind. No longer would she depending on Hector to convince that fool Bow Street Runner that she didn't kill anyone.

If she hadn't heard young White leave in answer to someone's call for assistance, she might not have gone to the door. She turned from the uninteresting view, wondering where he'd gone. Voices, muffled by the thick oak panels of her door, came, faded, then came again, accompanied by footsteps. She turned back to the frozen lawn, trees with their ice-crystal branches, and blue, blue sky.

The footsteps came back. She expected the footman to come down the hall, back to his duty. He stopped long before he reached her room.

That drew her to the door. She pressed her ear to the planking then bent and peeked through the keyhole.

It was blocked.

By the key on the other side.

The idea flashed, and she grinned.

Bee flew to her desk. A strong piece of parchment with a rough texture, not yet rubbed smooth for writing. Long enough to extend well past the door if the key bounced when it landed. That's what she needed. She jammed the drawer into place and hurried back.

Before she slid the parchment under the door, she peered through the gap down the long corridor. Feet. Black boots and the dark grey of the servants' livery. Into William Kennington's room and out, hurrying in, slower out. As they neared the landing and turned to the servant's stair, she realized they had the posts and upper tester support separated from the bedframe.

She sat back on her rump and considered.

Then she returned to her desk and once more rummaged through the drawer and cubbies, looking for something thin yet sturdy that would push the key out. She rejected a letter opener and a quill, too thick for the narrow keyhole. Long, thin, much thinner than the weapon that punched into the men's necks. She shuddered at the thought and kept looking. The desk yielded nothing that would work. She crossed to her dresser and delved into the sundries drawer. There, a long stick pin, a pretty little enameled ornament topping a sharp length of copper. She hadn't used it since last she wore her wide-brimmed straw hat. Sturdy, not easily breakable, long and sharp. Bendable. She would have to be careful not to jam it in the lock with the key. Then she would be truly stuck.

Bee applied the stickpin to the task.

Steps came back. She quickly pulled the parchment back in and peered under the door again.

Two footmen. Bumping, knocking, dropping wood on wood. They emerged with the slats and sideboards for the bedframe, charred by the fire. The headboard and footboard were all that would remain. If they were removing the ruined bedframe only, she had only this time and the next to escape.

She positioned the parchment, applied the hat pin, and wiggled and jiggled.

The key fell with a satisfying clink.

Bee carefully drew the parchment back. She stared at the key. Letting herself out of her room, after Hector asked her—ordered her to remain inside seemed momentous. She loved Hector. She trusted him— but she didn't trust her great-uncle or that Mr. Henning. Trusting Hector was as momentous as her recent letter to Mr. Cosgrove, begging him to retain control of her finances rather than give control to her husband upon her marriage. As momentous as deciding that she would leave Chalmsley and set up a new life for herself elsewhere.

On her knees she unlocked the door. She peered through the keyhole and watched.

Mad Aunt Beth slipped down the stairs. She darted a glance along the corridor then flitted across to the next flight.

Bee waited, certain the footmen would soon return. She didn't want to be caught in the corridor. If someone appeared and she tried to dash into an empty bedchamber, she might find herself plastered against a locked door. After a house stay, Mrs. Lovell usually shepherded a covey of maids behind her, unlocking a whole wing of doors while they stripped the beds and freshened the rooms before moving to the next wing. Bee had heard none of that usual activity since her arrival upstairs. The morning's departures would soon see the linens as next on the housekeeper's list.

She heard footsteps. The footmen came back. She sprang to her feet and waited. Yes, each man lugged out the last two portions of the bedstead. She eased open the door, but she didn't slip out until they turned for the servants' stairs. Then she whipped out, closed the door, locked it and left the key in the lock, just as it had been, and sped down the corridor.

An original plan had never formed. Queen Mab would give her direction. She would find the old woman, get her to tell what she knew. Once she'd said the words to Bee, perhaps she would be willing to repeat them to Hector. Even Henning scowling over his shoulder shouldn't intimidate Mab if she'd spoken the words already.

She reached the landing and turned to follow Aunt Beth.

"Miss Seddars. Miss Seddars."

Bee's heart jumped then thumped at a stampede beat. She turned slowly.

Nurse Gregg stood halfway down the flight to the nursery level. "Miss Seddars."

She gathered calm. "Nurse Gregg, how may I assist you?"

"It's that Miss Quenton. She's done slipped off, again. Have you seen her?"

Did she enlist the woman's aid or not? *Not.* "I did see her. She came down only a little while ago. I should have stopped her, I know, but I was attending to the removal of furniture."

An aggrieved sigh filled the air. "Which way was she heading, Miss Seddars?"

"I believe she nipped down the servants' stair to go for the kitchen. Mrs. Shelton normally has a few hot treats coming from the ovens about this time." There, a lie with a distraction. Nurse Gregg never passed up a sweet pastry. When the woman started down the flight, Bee said the first order she'd ever given of that sort. "Use the servants' stairs, Nurse Gregg, not the front stairs." She didn't want the woman to find Mab before she herself did.

"Oh. Of course, Miss Seddars." She retraced her steps.

Bee nipped down the flight. She paused, wondering which way Aunt Beth had gone. Thudding steps heralded the return of the footmen. Quickly, she sidestepped out of view then pressed her hands to her breast, trying to hold in her racing heart. She waited, expecting a *tally-ho* when her absence was discovered. Nothing came.

The corridor remained empty. No Mrs. Lovell with her master keys, opening doors then locking them back, no maids removing linens and freshening the deserted chambers. Where was everyone?

The first door she tried was locked. The second one, the third and fourth.

The doorknob that turned when she jiggled it opened to Mr. Pierpont's room. With a shudder Bee stepped in. She wondered why she had come into the chamber even as she saw the bed, stripped of its mattress. Was that the reason Pierpont's bed hadn't burned last night? Had Mrs. Lovell been too efficient for the murderess?

A screech came, not loud, not muffled, on the corridor but not nearby. Bee poked her head out.

"Give that back, you old bat. Give it to me!"

Aunt Beth darted from a chamber on the family wing. With winged feet she sped to the stairs. Grey hair flew behind her. She clutched something to her breast.

Portia shot from her room. Her tousled hair looked like she'd tussled with the old woman. Bee had had her own scuffle with Aunt Beth and come out the worse. The old woman was tricksy, quick of feet and ruthless with shoves. Portia had clearly wound up exactly as Bee had, on her rump while Mab escaped with her treasure.

"Give it back," her cousin shouted.

Aunt Beth saw Bee peeking out of the doorway and slowed.

She stepped into the corridor and motioned down the stairs. "Go, go. Find Hector, Queen Mab."

She laughed with delight and flew down the stairs.

Portia slid to a stop. "You! You should help me! I helped you!"

The horrid idea slipped in the keyhole and unlocked itself. Three murders, the last one was Edmund's. And Portia had thought it was a help to Bee. "How did you help me, Portia?"

"You won't go away from us now. But that old bat has to give it back! I need it."

"She's an old woman. She won't run far. What does she have? A steely pick?"

Her golden hair seemed to crackle with energy. "You know! I thought you did. Papa didn't think so, but he listened when I told him he had to choose. Me or you. And you sent her to Hector. He *never* liked me, *never*. I thought he'd come back to the family, but he *never* wanted to be with us. Look how long he stayed away. He *never* liked me. He likes Cordy more than he likes me."

"Too bad, so sad," Bee chanted, feeling a little like Mab.

She screeched again. She glanced down the stairs, stared hard at Bee, then hurried after Aunt Beth.

And Bee ran after both of them. Aunt Beth's surprise escape wouldn't work a second time. With Portia now murderous, Aunt Beth wouldn't stand long against her younger and more ruthless niece.

.~.~.~.

The door opened. Cold air gusted in with them.

"We tell his lordship first, I suppose," Henning said.

A screech echoed from the entrance hall.

They ran, Daniel on their heels, light-footed for a big man. His father lumbered after.

They arrived as Mad Aunt Beth jumped from the last steps. She stumbled her landing then darted for the drawing room. The footman refused to open the door. She bounced back then spun on her heel. Hector saw her eyes dart around, as if she searched for something. She grasped something in her hands and held it tightly to her chest. Something shining. Something silver.

"Here," he coaxed. "Queen Mab, come here."

Her frightened expression landed on him and turned into a manic beam. "I found it."

"What? What did she find?"

Her gaze shifted to Henning, and she backed up a step.

"Give it to me, your majesty. I'll keep it safe."

She hesitated, her gaze darting to the giants behind the two officers.

Lord Chalmsley appeared. "What is that infernal racket?"

Another screech sounded. Footsteps hit the stairs. As one, the men looked up and saw Portia racing down the stairs.

"Give that to me, you crazy old bat. It's mine."

More footsteps.

Mab had darted to Hector and pressed something against his chest. "Carrion Crow, catch your murderer."

"Don't give it to him! It's mine!" Portia reached the landing as Hector examined Aunt Beth's gift.

A silver ice pick, the kind used in the dining room. Just as the old woman had predicted. This one had dried blood stains marring the thin blade.

Portia fetched up behind the old woman, grabbed her hair and gave a hard jerk. Aunt Beth went sprawling.

"How dare you!" Bee cried and skidded her last few steps to reach the old woman.

Hector wasn't surprised Bee had slipped away from her guard.

She knelt beside Aunt Beth, trying to urge her to her feet, but Aunt Beth had frozen herself in a curled-up ball.

"Interfering old bat!" Portia aimed a kick. The old woman wailed.

Bee surged up and stepped over Queen Mab. "Stop. Do not touch her. Do not harm her."

"She took it!"

"And she gave it to Hector. Talk to him."

Portia started to argue, but she suddenly seemed to realize how many people had crowded into the entrance hall. She dipped her head, lifted her lashes, and the little termagant turned into a seductress. "Why! I didn't see everyone here. Papa, I'm—." Then her gaze fell on the giants. Words failed her. She fell back a step. "What are you doing here? Papa, why are they here? They're supposed to be with George. Is George back? Where is George?"

Lord Chalmsley stepped forward. He had ignored the men until his daughter called attention to them. "Sampson. Daniel. When did you arrive?"

"Just came to the house this moment, your lordship," Daniel supplied, obscuring their time of arrival with a different truth.

"Where is my son?"

"Well, your lordship, that's hard to answer."

"You've lost track of him!"

"No, no, we ain't. He's—." That first comment had apparently used up the only deception he had ready. Daniel rolled his eyes to his father.

Sampson cleared his throat. "Truth is, your lordship, that your son is at Chalmsley Church."

"Why isn't he here? Why did he stop at the church?"

"He should be here," Portia declared. "I fixed everything for him," and that claim had Hector wanting to ask his own set of questions.

"Hear that?" Henning hissed.

Hector nodded as Sampson sighed heavily. "Truth is, your lordship, your son is dead."

Lord Chalmsley fell back a step. Before he could speak, Portia screamed "No! No, no, no! I did what he asked. I did it! He can't be dead! He can't! He promised me." Her eyes darted about. "I have to—I have to go to him. I have to—." She started to fly past.

Henning grabbed her arm. "Easy now."

She struck at him. He cursed and released her. She grabbed for the ice pick. Hector snatched it away.

Her resistance suddenly collapsed. She looked at the two giants. Tears trickled out of her eyes. "You were supposed to guard him until he comes back to me. He said he was coming back. And that we would all be together."

A slight figure moved behind Daniel then stood still, waiting.

"What happened, Sampson?" Chalmsley asked. "The doctor sent a report right after Christmas. He said his treatment was successful."

"Not so successful, your lordship, since that treatment's what killed Master George."

Portia sobbed. "Don't say it. Don't say it. He's coming back to me. He loves me. He's the only one who's ever loved me."

Lord Chalmsley looked at his daughter, but he didn't move to offer the comfort of an embrace. Nor did Bee, and Hector noticed that she held something in her hand, pressed against her lower limb, some wire-like stick.

The servants were staring at the golden angel. "Aye, makes sense now, don't it, Da?"

The older giant nodded.

"What *makes sense*?" Chalmsley demanded.

"Something Master George harped on, every day we traveled, every day he was in that there hospital. Every day he saw us. Kept saying he had to get back here, to get back to his girl, to keep watch over her and what was theirs together. Didn't make sense then. Now it does."

A throat cleared. The giants turned to see who stood behind them then moved aside.

The head gardener stepped forward. He cradled a soil-covered bundle in his hands. Bee gasped and covered her mouth. Henning stood very still beside Hector.

"It were there, Constable," Peters said, "just like ya said it would be. This is it."

"Peters!" Chalmsley barked. "What is this?"

The gardener looked down at the bundle in his hands and said nothing. "Every year," Hector explained, "for the past five years, Miss Portia has burned a particular spot in the garden. I asked Peters to dig up the spot and bring what he found. Where, exactly, Peters?"

"The lower garden, sir," Peters answered.

"I asked what this is." Yet Chalmsley's words lacked their normal strength. He sounded and looked like a man far beyond his years. His gaze shifted from the bundle to his daughter.

"Miss Portia burned the patch, sir. I asked what she were up to. She said burning a memorial for the little lost one."

"My little lost one, mine and George's," she murmured. She held out her arms. "She belongs to me, to me and George. He helped me, before he went away, but she's mine. You dug her up. You dug up what

I told you to leave alone, didn't you? Why did you do that? Poor little one. My poor little one. Give her to me."

Peters hesitated. He looked from Portia to Chalmsley and then to Hector. After another second, he nodded.

"You don't want her, Miss Portia." Henning, voice pitched low and easy, used a hand to block Peters from moving forward. "She needs a proper burial. Peters will just put her in the chapel along with Mr. Tretheway."

The words fired Portia. "No! My little lost one will not be in the room with that man. He will hurt her."

"He can't hurt her, Miss Portia. He's dead."

She glared at him. "Not in the chapel. Not near that liar. He swore he loved me, do you believe that? He lied, just like they all lied. The only one who ever loved me was George. But we couldn't be together, not like husband and wife. Because we are sister and brother."

And although he knew it was cold and as merciless as her murders, Hector asked, "What did you do to the men who lied to you, Portia?"

"I jabbed them in the throat, where their lies came from. I jabbed them with that." She pointed at the silver ice pick Hector held. "They won't lie to me anymore, will they? They swore they'd love me, no matter who they married, then they said we couldn't be together, not anymore. George says people who lie have to be punished. I punished them. I jabbed them in the throat."

No one spoke. She continued to stare at the soil-covered bundle. "Give her the babe, Peters," Hector ordered.

Chapter 20

"You can't leave her in that cellar," Bee demanded. "It's not right."

"It's the only lock she won't be able to open. I'm not leaving her to slip away in the night or kill someone else, anyone that she thinks may have lied to her."

Bee rubbed her arms, as if she remembered the freezing darkness she had endured. "You can't leave her there," she whispered. "Hector, please."

"Lord Chalmsley and Hennings thought it good enough for you," he gritted.

. ~ . ~ . ~ .

At dinner, Lord Chalmsley looked broken. Cordelia had refused to leave her room. The officers seated themselves across from Bee. Hector took smaller portions and wondered if he would finish anything at all. Bee refused what she could then pushed the rest around her plate. Henning, unaffected by family connections, made as hearty a meal as usual.

Lady Chalmsley said only, "Portia would get these ideas in her head." Then she continued with her meal as if her younger daughter hadn't murdered three men and her only son wasn't a corpse in the village church a few miles away.

Bee choked.

Richardson entered. He bowed to Lord Chalmsley, who didn't notice. After a long pause, he approached Bee and whispered.

She gasped. Tears sprang to her eyes. When she started up, the butler pulled out her chair.

Her great-uncle didn't react.

She stared at him then looked away. "Hector, Mr. Henning, please come with me."

They followed Richardson to the cellar. Two footmen stood outside the room where they had secured Portia, the same room where Bee had waited for long, long hours. The unlocked door stood open.

The butler paused. Then he took up a candelabrum and led them inside.

The smell of wine was astringent, the rich fermentation filling the room, overpowering the musty smell that Bee had had to inhale. Broken bottles covered the wine-stained bricks. Blood stained the bricks as well.

Portia leaned against one of the support columns. She sat like a rag doll, her head dipped to one side, her golden hair spilling over to hide her face and her breasts. Her legs stretched out before her. In her lap was the little bundle that she had gathered close when Peters handed it to her. Bloody gashes covered her limp arms.

"Good lord," Richardson said then crossed himself.

"Well. That's for the best." Henning sounded as unaffected as he was unconnected. "Better that she doesn't stand trial. His lordship wouldn't want any of this getting around, with the trial like a circus, that's my way of thinking."

"Are you mad?" Bee snapped. "How can her suicide be for the best?"

"She won't have to hang."

Bee sobbed. Hector wrapped an arm around her and steered her out of the room.

. ~ . ~ . ~ .

Cordelia emerged from her self-imposed isolation before breakfast. She sat at the table, neither eating nor drinking, just staring out the windows at a wintry landscape she couldn't see for the glare of the bright morning sun.

Hector had waited until Bee was ready to descend. Henning had waited for Hector. He talked about returning to London. He talked about Hector's work as a constable. He didn't talk about Hector being right.

The footmen sprang to work as soon as they entered, pouring preferred coffee and tea, lading plates with a good breakfast, pulling out a chair for Bee.

Cordelia didn't acknowledge them, not until they three were seated. Then she stood so abruptly her chair toppled. A footman caught it then stood holding it, not certain what to do since she wasn't moving.

"Cordy?"

Her cousin turned her gaze from the sun glare to look at Bee. "I have something for you. No, for Constable Evans. He should have it."

She thrust a small book across the table, aiming it toward Hector without once looking his way. "What is it?" he asked.

She heard him even if she didn't want to see him. "The record of my sister's sins. My last good deed in this world, to give you the proof of her evil." Then she turned and walked out of the room. A footman opened the door then shut it behind her.

"Well, man," Henning said around a mouthful of sausage, "open it up. Start at the back."

Hector held the journal between his palms. He looked at Bee, waiting for her nod.

"Perhaps it would be better just to burn it?" she suggested.

"Burn it?"

"What good will it serve? She's dead."

Hector winced, knowing that the anguish would have to continue. "The families will want evidence that justice was served. The magistrate must record a reason for the murders. The constable must report his findings to the magistrate."

She nodded.

He turned to the last entries. Tretheway's murder was there, Pierpont's, Kennington's. Described in simple, flat sentences without emotion. Portia reserved her emotion when she wrote about George and his letter. Portia's looping, open scrawl reminded him how young she had been even as she described her trickery and her murders, her plan that duped her mother. On a chance, he looked back several years, searching for a single entry. He found it easily. Only two words were written on the page: *She died.*

Bee caught back a sob when he read that little entry. "How could Portia have been so broken and I never knew it?"

He clasped her hand. "We all hide our brokenness from the world. We need others to heal us. Perhaps George healed her."

She shook her head. "No. He was so—no. Besides, she tried to kill her own father while George was still here."

"Because her father planned to send George away."

Bee shuddered. "I can't believe I knew nothing. Portia gave birth to a child!"

"While her brother impregnated her and somehow convinced her to keep that secret."

She suddenly gasped. Her eyes lifted to the ceiling. "Cordelia. Her desperate need to escape. Hector—."

She didn't need to complete her thought. "Yes," he agreed firmly.

Henning slurped his coffee. "Now here's something I don't understand. She killed those three men because she said they lied to her. She said she loved George and he loved her. But he got the upstairs maid with child. So, why didn't she call *him* a liar?"

"He didn't lie because he didn't make any promises," Hector supposed. "He did say they couldn't be together as husband and wife, remember. She had to keep it quiet."

"And out of all that, which event turned her mind?" Bee still tried to fit the puzzle pieces into a coherent whole. "George's rape, then the death of her baby, and then George and the chambermaid, and his drowning that baby. When my great-uncle decided to send George away, because his violence was only increasing, Portia tried to kill her own father by cutting the girth strap on his riding saddle."

"Tried and failed. She only hastened George's departure. We'll never know everything, but we know enough."

"It breaks my heart."

.~.~.~.

It was breaking his heart to leave Bee in this house of anguish. He had written his official report. The servants had brought his horse around and loaded his saddlebags. Hector held Bee's cold hands in the entrance hall and knew he couldn't just leave. He couldn't wait for his next opportunity to see her. He couldn't wait for a return of his letter from the newest magistrate at Bow Street, hand-carried by Henning when he left after breakfast.

Richardson stood at the entrance, waiting to open the carved door. Two footmen stood statue-like at the opposing doors. He had an audience he didn't want, but if he said nothing now, he would never have a chance to say it.

He could argue that she didn't need stay with people who had been willing to sacrifice her. He could argue that she needed to get away, to free herself from the stifling atmosphere of grief that would linger here for years. Those arguments wouldn't win her.

"Come to London, Bee."

Her gaze drifted to Richardson, whom Hector knew watched without watching. "I do love the country. So much better than sooty, grimy London."

"I know." He wouldn't win unless he risked. The memory of their kiss gave him courage. "I know we haven't talked courtship, but I love you, Beatrice Seddars. I have loved you for eight years. I thought you broke my heart when you didn't write; I know now that your great-uncle interfered. Come with me to London. Once I have a special license, we'll marry. We'll make a life together. A sane, rational life."

She stared at their joined hands. "Married by special license. That sounds hurried."

"If you would rather wait."

She glanced up. Her eyes looked like stars. "Oh no. I'd rather be hurried. Let us break the norm."

The butler, at his station, nodded and smiled. Hector's heart began its climb out of the abyss. "If you want to live here still—. I can support us in London."

"Hector—." Then she hesitated. Her gaze searched his. "I will have access to my capital in three years, Hector."

"No. I'll support us. I can make a good living as a Bow Street officer. They've asked, twice now, that I return and take a position higher in what is becoming an organization. Teach my methods to new officers. There's talk of becoming more official although that's likely years down the road. Will you marry me?"

"I had thought to go to my mother's maiden aunt in Piggoty." She tugged her hands. He released her immediately, not certain what she wanted. Piggoty sounded like an escape from him. Then she smiled. "I really don't like the sound of Piggoty. London with you is much more interesting." And she looped her arms around his neck and drew him into a kiss.

Epilogue ~~ January 1814

Baby Macsen nuzzled his mother's neck, blowing bubbles that would dampen her collar. Bee patted his back as she led her man-of-business to the front room with its boxed bay window. The radiant light warmed the room more than the fire in the little hearth did. She chose to sit in the bright sunlight and gestured for him to take a similar chair. "What brings you to us on such a fine day, Mr. Cosgrove? Have you lost my principal on speculations?"

"Never," the old man said fervently. As Hector entered, he half-rose from his seat then subsided as Hector lifted the baby from Bee's arms then joined her on the settee. Mr. Cosgrove watched father with son and gave a decided nod. "I bear both good and bad news."

"We'll hear the worst first," Hector said. "If you've not been speculating, has the bank failed?"

He looked horrified. "No, no, nothing like that. Never. I am very careful with my clients' money."

"I think we have teased him enough, Hector." Bee smiled at the old man, and Hector—knowing the radiance of that smile—wondered how Mr. Cosgrove managed not to declare his love. Hector declared it, every time he saw that brilliance. Maybe that was the reason her man-of-business did everything she wanted, even when she didn't know to ask for it. "But I am now very curious, sir. If you have not come to talk about my principal or investments, what brings you here? Not that I do not enjoy our visits."

Mr. Cosgrove leaned a little forward. He gripped the head of his cane with both hands. "Lord Chalmsley's solicitor has contacted me and asked me to speak with the both of you."

The radiance cooled, almost as if a dark cloud obscured the sun. "We severed contact with my great-uncle a year ago, after he blamed me for his younger daughter's death."

"If Chalmsley wants a reunion," Hector ground. The baby in his arms began fretting. He patted the boy. "Hush, hush."

The old man looked unhappy. "I do remember those circumstances. A tragedy all round, and his lordship has never truly recovered."

"He had only to apologize to my wife."

Bee shook her head. "He is proud. And he had lost a daughter and his only son and his reputation. When I left with you, he lashed out."

"He won't treat you like that ever again, not in my presence." He lifted the baby to his shoulder and patted his rump. "Don't ask us to visit him, Mr. Cosgrove. That won't happen."

"No, no, that is not Mr. Atkinson's request. Mr. Atkinson is Lord Chalmsley's solicitor. He understands the difficulty that his lordship's accusations caused."

Hector snorted. "More than once, and much more than on that last day at the Court."

"Well. You informed me of this estrangement, Mrs. Evans, when you arrived in London, and I agreed then with your decision. I still do, although his lordship does appear to regret what occurred."

"He does not regret it. I know my great-uncle very well, Mr. Cosgrove." Bee rose and glided over the floor to stand before the hearth. She stared down into the fire. "He never regrets. He just continues on and hopes no one remembers his mistake. Let us not talk of him."

Mr. Cosgrove cleared his throat. "That may be a little difficult. I confess that I did not foresee—but then I am not that acquainted with your extended family, Mrs. Evans. I did know that your father was Lord Chalmsley's cousin, but I was not aware of the lack of male cousins in the family. With his lordship in such ill health—."

She looked around, a crease on her smooth brow. "You have me confused and a little worried, Mr Cosgrove."

"He means," Hector said, "that your great-uncle's title will lapse when he dies."

"Not lapse, not truly. The title will go to the next male heir, following the patrilineal line and then the matrilineal line."

"You've lost us."

"No, he hasn't." Again Hector knew, and the meaning made him want to shout at the irony. But his son slept on his shoulder, and he didn't want to wake him. "Macsen is the closest male descendant in the Seddars line to the barony of Chalmsley."

Bee gaped at her husband and then at her son. "Good lord."

"Exactly," Mr. Cosgrove said. "Your son will inherit not only the title but also the whole of Chalmsley Court, manor and estate. Lord Chalmsley has also made over to him the remainder of his funds. He will draw upon the interest until his death, then the monies will revert in their entirety, to the estate and thus to your son. With you and your husband as executors until your son comes of age. Age twenty-six," he added, with a nod to Hector, "as apparently is common in the Seddars family. That was how the will of your father was read. Lord Chalmsley's will reads much the same. Mr. Atkinson and I poured over the document itself just this morning."

"This is all very well, Mr. Cosgrove, and I confess that I am shocked by this news, but I do not see how this is relevant at this moment."

"Mr. Atkinson should explain this to you, but he preferred that I break the news to you. He stands ready, Mrs. Evans, to speak with you and your husband, at your convenience, to explain all the particulars related to your son's inheritance as well as the roles that you and your husband will play at Chalmsley Court. He understands that you may wish my presence at this conference, to serve as legal adviser."

Bee had heard only one thing. Knowing the cynical view of her great-uncle that she had developed, Hector had leaped to the same conclusion. He was glad his wife spoke before he roared. "Mr. Cosgrove, I do not care what stipulations he has imposed, I will not be separated from my son."

"No, of course not. Mr. Atkinson states that your great-uncle is well aware of this."

"Nor do I have a desire to return to the Court, not while—not at the moment."

"That is also understood. Lord Chalmsley's health is failing. With the death of his daughter Cordelia last October and his wife's death from illness last summer, he will remove to Brighton. That will leave Chalmsley Court vacant. You may repair there, without fear of his return, at any time. Mr. Atkinson wished me to convey that the servants and staff are eager for your return, Mrs. Evans. There can only be great benefit to your son and to the estate and its people when your family, a stable and compassionate family, is in residence there."

Mr. Cosgrove left not long after that. After Bee escorted him to the door, she found Hector putting the baby in his bassinette near their bed.

He turned. Seeing Bee's perplexed frown, he wrapped her in his arms and leaned his forehead against hers. "Our life is changing yet again."

She splayed her fingers on his shoulders. "This is not a change I ever expected."

"Nor did I. Did your great-uncle anticipate it, when he separated us all those years ago?"

She leaned into his embrace. "He must have."

"And didn't want a barrister's son to father the heir to Chalmsley."

"Well, I wanted that barrister's son." She looped her arms around his neck. "And I got him."

.~.~.~.

The Singing of Mad Aunt Beth, beginning with 2 Nursery Rhymes

Counting Magpies
https://en.wikipedia.org/wiki/One_for_Sorrow_(nursery_rhyme)
One for sorrow,
Two for joy,
Three for a girl,
Four for a boy,
Five for silver,
Six for gold,
Seven for a secret,
Never to be told.
Eight for a wish,
Nine for a kiss,
Ten for a bird,
You must not miss.

Heigh-ho A Carrion Crow
https://www.surfnetkids.com/early/5803/heighho-the-carrion-crow
A carrion crow sat on an oak,
Fol de riddle, lol de riddle, hi ding do,
Watching a tailor shape his cloak;
Sing heigh-ho, the carrion crow,
Fol de riddle, lol de riddle, hi ding do!

The rhyme covers three more stanzas of poetic justice on the tailor for trying to kill a crow.

Lord Randall
The classic ballad of love, betrayal and murder
https://www.poets.org/poetsorg/poem/lord-randall
"Oh where ha'e ye been, Lord Randall my son?
O where ha'e ye been, my handsome young man?"
"I ha'e been to the wild wood: mother, make my bed soon,
For I'm weary wi' hunting, and fain wald lie down."

"Where gat ye your dinner, Lord Randall my son?
Where gat ye your dinner, my handsome young man?"
"I dined wi' my true love; mother, make my bed soon,
For I'm weary wi' hunting, and fain wald lie down."

"What gat ye to your dinner, Lord Randall my son?
What gat ye to your dinner, my handsome young man?"
"I gat eels boiled in broo: mother, make my bed soon,
For I'm weary wi' hunting, and fain wald lie down."

"What became of your bloodhounds, Lord Randall my son?
What became of your bloodhounds, my handsome young man?"
"O they swelled and they died: mother, make my bed soon,
for I'm weary wi' hunting, and fain wald lie down."

"O I fear ye are poisoned, Lord Randall my son!
O I fear ye are poisoned, my handsome young man!"
"O yes, I am poisoned: mother, make my bed soon,
For I'm sick at the heart, and I fain wald lie down."

The Maid and the Palmer
   http://lyrics.wikia.com/wiki/Steeleye_Span:The_Maid_And_The_Palmer
A long ballad. The pertinent lyrics are these:
   You lie, you lie, you are forsworn
   For nine children you have born
   For nine children you have born
   As the sun shines down so early

   Oh, there's three of them lying under your bed-head
   Three of them under the hearth are laid
   Three of them under the hearth are laid
   As the sun shines down so early

   Three more laying on yonder green
   Count, fair maid, for that makes nine
   Count, fair maid, for that makes nine
   As the sun shines down so early

   Palmer, oh, Palmer, do tell me
   Penance that you will give to me
   Penance that you will give to me
   As the sun shines down so early

   Penance I will give thee none
   But seven years as a stepping stone
   But seven years as a stepping stone
   As the sun shines down so early

Seven more as a clapper to ring in the bell
Seven to run from the apes of hell
Seven to run from the apes of hell
As the sun shines down so early

The Forlorn Lover
More love, betrayal, and death, this ballad is also known as "The False Bride".

http://www.justanothertune.com/html/ilal.html

I once loved a lass, and I loved her sae weel
I hated all others that spoke of her ill;
But noo she's rewarded me weel for my love,
For she's gaun to be wed till anither.

When I saw my love to the church go,
Wi' bride and bride-maidens, they made a fine show;
An' l followed them on wi' a heart fu' o' woe,
For she's gaun to be wed till anither.

When I saw my love sit down to dine,
I sat down beside her and poured out the wine,
An' I drank to the lass that should ha'e been mine,
An' now she is wed till anither.

The men o' yon forest they askit o' me,
Hou many strawberries grew in the saut sea?
But I askit them back wi' a tear in my ee',
How many ships sail in the forest?

O dig me a grave and dig it sae deep,
An' cover it over with flow'rets säe sweet,
An' I'll turn in for to tak' a lang sleep,
An' may be in time I'll forget her.

They dug him a grave an' they dug it sae deep,
An' covered it over with flow'rets säe sweet,
An' he's turned in for to tak' a lang sleep,
An' maybe by this time he's forgot her.

"Lady Bothwell's Lament"
More love, no betrayal, but definitely death
http://www.musicanet.org/robokopp/scottish/balowmyb.htm

From Stanza 12 of the 13:

If linen lacks, for my love's sake
Then quickly to him would I make
My smock, once for his body meet,
And wrap him in that winding-sheet.
Ah me! how happy had I been,
If he had ne'er been wrapt therein.

The Twa Corbies
The classic ballad triad / love, betrayal, death
http://www.twocrows.co.uk/twa_corbies.html   *This website provides the original lyrics.*

As I was walking all alone,
I heard two crows (or ravens) making a moan;
One said to the other,
"Where shall we go and dine today?"

"In behind that old turf wall,
I sense there lies a newly slain knight;
And nobody knows that he lies there,
But his hawk, his hound and his lady fair."

"His hound is to the hunting gone,
His hawk to fetch the wild-fowl home,
His lady's has taken another mate,
So we may make our dinner sweet."

"You will sit on his white neck-bone,
And I'll peck out his pretty blue eyes;
With one lock of his golden hair
We'll thatch our nest when it grows bare."

"Many a one for him is moaning,
But nobody will know where he is gone;
Over his white bones, when they are bare,
The wind will blow for evermore."

Giggle-Down Fair

https://books.google.com/books?id=8Zg9AAAAYAAJ&pg=PA28&lpg=PA28&dq=Giggle+down+fair&source=bl&ots=j9poI_JQsT&sig=D0WKqp9Ne5mTokf8Gvup--B8Q80&hl=en&sa=X&ved=0ahUKEwjEq4b39bLYAhWETCYKHc_1CHEQ6AEINjAD#v=onepage&q=Giggle%20down%20fair&f=false

First stanza of Four

> Come neighbours, awhile and leave your labours and care,
> And follow tight Andrew to Giggle-Down Fair,
> Such din and diversion you never did see,
> As to-day, if you give credit to me:
> Come away, come away, come away to the fair,
> In your holiday gear,
> Trim and dainty appear,
> Come away, come away to the fair.

The Murder Near Leeds

https://books.google.com/books?id=BSpZQOvH6_kC&pg=PA165&lpg=PA165&dq=ballad+about+bloody+young+man&source=bl&ots=cDLNj8BTvE&sig=XM-inRq7QX3pmnLn0EvhEs-Sm5k&hl=en&sa=X&ved=0ahUKEwiixJSm8cbYAhUGVyYKHWNuD5MQ6AEIVjAN#v=onepage&q=ballad%20about%20bloody%20young%20man&f=false

From stanzas 2:

> `Tis of a young man, I may say,
> Which did his parents not obey,
> But like a crafty, cunning elf,
> Despis'd his friends, ruin'd his self.

From stanza 8:

> He valli'ed not her words that time
> But studied an inhuman crime;
> The Devil tempts him night and day
> How to take her life away.

The Unquiet Grave

http://www.sacred-texts.com/neu/eng/child/ch078.htm

> 'THE wind doth blow today, my love,
> And a few small drops of rain;

I never had but one true-love,
In cold grave she was lain.

'I'll do as much for my true-love
As any young man may;
I'll sit and mourn all at her grave
For a twelvemonth and a day.'

The twelvemonth and a day being up,
The dead began to speak:
'Oh who sits weeping on my grave,
And will not let me sleep?'

'`Tis I, my love, sits on your grave,
And will not let you sleep;
For I crave one kiss of your clay-cold lips,
And that is all I seek.'

'You crave one kiss of my clay-cold lips;
But my breath smells earthy strong;
If you have one kiss of my clay-cold lips,
Your time will not be long.

'`Tis down in yonder garden green,
Love, where we used to walk,
The finest flower that ere was seen
Is withered to a stalk.

'The stalk is withered dry, my love,
So will our hearts decay;
So make yourself content, my love,
Till God calls you away.'

Thank You*!*

Thank you for reading *The Key to Secrets*.

This story fascinated me, from the first idea to write a story of Hector Evans and his lost love. That fascination sustained me through the agony of trying to get the envisioned story onto the page.

From vision to manuscript is always a difficult transition. I remember being so pleased that my original concept and characters poured onto the page. While I find it difficult to rank the 12 books in the **Hearts in Hazard** series as top favorite and second favorite and so on, I do know that *K2Secrets* is definitely in the top five. It's one of the stories that I always recommend to new readers.

Now, several years after *K2Secrets'* first publication, I confess to having forgotten certain elements of the story and being surprised all over again by the method of and reason for the murders. Several details about Bee and Mad Aunt Beth and Cordelia had also escaped my memory. I dashed through my first re-read and had to keep backing up to insert the formatting changes associated with this re-read of all 12 books in the **HnH** series.

Meeting the story again was like meeting an old friend and being reminded of those clever details and precious emotions that bound our friendship together.

For any questions, comments, and speculations, please contact winkbooks@aol.com.

You can find my books on my Amazon author page or my website ~~ www.writersinkbooks.com

To receive monthly information about all of my books, please join my monthly newsletter list. Contact me at winkbooks@aol.com and receive a free peak of the book I am currently writing. I won't pester you with affiliate links or pass your email to any other person or institution.

Indie writers thrive on reviews. With *any* book that you enjoy, please share with other readers looking for escape from the stresses of life.

Dream it. Believe it. Do it.
~~ *M.A. Lee*

Hearts in Hazard by M.A. Lee

Mysteries and Suspense with a Dash of Romance
Set during the Regency Era of England

1 ~ *A Game of Secrets* ~ Smugglers, secrets and spies: Kate tries to hide in plain sight; Tony tries to catch a spy. First they fall in love, then they fall into trouble with smugglers. Will they survive?

2 ~ *A Game of Spies* ~ Salons and soirées, flirtation and dancing, gambling and spies: Josette and Giles fall in love over a deck of cards—and try not to die.
Spymaster Giles Hargreaves was introduced in *A Game of Secrets*.

3 ~ *A Game of Hearts* ~ **Two couples** :: One titled widow, one wealthy businessman: two hearts shadowed by their past. One bright young flirt, one hard-edged young man: two hearts crossed by circumstance. Mix in a courtesan and two rakes, all out for mischief, and murder bloody and foul.

4 ~ *The Danger of Secrets* ~ Deep in the wintry countryside, a house warmed by relatives and friends: secrets of family, secrets of hearts, secrets of blood and pain. Match a daughter to an unknown father; match a spinster to an earl; match a serial killer to his next victim.
Gordon Musgrove was introduced in *A Game of Spies*.

5 ~ *The Danger for Spies* ~ Impossibilities? Rakes don't lose their hearts. Spies don't give up the game. No one hides in plain sight. Codes are unbreakable. A man can't hold onto revenge for years and years. Impossibilities are designed to be shattered.
Toby Kennitt was introduced in *A Game of Spies*.

6 ~ *The Danger to Hearts* ~ A country manor in early Spring: older woman and younger man. Horses, cats, needlework, roses and afternoon teas ~ What could possibly go wrong in an idyll? Trouble in the past, trouble now, and murder.
The character Jess Carter was introduced in *A Game of Secrets*.

7 ~ *The Key to Secrets* ~ Debutantes should snare fiancés, not murder them. Constable Hector Evans must solve three murders. Is his former love guilty, of is she a convenient scapegoat?

Constable Hector Evans was introduced in *The Danger to Hearts*.

8 ~ *The Key for Spies* ~ Spies and traitors. Lies and treachery. Unexpected love where bullets fly. One traitor destroys loyalty. What will two traitors destroy?

9 ~ *The Key for Hearts* ~ A convenient marriage inconveniently causes murder.

10 ~ *The Hazard of Secrets*. Two hearts with dangerous pasts— Can they keep their secrets, or will murder force them to reveal all?

11 ~ *The Hazard for Spies* ~ Disguised to spy. Will murder destroy their chance for love?

12 ~ *The Hazard for Hearts* ~ Two wives haunt the castle. Will she be the third to die?

The **Into Death** Series, set after World War I

Digging into Death ~ A governess seeking refuge, a handsome young man, an archaeological dig: romance is inevitable; murder is not. Suspicions escalate, artifacts are stolen, and then a second murder. Has the love of her life beguiled her straight into death? Available in paperback and e-book

Christmas with Death ~ Christmas is for miracles, merriment, and murder. Set in 1919 at an English country manor for a party throughout Christmastide. Available in paperback and e-book.

Portrait with Death, publishing soon ~ the conclusion of the Isabella Newcombe series

Nonfiction by M.A. Lee

Think like a Pro Writer series

Think like a Pro: New Advent for Writers ~ Seven lessons to guide your growth from newbie writer to "thinking like a pro writer". Now available in paperback and e-book.

Think / Pro: A Planner for Writers ~ An undated planner with daily word counts, progress meters, project planning, and goals analysis. Paperback only. How else will you record your goals and progress?

Old Geeky Greeks: Write Stories with Ancient Techniques ~ Storytelling has its roots in the strong foundations of classical antiquity. Avoid the re-packaged "exclusive insights" and "wham-pow webinars" and return to the source, organized as a seminar in book form.

Discovering Your Novel ~ a 52-week course for new writers, offering guidance from original idea to publication and marketing.

Discovering Characters ~ Delving deeply into your primary characters entails more than just templates and character interviews. You also need to know your secondary characters. Focus on more than appearance, more than intellect, and explore your characters hearts and souls. Discover them!

Discovering Your Plot ~ What writers need and want for plot structures and genre expectations. Control pacing, tension, and suspense with a stronger comprehension of the major sections of a novel.

Discovering your Author Brand ~ The greatest secret to catch the attention of fly-by readers? Branding. Writers need to brand their books, their series, and themselves as the author. Packed with examples and explanations from past successful marketing efforts.

Discovering Sentence Craft ~ Zeug-what? Chiasmus? Auxesis? Are those spelled correctly? Well, yes. These are literary devices used for centuries by the best writers to make their works memorable. Writers are artists, seeking ideas from the creative muse. We're also crafters, looking for the best ways to present those creative ideas. *DiscS~Craft* presents techniques for using figurative & interpretive concepts as well as the structures of inversions, repetitions, oppositions, and sequencings.

Just Start Writing :: Inspiration 4 Writers, book 1 ~Writing can be a dizzy whirl of a carousel, all colors and mirrors with unicorns and griffins and dragons to ride. How do you get your ticket, climb on the carousel, and join the writing ride? If you want to pursue your writing dream, *Just Start Writing* will help you start.

Pen Names of M.A. Lee

Remi Black ~ Fae Mark'd
Fae Mark'd Wizard
Weave a Wizardry Web
Dream a Deadly Dream
Sing a Graveyard Song
Kindle a Fae's Wrath (coming soon)
Quench a Dragon's Fire (in the sketching stage)
Dance to Bone-Edged Music (in the sketching stage)

Fae Mark'd World
To Wield the Wind :: Spells of Air 1
To Charm the Air: Spells of Air 2 (coming soon)
To Curse the Wyre: Spells of Air 3 (sketching stage)

Edie Roones ~ Seasons in Sansward
Summer Sieges
Autumn Spells
Winter Sorcery
Spring Magicks (in the sketching stage)

All books from Writers' Ink are available at Amazon.

For any comments, questions, and speculations, contact
winkbooks@aol.com. Use the subject line to direct your email to a
specific book or series.